## A MAN WITH A PAST

He grew grave. For a moment, she thought she had angered him but he replied with resignation. "I was once the kind of man mothers warn their daughters about and rightly so, but since—" He paused. "I have changed somewhat," he amended. His mouth smiled but his blue eyes did not. "However, I still appreciate a pretty girl."

Elisabeth blushed. Her weariness forgotten, she longed to learn about this man's past. She didn't dare ask, afraid to awaken the dangerous rake he said he had been. Was he trying to lull her into a false sense of security so that he could—well, do whatever it is that rakes do to susceptible young maidens? "I cannot think you much changed then," she said.

"Have you had much experience with men?" he asked dryly.

# BOOK YOUR PLACE ON OUR WEBSITE AND MAKE THE READING CONNECTION!

We've created a customized website just for our very special readers, where you can get the inside scoop on everything that's going on with Zebra, Pinnacle and Kensington books.

When you come online, you'll have the exciting opportunity to:

- View covers of upcoming books
- Read sample chapters
- Learn about our future publishing schedule (listed by publication month *and author*)
- Find out when your favorite authors will be visiting a city near you
- Search for and order backlist books from our online catalog
- Check out author bios and background information
- Send e-mail to your favorite authors
- Meet the Kensington staff online
- Join us in weekly chats with authors, readers and other guests
- Get writing guidelines
- AND MUCH MORE!

**Visit our website at
http://www.kensingtonbooks.com**

# DANGEROUS TO KNOW

## LEANNE SHAWLER

## ZEBRA BOOKS
### Kensington Publishing Corp.
www.kensingtonbooks.com

OCT 1 1 2005

ZEBRA BOOKS are published by

Kensington Publishing Corp.
850 Third Avenue
New York, NY 10022

All Kensington titles, imprints and distributed lines are available at special quantity discounts for bulk purchases for sales promotion, premiums, fund-raising, educational or institutional use.

Special book excerpts or customized printings can also be created to fit specific needs. For details, write or phone the office of the Kensington Special Sales Manager: Kensington Publishing Corp., 850 Third Avenue, New York, NY 10022. Attn. Special Sales Department. Phone: 1-800-221-2647.

First Printing: April 2005
10 9 8 7 6 5 4 3 2 1

Printed in the United States of America

*For Dan,
and in memory of my grandmother, Avril,
who encouraged me to write.*

# CHAPTER ONE

Pleasantly aching from a hard ride, Miss Elisabeth Stockwell led her chestnut mare into the stables. She bid her girls, two Irish wolfhounds, to remain outside. Jade and Sapphire sank to the ground, whining softly, their large heads resting on their paws.

The few horses in their stalls pawed at their straw bedding. Who could blame them for wanting to be outside and free of the dark?

Not Elisabeth. She swung open a stall door, murmuring encouragement to her reluctant mare.

"Don't move," a deep, masculine voice growled from the depths of the stall, "or I shall shoot."

His clipped, gentlemanly tones conflicted with his harsh words. Dropping the reins, she turned very slowly to face him. Had her brother come back, unannounced as usual? Was it one of her brother's friends playing a trick?

Grunting, a fair-haired man levered himself up from a sitting position against the far wall, his face an ugly rictus of pain.

Not a friend. A stranger. And armed.

He pointed an unwavering pistol at her chest.

The barrel's mouth seemed like an endless well. She sucked in her breath, frozen by the deadly weapon. How could she be so gullible and think it to be no more than a prank? When would she ever learn?

Would this be the end? Her life had been destroyed once by

a man. Had another come to hammer the final nail into her coffin?

She swallowed the rising panic and forced herself to look beyond the small black eye of the pistol and at the intruder. The usual smells of warm horses and sweet, fresh straw did little to reassure her.

He slumped against the rear wall, a hand pressed to his side. His dirty and wet shirt stuck to him in a way that revealed the athletic muscles beneath. Judging by his fine linen shirt and cravat, albeit in ruins, her attacker was a gentleman.

"You're no stable boy," his voice grated, laced with pain. "Who the devil are you?"

She knew she couldn't tell him. If she revealed herself as lady of the house, he could take her hostage—or worse. But that fate may await her yet. She would not give him the satisfaction of a higher prize.

"My name is Elisabeth."

He grunted. "I suggest you turn around and leave, woman." She hadn't given him any title, and he refused to give her a term of respect. "Let me die in peace."

"Die?" With a start, she saw the smudge on his shirt was not dirt, but blood. His blood.

"You're hurt," she said, rather stupidly. Surely he knew.

"Very observant of you."

The pistol in his hand vibrated. She saw sweat upon his brow. It was sweat, not water, that soaked his shirt.

Fever. His wound must be infected.

"Put the gun down," she advised, her voice trembling only a little. "You need help."

"I'm beyond help," he snarled. His aim grew less steady. She couldn't begin to imagine the sheer amount of will and effort that kept him upright. "Who are you? Not the lady of the house."

"Her companion," she lied. She held out her hand. "Please. You need assistance."

He shook his head, looking dazed. "No. I am not worth it."

"You are a gentleman, sir," she observed.

He snorted.

"Fallen on hard times, perhaps, but a gentleman nevertheless. Besides, any human life is worth saving. Even yours."

"Go," he managed to gasp out. "Let me expire in peace. I need no more interfering women."

She ignored the bite of his insult and stepped forward, pausing when she saw his grip tighten on the pistol.

"I am damned already," he said. "Taking your life won't make a difference."

She covered her heart, his target, as if leather gloves and fine bones could stop a bullet.

The pistol slipped from his grasp and into the straw. "Damn," he muttered. He toppled to the ground.

She rushed forward, bending to touch the pulse point at his sweaty neck. She felt the thready beat of his heart. Not dead, then.

Nor would he be, if she had anything to do with it.

The stale odor of his sweat masked any sickly sweet stench of putrefaction, but she would need to check his wounds more closely.

Did she know him? Leaning closer in the darkened stall, she examined his even features. Past the first flush of youth, his dark blond hair lightened at the ends from exposure to the sun. Lines creased the corners of his eyes and mouth.

She had the tingling sensation she knew him but not from this area. Where? London?

Unconscious, he looked vulnerable, lost. Her fingertips brushed his cheek, lingering. She jerked away. What was she thinking? She refused to become attracted to yet another gentleman down on his luck. She would not!

She hastened out of the stables, dragging her mare behind her and calling for help. Her girls' frantic barking added to the uproar. In moments, she had her mount rehoused in another stall and the unconscious intruder carried into the house on an improvised pallet.

"And where do you think you're going with that?" boomed

Mrs. Peters, a buxom woman and her former childhood nurse, now housekeeper.

Elisabeth flashed her an annoyed look, batting away a hound's curious nose from the stranger's face. "To one of the guest rooms. He's badly hurt."

Mrs. Peters bent to take a closer look. "He's a vagrant. There's no place for him here."

"A gentleman," Elisabeth corrected. In better light, she saw dirt encrusted his face. "Down on his luck."

"A vagrant," Mrs. Peters confirmed. "You can't be suggestin' we take him in?"

"I should have left him to die?" She didn't conceal her ire.

"Of course not. You should send him down to the poorhouse."

She shuddered, the image of those gray walls and the gray half-starved people contained within them leaping unbidden into her mind. "I will not!"

"For heaven's sake, Miss Elisabeth, he's not one of your stray kittens. Having a man in the house without a proper chaperone will ruin your reputation."

*What reputation?* she thought, glowering. "The blue guest room," she ordered the waiting footmen, who sagged from the man's dead weight.

"If you're going to insist, he should go into the west wing. What if guests arrive and we need that room?"

"Are guests likely to arrive?" she shot back.

Mrs. Peters folded her arms over her expansive bosom. "You never know with your brother."

True enough. Since coming into his inheritance, James spent the majority of his time in London, returning with a gaggle of friends. The Season was in full swing and she didn't expect him now until the end of it. However, you could never tell when he might appear.

"Very well," Elisabeth conceded. "The west wing. I'll need my medical supplies." She followed the burdened footmen.

Stockwell House's western wing had fallen into disuse. Income had decreased over the years, little helped by the incessant gambling of both father and son. Most of the furniture in the wing had been sold off, but a couple of bedrooms nearest the main hall remained intact.

The footmen shifted the unconscious gentleman off the makeshift pallet and onto the bed.

"Shall I send for Dr. Harris, miss?" the senior footman asked.

She considered the decrepit doctor's reputation. "Let me see if I can staunch the bleeding. If not, then we must send for him."

The senior footman awaited her further orders at the foot of the bed. Another entered with her medical bag and withdrew to stand by the door.

She concealed a smile, certain that Mrs. Peters's rant about reputation had her staff hovering to protect her.

She opened the small leather bag, which contained the basics needed in case of an accident. It would do until she ascertained the severity of his injuries. Using scissors, she slit his shirt in half, peeling the bloody fabric from his skin.

The wound scored his left side, just above the hip. A recent wound, it had started to mend, but had never healed. The angrily inflamed wound was open but not deep. Crusted pus edged the gash, melting from the flowing blood.

She gathered a wad of linen and pressed over the wound, but not before the senior footman had leaned in to get a good look. "Looks like a pistol shot," he opined.

She darted a shocked glance at her footman. A bullet wound? Had he been shot fleeing a crime scene, or had he been in a duel? Whatever the reason, such a lawless injury meant trouble. She gestured the footman closer and peeled back the pad for him to take a closer look. "Are you sure?"

The footman scrunched his nose. "Yes, miss. He's lucky he didn't die when he got it."

"We will just have to see he does not die from it now, won't we?" She covered the wound with a fresh lint pad and placed another on top. The bleeding had slowed, but only a little.

She tried to keep her mind on her work, but it raced ahead. Who was he? What had happened to him?

She glanced at his still, pale face. Whoever he was he was no danger to her now.

His chest rose and fell evenly. A few hairs sprinkled the upper chest area, but it was otherwise smooth and well formed. His chest could have belonged to any of her farm hands, except it lacked the tanned, sunburnt look. Whoever he was, he took care of himself. Except for this wound he'd received. She'd never seen a man's chest this close before, and she longed to touch him, just to feel what it was like, but she'd rather stop the bleeding and save his life first.

Satisfied the bleeding had stopped, she rose, brushing the creases from her crushed skirts. In a low murmur, she asked the footmen to follow her outside.

"That man in there may be a gentleman," she told them, closing the door behind her, "but I don't wish whatever misfortune that has befallen him to land on our doorstep. If he knows my name, he may use it in the future to our disadvantage. Therefore, he shall know me only as Miss Elisabeth, a companion to the lady of the house. Is that clear?"

The elder of the two footmen disagreed. "But that isn't proper, miss. You can't be on a first name basis with a ruffian!"

"I do agree we should not." She chewed at her lip and raised a hand, forestalling further protestations. "But I do not see any other choice."

She left to change out of her stained riding habit, leaving a footman on guard with strict orders to call her if the fellow worsened. She did not plan on being away for long, but her duties as mistress of the house called.

* * *

A few hours later, she returned. A footman took his ease at the stranger's bedside.

"Has he woken?"

The footman leaped to his feet. "Hasn't stirred, miss."

"Good. You may go. He is no danger to me unconscious. I shall ring if I require anything."

She dismissed the maid also and sat. Streaks of sweat scaled his face, revealing white-pale skin beneath a dark gray layer of grime. Further black smudges marked his pillow and sheets.

He needed a wash. In his precarious state, washing him could endanger his health even more, but surely he would feel better for it? Elisabeth knew she would.

She rang for hot water and a sponge. When it arrived, she rolled up her sleeves and got to work. It seemed safest to start with his hands. They lay limp on the bedcovers, the nails black with dirt.

She picked up the one nearest to her, cradling it in her hand. It engulfed her small hand, making it appear he held it, although his fingers lay limp. His hand, she felt certain, would squeeze the life from her, had he been conscious and fully healthy. Even now, she thought it might yet be strong enough to grind her bones in a tight grip.

She sponged the back of it first, cleansing away the grime. She curled the sponge around each of his fingers, drawing the dirt free. For the time being, she left the dirt beneath his fingernails alone.

She pushed back his sleeves, the wrist ties long since broken, and cleaned his forearm. No idle fat wasted here either.

She glanced at his face. He slept, undisturbed by her ministrations. What if he woke? She hurried to wipe the dark smudges from the hand and arm farthest from her. She leaned over him, growing aware of their close proximity.

Reminding herself she was safe, she turned her attention to his face. The water had turned tepid, an ideal temperature for bathing a fevered forehead.

She dipped the sponge into the water, squeezing the dirty

water out and then dipped it in again. The water turned a smoky gray color. She wiped his cheeks and forehead. He looked much better without the gray cast to his features, flushed pink from the fever.

She washed his neck, and the vee of darker skin below it. He had been out in the sun recently, with no cravat and his shirt destroyed. Her hand slipped off the sponge and onto his damp chest. His hot skin felt hard beneath her cool palm, rising and falling with his breathing. Taking a deep breath, she let the sponge be her only contact with him. She couldn't afford to get too close.

She avoided getting the bandages wet and sat back, satisfied. Surveying the length of her patient, she saw he seemed comfortable. Should she wash the rest of him?

She peeled back the covers. He still wore his muddied breeches, although the buttons were unfastened. A dark golden line of curling hair ran from the bandages before disappearing under his breeches.

Taking a deep breath, she twitched the covers back over him and made her escape, carrying the bowl of water with her.


The afternoon drew to a close before Elisabeth visited her patient. Attired in her simplest muslin gown, she took the footman aside for the latest update. "Has he woken yet?"

The footman nodded. "Yes, miss. He stirred a little while ago. I gave him something to drink but he wasn't hungry."

She smiled with relief. That he regained consciousness was a positive sign. "Has he said anything?"

"Didn't seem like he was happy to hear ye was behind it all—not that I told him who you were, miss"—he hastily interposed—"but I reckon that's 'cause he got himself hurt over a lady."

"A lady? Not smuggling, you suppose?" They were not that far from the coast, after all.

The footman shrugged. "He gave a name. Calls himself Henry. He's as cagey as you are."

She muffled a grin, turning it to a frown. Finding commonality with a vagrant gentleman was not a good idea, no matter how handsome. "I wonder why he doesn't want us to know his identity? Is he a criminal?" Did her shudder came from fear or excitement?

"Couldn't say, miss."

She dismissed the noncommittal footman. "The man is too weak to be a threat. A guard is not needed."

The footman bowed. "I'll wait outside, miss."

Taking a seat by the bed, she studied his face, wondering if he really slept. Two deep creases ran perpendicular to his stern mouth, disturbing his angelic expression. His strong aquiline nose hinted at his noble heritage and faint crow's-feet ran from the edges of his eyes.

His blue eyes.

"I was just wondering whether you were . . . asleep or not," she stuttered, embarrassed to have been caught in her frank perusal.

"As you can see, I was not. Do you like what you see?" he asked, affecting a slow drawl.

"It is pleasing enough," she replied coolly, burying her heart's sudden accelerated response to the stranger's languorous voice. A servant entered with a bowl of hot water, placing it by the bedside and bobbed a curtsey before leaving.

She turned her attention back to her patient, catching him eyeing the room with wary curiosity. "How d'you do. My name is Elisabeth." She grasped his proffered hand. It was hot and dry. The man's eyes glinted feverishly.

"Call me Henry," he croaked. "May I have a glass of water?"

"Of course."

She poured water into a tumbler. Helping him into a sitting position, she watched him sip the water, holding the glass with an unsteady hand. When he finished, he returned the tumbler to her. With a grateful expression, he lay back.

"I cannot believe my luck in having such a pretty nurse," he said.

Her eyes narrowed. If the man could flirt when ill, she didn't want to know what he'd be like when healthy. "Flatterer," she accused. "My appearance won't get you well, sir. You have a better chance with my nursing."

His wicked smirk, quickly smoothed away, prodded her memory. She *had* seen him before. In London? There had been so many faces at the assemblies and balls during her coming out two years ago, she couldn't be sure. She hadn't been back since.

Disturbed, she rose and immediately wished she'd chosen a gown with a higher neckline. His gaze shifted at once to her bosom while she leaned over him in rising. She flushed, turning away. He was no gentleman!

"Would you care to tell me what happened to you?" She wanted to hear it for herself.

He grimaced. "It is not suitable for a young lady's ears."

"I am not a lady, sir, I work for a living." She hoped her lie convinced him.

He snorted in disbelief. "I think not. You are far too refined to be a servant."

"As I told you in the stables, I am a companion," she hastened to assure him, feeling her cheeks grow warm.

His eyes narrowed. "I remember you now. You are that stubborn woman who would not let me die."

His speaking of death with such yearning gave her chills. "Why do you long for death, Mister Henry?" she murmured.

"None of your damned business. My tale is not suited for a gentlewoman's ears." His eyelids drooped. "Even for one who has to work for a living."

Silence fell. She wished he'd tell her the truth. That he refused did not bode well. Perhaps she ought to call in the magistrate and let him deal with this Mister Henry.

Henry resumed the conversation. "Whose house is this? Who do you work for?"

She eyed him. "I do not see that it is any concern of yours, Mister Henry." She noted the shadows under his eyes and his resigned, wary expression. Despite his uncomfortable questions, she couldn't turn him over to the authorities yet. He wouldn't last very long in a jail cell without proper care.

His penetrating gaze made her look away. It was almost as if he could read her mind, see that already she harbored a softness for him. She had to remember he was not a sick puppy she could grow fond of, but a man, treacherous and deceitful.

She'd nurse him back to health, then the magistrate could take care of him. She flung back the bedclothes, intending on doing just that.

He gasped. "What are you doing?" He looked down. "What have you done to my shirt?"

She raised an eyebrow. "Your shirt was already ruined beyond all hope," she told him, flushing. "I am changing your bandages. This may hurt a bit." She noticed that someone had changed them in her absence. With care, she pulled them from the wound. She needed to clean the area now that the bleeding had stopped. It would make it easier to change bandages without as much damage.

His breath hissed out in pain. "What is your real name?" His voice sounded strained.

"I have told you my real name." She glanced to find his gaze riveted upon her face, his mouth pulled into a tight line. He needed distraction from the pain. "What is yours?"

"You know that it is Henry," he replied.

"And you know that mine is Elisabeth. There, we are even. Unless you care to enlighten me as to your surname?" She dabbed at the wound. Henry's breath hissed out again, but he made no reply. "You cannot tell me yours, and so I have no intention of telling you mine."

The wound didn't bleed but oozed pus. No wonder removing it had hurt. "Why not? What do you have to fear?"

She smiled. "I could ask you the same question." She dipped a cloth into the hot water. All conversation ceased, Henry gritting his teeth as she bathed his wound to clear it of all the oozing muck.

She scattered basilicum powder over it before placing fresh bandages over it. With some assistance from him, she wrapped a sturdier bandage around his torso. His fingers reached to scratch his back.

"The bandages itch?" she asked, craning to see.

He nodded, his hand slipping away from his back. " 'Tis nothing."

She frowned. "I have some lotion, perhaps it will help soothe . . ."

He shook his head. "No."

"Are you sure?"

He nodded, thin-lipped.

She pulled the covers over his stocky, athletic chest, longing to linger there. "There. All done. Do you want something to eat?"

He refused.

"You're not trying to starve yourself to death, are you?" The thought blurted out before she could stop it.

A ghost of a smile crossed his face, but again he refused. "Too tired," he said.

"Then you will eat tomorrow," she told him in a firm tone that brooked no argument. "Would you like some chamomile tea to help you sleep?"

Again, he demurred.

She retreated to her parlor, the dining room too large and empty for her to dine in alone. She turned her mind to the mystery that surrounded him.

Who was he? He had the bearing of a gentleman, although from his few comments, she wasn't sure if he was a well-bred one. Perhaps boredom brought forth those few flirtatious words?

What was he doing on Stockwell lands? Her home was

close to the coast. If smuggling was his crime, was this as far as he could make it?

It was not in her nature to pry into other people's business but Mister Henry was an enigma just begging to be solved. She would find him out.

# CHAPTER TWO

Morning sunlight streamed through the cracks in the curtains, threatening to dispel the coolness brought by the night.

Mister Henry's temperature soared, heat emanating from his prone body. Worse, his wound seeped more foul pus, forcing frequent changes of his bandages. She found his lack of protestation while she did so even more disturbing.

She remained beside him, shirking her other duties. She didn't dare leave him with the grip of fever so strong upon him. A moment's neglect could lead to his death.

She settled by him, bathing his brow, her soothing hand lingering. Unconscious, he kept plucking at his bandages and trying to scratch his back.

As soon as he was well enough, she decided, she would have his fingernails cleaned before he did any further damage to himself by scratching with such noxious fingers.

"Nearly had you . . ." he muttered. Although she felt uncomfortable listening in to his disjointed utterances, she had no choice but to hear. "Damn you, Harriet . . . I'll get even . . ." His words slurred and grew unintelligible. He tossed and turned with increasing violence, as if he fought the demons that plagued him and made him wish for death.

It took all her strength to keep him in the bed. She leaned her body against his, forcing all her weight onto his shoulders to keep him down. A number of times, he threatened to shake her free, but she held on. Her head pressed against his chest, she heard his heart racing.

At last, the violent movements reduced to twitches and then to stillness. She bathed his hot face, murmuring soothing nonsense.

Who was this Harriet? Was she some girl who had once broken his heart? A woman who had somehow brought about this terrible wound of his? He had spoken of revenge after all. Was the agony in his voice only from the wound and fever, or from betrayal, or an unhappy loss?

The day drew to a close. She sat by him, trying to read. Again and again, the book's words blurred and she glanced over at Mister Henry's sleeping form. In this state, he was of no danger to her. She kept telling herself that, but if that were so, then why couldn't she stop thinking about him—and not purely in a doctor-patient manner either. She had treated half-naked farm hands before without feeling this strange quiver inside. Why now? Why him? Why such an unsuitable subject?

She glanced at Mister Henry and found him awake. "Welcome back," she whispered, smiling, resisting the temptation to brush back the damp hair from his face.

He managed a listless smile in response.

"Would you like something to eat?" A faint shake of his head told her no. "Something to help you sleep, perhaps?"

"I have slept enough," he muttered, his voice hoarse. "I am thirsty." She poured him some water. She held out the glass to him. He struggled to raise his head from the pillow. Understanding, she held his head while he drank from the glass.

She busied herself with putting the glass back on the side table.

A small crooked smile faded from his lips. "Could you perhaps read to me? I do not wish to be alone with my thoughts."

She didn't blame him. "Of course. I have a book of poetry. Would that suit?" At his slight nod, she opened her book to a random page. His listlessness concerned her. She had sensed such vitality in him before.

Murmuring Byron's words, she felt his hand move to rest upon her knee. She tensed, ready to remove the offending hand, preferably with a blunt instrument.

She shot a glance at him. His eyes were closed, oblivious of her silent outrage. She took a steadying breath. Perhaps all he wanted was a bit of human comfort. She huffed a soft snort. Not likely!

The weight of his hand burned through her thin skirt. The warmth of his skin reminded her that he was ill, still feverish and thus not in his right mind. She decided not to protest.

In a short time, she found him asleep. Who would have thought Byron to be so boring? Closing the book and placing it by the bed, she carefully removed his hand from her knee.

A shout from the hallway startled her. The door creaked open and the footman stuck his head in. He glanced at the sleeping patient and hissed, "Your brother, miss."

Wearily, Elisabeth closed her eyes. Why did he have to show up now? How was she going to explain Mister Henry's presence?

She rose and nodded in Mister Henry's direction. "Keep an eye on him. He's sleeping. I will send someone along shortly." She stepped out into the corridor, closing the door behind her.

"Elisabeth! There you are!" boomed her brother. Her former guardian, Mr. Jeremy Radclyffe, and his brother-in-law, Lord Hampton, flanked him. "What are you doing lurking in the west wing?" Having come into his majority, James had since taken over as her guardian, although he left her to her own devices.

She hurried closer before James's shouting woke her patient. "Spring cleaning," she improvised. That would explain her flushed face, she hoped.

"It is not your place to do such things," Mr. Radclyffe observed. "Do you not have a housekeeper to take charge of such matters?"

"Of course." She linked arms with her brother and guided them back to the main part of the house. "I wish you would be grateful I am not gambling the family fortune away or—" She halted in her usual sisterly litany against her brother's ways. She was indeed on the verge of causing a scandal.

"This behavior is scandalous," her brother disagreed, his blue eyes flashing. "Look at you! You look like a washerwoman!"

"Well, maybe so," she admitted. "But I hardly think it is anything to get into such a flap about. Particularly from you, brother dear."

Radclyffe walked alongside and gestured at her creased gown. "It looks like you have slept in it. This is not the attire a lady wears to greet her guests." It seemed he had yet to shake himself of his guardian habit. She was in her brother's charge now.

"I was not expecting guests." She shot a dark look at her brother. "We were not sent word you were coming." She smiled at Lord Hampton. "I am sure I am excused for being caught so unawares."

Lord Hampton bowed. His untidy auburn hair flopped over his pale blue eyes. His rather wide mouth smiled in an effort to placate her. "Indeed, Miss Stockwell. You are forgiven. Your brother is much in the wrong for not giving warning."

She flashed a look of triumph at her brother and followed through with a dig of her own. "How much money have you lost this week?"

James scowled. "What makes you think I have?"

"You are home, are you not?" she asked, all sweetness.

"It's not his sole reason," Radclyffe interrupted. "We had expected you to come to London for the Season."

She scoffed at the idea. He'd expected her in London last year too. "What would be the point of that? I am off the marriage market."

"Elisabeth!" James exclaimed, reddening. "You are being ridiculous. You are no spinster! There is a husband for you. I'll bet money on it."

"You would bet money on anything," she responded, unable to hide a smile. She caught his embarrassed look at Lord Hampton. Her heart sank. Oh, Lord. It looked like James thought he was on to a sure thing.

They entered the old great hall of the house. Radclyffe excused himself. "I should see to my wife. The journey from London has been long for her. Do come up and say hello when you have changed."

Elisabeth agreed with a nod. Before she knew it, her brother had disappeared also, "to see about dinner."

Leaving her alone with Lord Hampton.

Oh, Lord.

"Miss Stockwell?" Lord Hampton asked with a tentative touch to her sleeve.

"What is it, my lord?"

His beaming mouth almost split his face. "I came up from London especially to see you."

She gasped. "Me?"

"Yes." The reddened cheeks of the usually unflappable Lord Hampton surprised her. "I hoped to spend some time with you. When you didn't come last year . . . I . . . quite enjoy your company."

She felt her cheeks go hot in turn. "Why thank you, my lord," she murmured, her eyes downcast.

"I have asked Mrs. Radclyffe if she would ask you to come to London. It is not right for you to be buried out here in the country like this." He fidgeted with a button on his waistcoat.

"I like the country," she replied, "but there are times I wish I could be in London if only to keep an eye on my brother."

"There would be no other reason?" His pale blue eyes held a hopeful gleam.

"I miss the dancing," she replied with honesty.

"I will dance every dance with you," he declared, his gaze intent on her. "When Mrs. Radclyffe invites you, do say that you will come."

She smiled, shaking her head at his outrageous statement. "But who will mind the estate?"

"I am sure the estate will survive without you for a season. I do not think I can."

She repressed her astonishment at his intensity. Where did this come from? He was a friend of the family, nothing more. "My-my Lord Hampton," she stuttered, "I never realized you felt this way."

"I have not been able to get you out of my mind since I spent Christmas here at Stockwell House. I was never happier."

"But—" Her mind whirled. She swallowed, her gaze darting about for an avenue for escape. She never expected this romantic outburst. A niggling suspicion occurred to her. With pretended lightness, she asked, "Are you sure you are not on the rebound from Lady Sophie?"

"If you are inferring this is some infatuation, Miss Stockwell, you are much mistaken," he replied, unmistakably indignant. "Please try and remember that I am not like your brother!"

"I beg your pardon, my lord," she soothed, "but this has taken me completely unawares. I had no idea until today of your . . . your feelings toward me."

"Then come to London for the Season and I will show you how much I care for you." His expression turned indulgent. "I shall let you change into more suitable attire. Think upon what I have said."

Alone in the great hall, she smiled after the retreating figure. Lord Hampton's declaration of love had been peculiarly touching. Would he have proposed to her if she'd stayed for her entire first Season in London? If only she hadn't hightailed it back to Stockwell House when—She banished that unpleasant thought.

She strolled upstairs to her rooms to change for dinner and think about Hampton's declaration in relative peace. He moved her not, but such a match would not be unpleasant. He seemed nice, polite, the perfect gentleman. It would be a safe, secure match. She could expect little more than that.

"Miss Elisabeth," Mrs. Peters called, entering her room. "Have you seen Mrs. Radclyffe yet? It is said she looks well."

Elisabeth looked up from brushing out her hair. Her maid hovered, ready to take over in dressing it up for dinner. "Why shouldn't she look well? She's happily married."

"She is a lucky woman." Mrs. Peters barged onto the next subject. "Is it true that Lord Hampton spoke with you alone? What news?"

"Why should there be any news?"

"Why everyone knows that Lord Hampton almost proposed when he was here at Christmastime, and here he is making a return visit to be sure of the match."

"That is not for me to say." Elisabeth managed to appear calm, while she boiled underneath. Had everyone married her off already? "Really!" she hissed under her breath. "How absurd!"

"It's not absurd at all." Mrs. Peters folded her heavyset arms. "After the scandal surrounding his sister's marriage, I'd have thought he wouldn't be champing at the bit to be wed."

"Who says he is?" Elisabeth's eyes narrowed. "What do you know of the scandal? Mr. Radclyffe forbade all mention of it."

"Got it from Mrs. Radclyffe's maid," Mrs. Peters pronounced, looking pleased with herself. "It was kind of Radclyffe to marry her anyway, in spite of her being ruined by Langdon."

Elisabeth prickled in her former guardian's defense. "Nonsense! I have it on the very best authority she was not harmed by—" She paused, her breath catching. Mrs. Peters had mentioned a name. She'd never thought to know the other person in the scandal. Radclyffe's gag order had seen to that. "Who did you say?"

Mrs. Peters beamed. "The Viscount Langdon."

Elisabeth's gasp mingled with her maid's. Even country folk had heard of the viscount's exploits. One of the worst rakes of London. How horrid for Odette Radclyffe!

"Never mind, dear," Mrs. Peters soothed, returning to her

pet subject. "I am sure his sister's misadventure will not affect Lord Hampton's suit."

Elisabeth gave an unladylike snort. "Really, you shouldn't be gossiping with the servants. . . ." Her voice trailed off at Mrs. Peters's grinning face. Elisabeth drew herself up primly. Isn't that exactly what she had been doing? "Yes, thank you for the information. Let us hope it is reliable."

At last she knew Odette's abductor's identity. Why had she not been told it before? She grimaced. Didn't she know, better than anyone, how important it was to keep scandal hidden? Shivering, she pushed away the old, unpleasant memory and dwelled on the new scandal brewing in the west wing of her house. What was she to do about that?

Mrs. Peters lingered. "What are we to do about the ruffian in the west wing?" It was as if Mrs. Peters had read her mind.

"His name is Henry," Elisabeth reminded her. "What do you suggest we do?"

"Have him moved to one of the farmers' cottages. Your brother won't be impressed to learn you've been entertaining a man in his absence."

"Entertaining? Mister Henry was at death's door. Nobody goes to the west wing. We say nothing about him. He does not exist."

Mrs. Peters narrowed her eyes. "Why? What has he done?"

"I don't know what he has done," she explained with more patience than she felt. "But I'm not going to cause him any more trouble until he's strong enough to withstand it."

"Yer daft," the housekeeper responded, shaking her head. "Yer riskin' the life of everyone in this house, not to mention your reputation."

"Hardly." They wouldn't all be sent to the gallows and he didn't seem the type to murder everyone in their beds. "I have made my decision. He's too sick to hurt anybody. He stays and that's final." She swept downstairs to dinner before Mrs. Peters could continue the argument.

She couldn't think about Henry any more. *Think about*

*Hampton.* Practicality came to the fore. She liked Hampton, but sisterly feelings were not enough on which to base a marriage, were they? She wondered whether her first suspicion was correct: Had he latched onto her kindness last Christmas after he had been cruelly snubbed by Lady Sophie?

She sighed. She had wanted to marry for love. Her first attempt at this had been an utter disaster. She doubted such strong emotions were what the poets meant when they wrote of love. Was love this friendly affection she held for Hampton? She wished she knew.

Darkness.

Henry longed for the dream that slipped away. He and an unseen woman coupled with abandon. His eyes felt stuck together. Abandoning the attempt to open them as too much effort, he reached out with his other senses.

His pinkie finger twitched along smooth cotton. Not dead yet, then. Not lying in a ditch either. The air smelled musty and still. He recalled wanting to curl up in some dark corner to die, but the air had smelt of horses and fresh straw.

Ah. He remembered. He didn't need to open his eyes now. He lay in a rarely used bedroom, a guest of that woman, Miss Elisabeth of the secret last name. A woman who claimed she was a mere companion but appeared used to getting her own way, if the servants' reactions were any indication. Perhaps the lady she attended was elderly or ill and had left her to run the household.

A pretty thing. His jaded mind automatically recalled her soft, mahogany colored hair, a reddish glint adding fire to its lush, dark depths. He took a deep breath, hoping to catch a lingering whiff of her lavender-water perfume.

He had no time for mooning over any sweet miss, let alone the mysterious Elisabeth. Another scandal could kill him.

Like the last one should have.

Why had she insisted on rescuing him? A dank ditch would be far preferable to this mollycoddling he didn't deserve.

To his surprise, he rejected the idea of dying. Just a few days ago, it would've made things so much easier, to stop fighting for each breath and simply let go and accept whatever punishment lay in store for his life of misdeeds.

If the chit is unafraid of him, maybe there's a chance yet. If not to die, then to live a normal life, or failing that, to taste the sweetness of hers.

He forced open his gritty eyelids. The room was gray with early morning light. He tested his limbs, wishing he were a little stronger.

With effort, he sat up, ignoring his spinning head. He had to leave. If he were found and recognized, he'd bring ruin upon his pretty Samaritan. If he were to make a new start on life, then destroying the angel who wanted him so badly to live would be a very poor start.

He swung his legs around and felt cold, hard wood beneath his bare feet. What the devil had she done with his clothes? He saw an armoire standing against the far wall. If only he could make it that far, and dress. . . .

He stood and the world spun alarmingly. He grabbed onto a bedpost, as if to steady the world.

No good. He collapsed back into bed. He would have to wait until he was stronger and pray that no harm befell them in the meantime.

It would be an interesting exercise in willpower he hadn't used in years.

Later that morning, Elisabeth entered to find Mister Henry already awake. She urged him to eat from a bowl of beef tea.

His glassy, pain-filled eyes focused on her, but he managed only a small amount. His intent gaze sent an unbidden warmth to flush her cheeks. Although he said nothing, his determined consumption of the tea made her feel like he now willed himself back to health. There would be no more talk of death, she felt sure.

"My apologies for falling asleep, Miss Elisabeth," Mister Henry said, speaking at last, while she checked on his wound.

She didn't look up from peeling off the bandages. "There is no need to apologize to me," she replied. "To Lord Byron, perhaps." She flashed a smile at him. "You needed your rest. I am glad I could supply you with the means for it."

"When I am more attentive, I hope you will read to me again. You have a lovely voice."

She blushed, surprised by his flattery. "Your wound is beginning to heal."

He grimaced. "I am much relieved to hear it." His fingers slipped under his back to rub his skin.

She watched him scratch. "Are you sure you do not wish any lotion?"

"Quite sure." His voice sounded stronger. A night's sleep had done a great deal to heal him, she realized. Soon, he would no longer be a bedridden invalid but—dangerous.

"You do not want to get a scratch infected, Mister Henry." She started to rise. "I'll fetch that lotion. I will just be a moment."

"Miss Elisabeth!" Henry reached out to detain her. His hand catching her wrist. "There is no need."

She shook her hand free, letting his arm fall back to the bed. "No need?"

"There is an exit wound at the back," he confessed.

"An exit?" she exclaimed, her eyes wide. "You mean it went all the way through?"

He nodded.

She struggled to regain her composure. How had she missed it? She had failed him in not checking more thoroughly for other wounds. "Is it infected?"

He attempted a shrug, constricted by his horizontal position.

"Do you think you can roll over so I can have a look?"

He tried to move. "I will need some help," he admitted with reluctance.

*I should call in the footman.* Instead, she offered her own strength. She pushed him at his shoulder and at his hip. She leaned in close to him, breathing in his maleness, more pungent because of the recent fever. Henry rolled, unable to restrain a groan.

Now able to see his back, she examined the exit wound. Not nearly as large as the entry point, a healthy scab covered it, the cause of the itching sensation. She sat back with a sigh. Her oversight had not been a catastrophic error.

Without her support, he rolled back. "That's one less thing to worry about, eh Mistress Elisabeth?" he said, correctly gauging her relieved expression.

"Miss Elisabeth," she corrected, placing fresh bandages on the wound in the front. The footman had thought it had been pistol shot, but they tended to be far messier. "What else should I be concerned with, Mister Henry? If I am not mistaken, I am treating a wound left by a sword, not a bullet." She had to make it clear that despite the enforced intimacy occasioned by her nursing him, she'd no intention of falling for any of his charms.

"Sword," he confirmed. "Do you want me to tell you all about the trouble I am in?" he purred. "I do not want a pretty girl like yourself becoming unnecessarily involved."

"What kind of trouble?" she demanded, covering him with the sheets. "How much am I risking my own neck by keeping you here?"

His hands covered hers and she snatched them out of reach. How dare he!

"I promise you will not hang for it," he said, apparently unperturbed by her reaction. "I have not broken any law. You see, it involves a lady." He turned his head away from her. "I am ashamed to say it."

"And you have paid for it too," she murmured. She stepped

away, putting distance between them. She mustn't soften. He was a rake, she must remember that. She couldn't trust him.

He looked up at her. "I will repay you for your kindness," he said. "No matter how menial the task."

She laughed at him. "You are a gentleman, Mister Henry, for all your lack of title. I will not have you climbing my roof or standing in as a footman." She held up a hand to silence his interruption. "Nor will I accept any money. Just accept my hospitality."

"It sounds like you regret your generosity," he murmured.

She flushed pink. "I—I, er . . ." She straightened her shoulders. "Of course not." She'd made her decision, knowing the dangers. She would stand by it and arm herself against him.

Her gaze met his. Without his saying another word, she felt he read her true motives. Did she imagine it or did his fervent, silent expression almost plead with her to reconsider?

"I—I have to go. My—my mistress will be needing me." Wits scattered, she dipped a curtsey and hastened away.

She could not trust him. She repeated the mantra to herself while in search of her guests. She could not trust him. No matter how sweet and helpless he appeared now.

To her relief, Elisabeth discovered the men had gone riding. James was, presumably, showing off all her handiwork on the estate and claiming it for his own.

She sat with Mrs. Odette Radclyffe in the sunny drawing room, the curtains drawn back to give a view of the verdant lawn. Odette, a tiny blond woman, fresh from her honeymoon, bubbled about the latest *on dits* from London society.

Elisabeth listened with half an ear, thinking about Mister Henry. The factual tidbits she'd gained added up rather worryingly. That her skin prickled and warmed when around him didn't bode well either. She couldn't trust him. It would be best for all concerned if he made a speedy recovery and left.

# CHAPTER THREE

Before Elisabeth could stop them, her two hounds bounded into the sickroom ahead of her. Sometimes they would just not listen. Jade, the bolder of the two, stuck her nose against Mister Henry's prone hand.

A muffled sound (was it a chuckle?) came from Henry's supposed sleeping form. She looked up and found him awake.

"Quite the welcoming committee," he remarked, stroking Jade's floppy ear. The hound licked him in reward for his efforts. Sapphire leapt up and demanded similar attention. Chuckling, he patted the second dog.

"They will wear you out." Elisabeth ordered the dogs down. They settled themselves comfortably on the rug beside the bed.

"They obey you," he remarked with a surprised tone.

"Most of the time," she admitted.

"They are yours?"

She flushed. "They belong to the lady of the house," she hedged. She hurried to change the subject. "Are you having difficulty sleeping?" she asked. The dark smudges under his eyes suggested it. He opened his mouth to reply but she interjected, "Be honest just this once, Mister Henry."

"I do not make a habit of lying," Henry informed her, his lips in a prudish twist.

"Good," she said. "Do you want something to help you sleep? There is some laudanum."

"A little of that would help," Henry confessed, adding with a wry grin, "I have never lied to you, Elisabeth."

She pinked at his familiar use of her Christian name. "That is true," she responded, tartly. "You have only withheld information."

"I have told you all I dare."

Unfazed by his ominous pause, she replied with a studied, careless air, "Now drink this up and try to get some sleep."

He tried to raise himself up. Seeing his difficulties, she propped up the meager pillows and he sank back in them to drink from the heavy mug that she held for him.

Finished, he lay down. She rearranged his bedclothes in an attempt to make him more comfortable. His groan halted her.

"Did I hurt you?" Worry creased her forehead.

He punched the mattress with a closed fist. "I hate being this weak. Damn this wound!"

"By the looks of it, you were lucky to survive it," she murmured. His eyes closed. Whether by cunning or a simple instinctive urge for a feminine touch, his hand nudged hers resting on the bed. She clasped it with her own, feeling its weight growing heavier as his breathing slowed and he slept.

Awed by the trust he had placed in her, she carefully slipped her hand from his. She rose, heading for the door. She patted her skirts, bidding her girls to follow. Sapphire leapt up immediately, but Jade remained behind.

"Oh, very well," she muttered, unreasonably churlish at the dog's defection. "You keep him company."

She returned to her guests, resolved to put Mister Henry from her mind for the rest of the day.

The next day, Elisabeth changed Mister Henry's bandages in silence. A scab had formed, fragile but there. She'd been firm in keeping all their interactions distant. She was his nursemaid, no more, no matter how often his heavy-lidded gaze beckoned her.

"And the other side?"

"You saw it yesterday." Grumbling, Mister Henry rolled onto his side, giving her a view of his back.

"I know," she murmured, unscrewing the cap of the small glass bottle she'd brought with her. "I brought you something to help with the itching." She poured a small amount into her hand.

"I can manage——" She smoothed it just above the old scar. "Oh, that feels good."

"It does?" She smoothed it in, her hand trembling. She skirted danger doing this for him. Soothing his irritated skin proved more intimate than she expected.

"Nice and cool. Soothing."

She laughed softly. "That is what the lotion is supposed to do." She handed him a gauze pad. "Here, place this over your wound and roll onto your stomach."

Their fingers brushed as he accepted the wad of linen from her. Her heartbeat pounded. She swallowed, watching him roll onto his stomach.

"Are you comfortable?"

"It is better than lying on my side," he confessed, his reply slightly muffled by the pillow. He lifted his head, turning so he could lie facing her.

She rather wished he hadn't. Unseen, she could hide her embarrassment at touching him so intimately. She focused on the lean lines of his muscles. *No, bad idea. He is your patient, not your husband.* She took a deep calming breath and tried not to think of him at all.

She examined the scab and the red marks of irritation around it. Her prime concern, outside of keeping her blushing under control from Mister Henry's intent gaze, was to be sure the scab would not soften and fester if she applied lotion.

Taking a smear of lotion, she smoothed it over the scab's edges, watching the skin absorb it. Another experimental smear appeared to result in no ill effects.

"Is there a problem?" Henry asked, low-voiced.

She darted a look at his face. "No, of course there is not. Should there be?"

"You are poking at my back and frowning. That would indicate a problem of some sort."

She flushed. "On the contrary, I was merely testing the scab to see if it would hold when softened." She darted another look at him. "It does. The bandages are irritating it. The lotion should help." She poured a small amount into her palm. "I am going to start now."

"You make it sound like it will hurt."

She huffed a breath of amused air. "You know it will not." Of course, it might hurt her heart. She rubbed her hands together, warming the lotion before applying it to his back.

With care, she worked the lotion into the scab making sure she didn't catch the edges and cause any new damage. The more lotion she applied, the softer, more pliable his skin grew.

At last satisfied she had done all she could for the scab itself, she turned her attention to the red area around it. It was not the red of infection, but caused by his scratching and the linen bandages moving over it.

Pouring more lotion into her hands, she smoothed it over his lower back. He moaned softly. At once, she jerked her hands away. "Did I hurt you?"

He chuckled. "On the contrary, Miss Elisabeth, you afforded me great pleasure." His voice grew husky. "Please, do not stop."

She should, of course. A few more moments to take care of his reddened skin and she would end this session before anything happened. She added more lotion to her hands and tentatively laid them on his back. She massaged the cream into the afflicted area, her touch light and gentle.

Mister Henry's eyes fluttered shut. She used more lotion, going beyond the irritation, across the rest of his lower back. That would be covered with bandages again too, and the lotion might help prevent friction from causing fresh problems.

He moaned again, more softly this time, so as not to startle her, she supposed. She ignored him this time, continuing to smooth the lotion into his back.

It was an oddly pleasant pastime, she acknowledged, but from her position on the chair, her shoulders ached. She rose, settling on the bed next to him, her hip nestled against his.

He lifted his head, looking back at her with an odd kind of wary expression. "Miss Elisabeth?"

She matched his cool tone. "Yes, Mister Henry?" Her hands resumed their gentle massage of his back and he subsided without further complaint.

Her hands roamed upward, feeling his muscles contract under her touch and then relax. He felt good under her hands, warm and strong. She almost forgot he was ill. Some hard balls of flesh refused to relax at her touch and intuitively she worked on them, rubbing her thumbs against them until they too seemed to dissolve.

"Dear God," Henry moaned, sounding drowsy. "Where did you learn to do this?"

She hadn't been taught at all. "Uh, my mistress likes to receive neck rubs once in a while. I assumed the same principles applied to your back."

"You are a clever girl, Miss Elisabeth." He grinned. "You would make some man happy one day, I am sure."

She sat up, realizing she had again exceeded the proper bounds. Where had her common sense fled to? "All done," she said. She placed a clean pad of linen over the old scar to protect it from catching on the bandage windings. "You may roll over." She held her hand over the pad to keep it in place.

"Give me . . . give me a moment." His amused expression seemed pained.

"What is it?" She leaned closer to catch his words.

His eyes closed, he didn't see how near she came to him. A flash of white teeth grazed his lower lip. "You see, Miss Elisabeth, your magic touch extends far beyond my back."

"I do not—" Puzzled, she stared at him.

His eyes opened, a dark sea of blue. He grinned to see her

so close to him. "I am sure you are far too respectable for this, Miss Elisabeth, but you have awoken a certain part of my anatomy, which is uniquely male and——"

"Oh!" She flew off the bed, not letting him finish. She retreated a few, horrified steps.

He remained still. "Miss Elisabeth, be calm. I am in no condition to ravish you. Give me but a moment and . . . and all signs of these . . . these feelings will subside."

She sat in her accustomed chair. "I only wished to give you ease. I did not intend——"

"Hush, my dear. I am sure you did not, and I see I have embarrassed you far more than by simply rolling over as you wished. I am sorry. I had wished to avoid that."

She wasn't altogether sure he'd wanted to do that at all. He seemed to enjoy seeing her discomforted. She laid out fresh bandages, busying her hands and her eyes elsewhere.

"I am ready. If you would hold those bandages?"

It felt too awkward to lean over from her seat, so she stood by the bed, bending over him. He rolled over by himself, and she caught a glimpse of a smile quickly hidden when he caught her eye.

"Mister Henry," she began, irritated.

"Please," he said, beaming, "I told you that you must call me Henry."

She ignored that and resumed bandaging him. "Why do you smile?"

His face transformed into a picture of innocence. "I always smile at pretty girls." He grinned, now unabashed. "It is my nature."

She gave a tired sigh and managed to smile back, playing his game for now. A nurse's duty included giving some amusement for the invalid, provided it didn't go too far. "Your nature?"

He grew grave. For a moment, she thought she had angered him but he replied with resignation. "I was once the kind of man mothers warn their daughters about and rightly so, but since—" He paused. "I have changed somewhat," he amended. His mouth smiled but his blue eyes did not. "However, I still appreciate a pretty girl."

She blushed. Her weariness forgotten, she longed to learn about this man's past. She didn't dare ask, afraid to awaken the dangerous rake he said he had been. Was he trying to lull her into a false sense of security so that he could—well, do whatever it is that rakes do to susceptible young maidens? "I cannot think you much changed then," she said, finished bandaging.

"Have you had much experience with men?" he asked dryly.

She flared, withdrawing. "What do you mean? What are you insinuating?"

His chuckling halted her. "All men—rakes, gentlemen, hermits—appreciate a pretty woman." She blushed at her naivety. His soft laughter resumed.

"I am sorry. I misunderstood your meaning." She pulled the covers up over him.

"I expect you will be glad to be rid of me," he drawled.

The lightheartedness transformed into something much more warmer and intimate. She struggled against it. "And miss all your delightful comments? Never!"

His sandy eyebrows rose in astonishment.

"And why not?" Elisabeth challenged.

"You want more than my comments." There was no mistaking the heat in his voice. She colored again under his intense gaze. "You want me."

"You?" she scoffed, pulling away.

He grabbed her wrist, hoisting himself into a sitting position. "Elisabeth," he murmured. "Why fight it?"

Booted footsteps sounded in the hallway. Shushing him, she gripped his hand tightly, aware that the stab of fear in her belly reflected in his face.

If she were found here with this man, a stranger . . . She would be undone and Mister Henry would be carted off to face justice for whatever crimes he had committed, at worst, and at best tossed out to fend for himself. She had no doubt of her brother's ire when it came to her reputation.

She focused on the door, willing the steps not to stop.

Henry turned over her arm and pressed his lips against her wrist. The heat of his mouth seemed to pulse through her veins, racing to her heart. Her breath caught in her throat.

She gazed down at his bent head, the blond hair tousled from the pillow. "The footman will deal with them," she murmured.

From outside the door, a man called. "Elisabeth!"

"Oh, Lord," she swore softly, recognizing the voice as her brother's.

She tried to ignore the tinge of fear in Henry's face. Had he also recognized the voice? Did he fear discovery too? Afire with curiosity, she didn't have time to find out. "I think I'd better deal with him before he tears down the wing."

She hastened out, smoothing her skirts and her hair. She had done nothing wrong, and yet appearance was everything. She left the door slightly ajar. She didn't want to be seen to be hiding anything.

Her brother and Radclyffe stood in the hallway. "We've been looking for you," James said.

She pasted on a smile. "I am right here, as you can see."

"Neglecting your guests," Radclyffe put in. "My wife in particular."

"I must apologize. I was under the impression she had gone upstairs to rest before dinner." She turned her bright smile to James, noting out of the corner of her eye that her girls had padded out into the hallway also. "I thought I'd continue with my spring cleaning while our guests were otherwise occupied."

"The country has made you most peculiar," her brother commented. She pulled a face at him and he grinned with mischief. "Lord Hampton is looking for you also. Will you not join us?"

She bobbed her head, closing the sickroom door. "Lead on. I'll not shirk my duty."

"I'd hope that attending Lord Hampton would be more than

duty, sister dear," James remarked as they walked toward the main part of the house.

Her cheeks burned. Hampton's attentions had been of polite interest, nothing more, since his earlier declaration. She found herself not caring that his interest had waned and wondered why.

It had become her habit to check on Mister Henry after dinner and before retiring to bed. Usually he was asleep—or pretended to be—when Elisabeth looked in on him.

She had no rationale for doing this. If his health took an abrupt turn for the worse, someone would fetch her. She'd ordered a footman to check on him hourly—with her unexpected guests, her limited staff were stretched to the limit.

She met the footman in the hallway. "Just checked on him, miss," he said. "He's well on the mend."

She understood his meaning at once. "And will be on his way soon enough. Get some rest, Charles." She waited until the footman was out of sight and continued down the corridor toward Mister Henry's room.

She opened the door and peeked in. One lamp remained lit, casting a golden glow upon his sleeping face. Now, when he was still, peaceful, she dared to look upon him and wonder what might have happened if her brother hadn't interrupted her.

She leaned against the door, dreaming of possibilities: that he would get well, reveal his identity, and offer for her. It seemed more than unlikely, improbable not knowing who he was.

"Come in, Miss Elisabeth," Mister Henry drawled, bringing her back to herself. "You're letting in a draft."

"I didn't mean to wake you." Instead of closing the door between them, she obeyed him and entered. Her heart thudded with unforeseen anticipation. "Are you in need of anything?"

"You really should not ask such leading questions." He delivered that crooked smile of his. She drew closer and his eyes widened. "You look enchanting tonight."

She glanced down at herself and cursed silently. Until tonight, she'd dressed plainly for him. Now she had come to him in all her evening regalia. The simple cut of the gown highlighted the white silk fabric and the fashionable lace trim. Too costly for a companion. "Thank you. My mistress likes me to look well during her evening suppers."

"She's entertaining guests?"

"You have heard them in the hallways." She sat on the bed beside him, hoping her proximity would distract him from the subject of guests. "Do you need something to help you sleep?"

"I am tired of sleeping." He rested his hand on her knee. "Will you stay and talk with me for a while?"

She let his hand remain, feeling the warmth seep through the thin fabric. "If you wish, Mister Henry."

He chuckled. "We seem to be going about this backwards, but isn't it time I learned all of your name, Miss Elisabeth?"

"And yours?" she challenged.

He grinned. "I wish I could oblige, but I cannot."

"Then I suggest we pick a different topic of conversation."

"Tell me, Miss Elisabeth, do you intend on being a companion all your life?"

She shrugged. "No doubt."

"You do not hope that one of the young men who fawns around your mistress will choose you instead?"

"Hardly." She laughed softly.

"You intend never to marry then?"

She shook her head. "I do not want to talk about this." She wasn't about to give him chapter and verse on her disastrous engagement. She rose, shaking off his hand. "Sleep, Mister Henry." She escaped the room.

The following morning with the household still abed, Elisabeth delivered her invalid his breakfast. He sat, propped up in bed, buffered by pillows. She noticed his grim visage. Were her early hours too much for him, or did another matter concern him? "The rest of the house will rise soon. You must eat your breakfast."

He glowered into the bowl of porridge, feeding himself. Between spoonfuls, he asked, "You know a Mr. Radclyffe?"

Ah, so it had been mention of her guests that had put him in a bad mood. Had he identified who had interrupted them yesterday? What did it mean? "Mr. Jeremy Radclyffe?" Henry nodded. "He is my former guardian."

He raised an eyebrow, but it didn't banish his frown. "A companion having a guardian of such stature?"

"I am honored to be included among his charges." She gnawed at the corner of her lip. He came close, too close, to discovering too much about her. "You have already guessed I am a gentlewoman, sir. Why then, should such a guardianship be so surprising?"

"I am surprised a man like Radclyffe would allow you to become a companion. Such an act must have destroyed your position in society."

She squirmed, trying to avoid the lie. "It is not yet known," she confessed. "I would appreciate it remaining that way."

"A career recently chosen, if I am to guess correctly from Radclyffe's bellowing." His voice held a note of concern. "Who was the other fellow?"

"My brother." She caught the disapproval flashing across his face. Her brother could afford to associate with Radclyffe and yet she had to work? Oh, dear. Things were starting to get remarkably complicated.

"And you have Lord Hampton interested in your person, despite your being a mere companion?" Henry persisted in his questions. "Have they come to rescue you from this pitiful fate of yours? And why do you resist it?"

She felt a chill settle into her bones. "For a gentleman who refuses to tell me anything, you ask far too many questions."

A short silence fell between them. A question burned at

her. She had to know. She had to know how close Henry was to discovering her identity. "Do you know them?"

"I have lived in London for a long time." Henry was a picture of studied nonchalance. "I thank you for not revealing my presence. It would have made things . . . unpleasant."

She shrugged off the compliment, searching for a clue in his face but found nothing to help her. She wished she knew why he didn't want her family or friends to know of his presence. If it hadn't been for his mentioning Harriet, she would suspect him of being the Viscount Langdon himself!

Perhaps it had been a well-publicized scandal and so everybody in London knew about it. Knowing it useless to further question him on it, she asked instead, "A long time in London? Goodness, how old are you?"

"Old." She laughed and he smiled in answer.

"You are not old," she said gaily. She felt freer in talking with him with no social conventions, no expectations, to bind them. So long as their identities remained a secret, she was safe. "You are . . . are" —she began to giggle— "why you are only middle-aged!"

"Middle-aged!" he spluttered. She laughed at his transparent attempt to look indignant, covering her mouth in an effort to quiet her chuckles. "I will have you know I am thirty-five."

She convulsed into more giggles. His look of patient humor might have appeared long-suffering were it not for the sparkle in his eyes.

She gasped out, "Thirty-five? You are old!"

He eyed her sternly. "If I am old, you are nothing but a baby."

She pouted, a smile lurking in the corners of her mouth. "I am not a baby," she said, playing his game. "You take that back."

He laughed but the laughter turned into a low cry of pain and he clutched at the bandages under the blanket. "You minx," he groaned. "Stop making me laugh."

She bit her lip. "I did not think . . ." she began. The apologetic tone left her voice and she became businesslike. "Let me see."

She drew down the blanket but he captured her hands, preventing her. They fit easily within his palms. She marveled at their potential strength, so carefully withheld.

"Leave it," he said.

"But it could have opened up again." She didn't remove her hands from his grasp but took them into her own, squeezing them a little. "Let me have a look, please."

"I am fine," he reassured her. He released her and pulled down the blanket, exposing the bandages, revealing more of his bare chest.

Her fingers trembling, she peeled back the bandages. The wound had improved since his enforced bed rest had begun. A healthy scab had formed, the weeping from infection gone. A tiny crack had formed across the surface, but there was no bleeding.

She smiled at him. "It is healing well."

"I told you it was fine."

She sat by his bed again. The way he looked at her made her head swim, every sense attuned to what he might say or do. She caught his gaze drawn to her décolletage as she bent over him.

She met his gaze and he winked—winked!—at her. She couldn't help it. She smirked back at him.

Backing away, she recalled her guests would soon be rising and expecting her to join them. "I have to go, Henry. The others will be awake soon." Leaving Jade with him, she hurried back to the main part of the house.

She wished she could dismiss thoughts of him just as easily, but he plagued her all through breakfast and during the walk up the hill with her guests. If Lord Hampton noticed her absentmindedness, he said nothing.

The edge of a memory stirred at the periphery of her mind. There was something about Henry, something she felt she ought to remember.

# CHAPTER FOUR

Flinging on a loose gown over her shift, Elisabeth raced down the servants' stairwell and headed for the west wing. She had a little time before dressing for dinner. She slipped into the sickroom and saw Mister Henry standing, gripping the bedpost.

She dashed forward as he weaved, putting a steadying arm about his shoulders.

He looked at her, taking a moment to focus, and another moment to realize how little she wore. She flushed, pulling her gown closer about her neck. "I came to check on you," she said in response to the amused question in his eyes. "If I hadn't, I am sure you'd be flat on your face by now."

"What would I do without you?" He sounded hoarse. His arm curved about her waist.

Warmth rushed through her, radiating from the heat of his arm through the thin fabric. She gave him a tight little smile. *I cannot show how he affects me.* "I cannot stay long," she said, gently disengaging herself.

He recaptured her. She ought to have moved farther away. Yet he was an opiate that brought her alive, instead of leaving her to sleep.

His thumb caressed her cheek. "I am tired of the sickbed." Despite his drawn features, she wondered what kind of bed he did want. "If I do not move, I will die in that bed." His gaze penetrated her defenses. "I no longer wish to die."

"I am glad to hear it." She sounded breathless.

His intent gaze didn't waver. "Help me."

"But your wound . . ." Her protest sounded weak to her ears. She bowed her head. "Very well," she said. "We shall try it."

He took one step and wavered. His hold tightened, gathering her robe into a tight-fisted grip. It revealed more of her, yet he seemed resolved to ignore her temptations and walk on his own. She held her breath, aware of their intimacy.

"Let's walk," Henry grated through gritted teeth.

They shuffled forward a few steps. He leaned heavily against her and she braced each step she took. They negotiated a turn. He let out an involuntary groan. She glanced at him, but he dismissed her concerns with a wave.

"Back to bed," she declared.

He didn't argue, slumping against her. She maneuvered him back into bed, swinging his legs around, pulling up the covers. He grunted, his eyes shut tight. "I think," he said through gritted teeth, "it has opened again."

Wincing in sympathy, she pulled back the covers and examined the wound. "Yes, it has broken open a little. Do not worry, Mister Henry, it will heal."

"It better," he ground out. His pained breaths came quick and fast. She took hold of his fist and massaged the back of it, not knowing what else to do.

At length, he relaxed, his fingers unfurling. "My pardon, Miss Elisabeth. I did not mean to be so surly."

She pinked under his warm gaze and readjusted the ties of her gown. "I understand the frustration, Mister Henry."

"Yes, I believe you do," he whispered.

Shivering at the hint of the forbidden in his soft, husky voice, she rose, giving a perfunctory check of the bedside table, making sure he would not want for anything before leaving.

He stirred her blood too much. She should hand off her

nursing duties to another, yet she felt no desire to put another at risk of scandal. Sighing, she hurried to change for dinner.

Henry had almost completely recovered by the week's end, doing small odd jobs suitable for a convalescent, despite her protests. He spent most of his time in the stables, polishing tack or grooming horses. Both her girls had deserted her for him, padding after him with big soulful eyes.

She dismissed the notion of following suit. She wasn't about to moon after him, when he was sure to leave soon. He still tired too quickly to make any journey possible, he claimed. She wondered why he delayed, when each day brought him closer to exposure. Closer to her.

She stepped into the back courtyard, a parasol slung over her arm. Everyone waited on the front lawn for their afternoon stroll, but she'd been drawn here, having found his room empty.

A movement in the stable doorway caught her eye. Henry approached, leading her horse.

Her eyes widened. He didn't wear a shirt. He stopped at the sight of her, but with a small grin, resumed walking toward her.

Even though she'd seen his bare chest before, the sight of it outside his sickroom and in broad daylight unsettled her for reasons she didn't care to examine. His compact figure stood slightly taller than she expected. Well-made for a "middle-aged" man, he showed no sign of gout or overeating, the ripple of muscle in arm and shoulder softened by his recent illness. Bandages masked his abdomen, for she'd insisted he keep it covered while he worked.

He inclined his head in acknowledgment of her silent examination. "Shall I pull up the bucket for you?" he asked, dropping her mare's reins.

She glanced around and saw he meant from the well nearby. He didn't wait for her reply but reached for the rope.

She laid her gloved hand on his forearm, halting him. "Mister Henry, that is not necessary. Surely it will be too much of a strain?"

He shook his head, delivering a disarming smile. "I am almost completely recovered." Releasing him, she watched him haul the bucket out of the well's depths, his muscles contracting and stretching. He proved his words, a light sweat breaking on his brow. He set the sloshing bucket at her feet.

She glanced down at her watery prize. "You will be leaving us soon." She sounded subdued. What was wrong with her?

His suddenly hooded gaze regarded her. "Perhaps."

"What do you mean by that?"

"You have done so much for me. I do not feel as if the debt has been repaid."

"Nonsense." She smiled. Her heart palpitated with the sorrow of losing him soon. Too soon. "It's the basic laws of hospitality."

He leaned against the lip of the well. "I must make my penance." He regarded her, arms folded. "Are you happy here?"

She blinked, startled at the real concern in his voice. Her feet became interesting items to peruse. She had to keep up the deception. What if he discovered her identity and ruined her reputation? "Happy? Why do you ask?"

He shrugged, looking uncomfortable. "I have talked to the servants. They all refuse to speak of your employer. Is she that much of a dragon?"

A burst of surprised laughter sprang from her lips. "I hope not! The people here are very loyal, Henry, including me."

"So you are happy."

Why did he care, now, when he was leaving her? If he cared, he would stay, but that was impossible.

"Henry, we all make do with what we have. I am happy enough. There is a . . ." She searched for the right word. "There is a security in living in the country that the city does not provide."

Good grief. He may be dressed, or undressed, as a servant, in public, but she should not be so familiar. "Uh, I mean, Mister Henry. Now, please get out of sight before someone sees you."

"Nobody thinks of me as anything but a servant, Miss Elisabeth." He smiled and bowed with mock servility. He picked up the reins and returned to the stables. She watched him for a moment, admiring his newfound health, before heading back inside.

She'd taken no more than a step, when Hampton appeared. "Elisabeth!" he exclaimed. "We have been waiting for you!"

She shot a frantic glance over her shoulder and found the courtyard bare. It appeared Hampton hadn't seen her Mister Henry. She gave a soft laugh of relief. "I had to check on something before I left," she said, accepting his arm.

He accepted her excuse, drawing her closer. "I understand the delights of your grandfather's folly awaits?"

"Truly, it's too beautiful to be called a folly, although it's in a sad state of disrepair at present."

They rejoined the others and Hampton persisted in remaining by her side, and she found that she didn't mind him so much. She nodded at his wildlife observations, but her mind ran a different course.

Mister Henry had said he remained as a penance. A penance for what? Could she help him? She required facts. She hoped he would agree with her.

"Miss Elisabeth?" Hampton prompted.

Blinking, she realized it was not the first time he wished her attention. She turned to apologize. Her booted toe connected with something solid. Arms flailing, she reached out to him, trying to regain her balance.

With surprising swiftness, he scooped her up in his arms. She hugged his neck, her muddied boots swinging in air.

She gazed at him, watching his emotions flit across his face, his initial concern transforming into an unreadable expression.

Mister Henry looked at her like that, sometimes, when he thought she wasn't watching.

It was more disturbing to recognize Hampton wanted her, in the way that Henry did, much more than realizing she understood and translated such expressions.

She managed a shaky laugh. "Thank you." She swallowed. "I think you can put me down now."

His cheeks turning a fiery red, he set her upon her feet. The others, walking ahead, had missed the entire interchange.

She rallied her thoughts and decided it would be safest to tease him. "That was quite the rescue. I thought you were going to be dreadfully romantic and carry me off!"

Her light teasing seemed to relax him. "Do not think the thought had not occurred to me," said Hampton, chuckling. "Would you want me to?"

"Do not be ridiculous!" she rebuffed him. Hampton drooped. She continued brightly, "Why, if you were going to carry me off, it would have to be done with style! Not just at the drop of a hat." She grew dramatic, hushed. "It would have to be at the very dead of night! You would have a coach and four waiting. . . ."

Hampton grinned, his face mischievous, a laughing light in his eyes. "I shall see to it, ma'am," he said, bowing low over her hand and kissing it.

"Pray do, my lord," she said, aware of a serious undercurrent in their funning. She ignored it, letting loose a theatrical sigh.

He laughed. "Elisabeth, you are the most absurd creature!"

"If it pleases, my lord," she replied in an arch manner. She accepted his proffered arm and they continued on their ramble, the balance restored.


Henry reclined on the bed, watching as Elisabeth entered her bedroom. He schooled his features to conceal his amusement at her shock at seeing him in forbidden territory.

"What are you doing here?" she hissed at him, clutching at the door handle behind her, looking ready to bolt.

How quickly shock turns to anger, he thought, giving her a devil-may-care smile. He admired the way her bosom heaved. "I had no choice."

"What do you mean?"

"I thought I would explore your fine house, and was surprised by your early return," he replied in a low voice. "I did not care to be discovered by your guests. You have a fine room for a companion, Miss Stockwell."

He didn't hide the loathing in his voice in speaking her true name. Damn the minx! The last thing he needed was another entanglement with *them*. If he hadn't come across the letters on her desk just moments ago, he'd never have learned the truth, although he'd had his suspicions with the combined presence of that damnable Radclyffe and his brother-in-law Hampton.

She raised her chin, a slight tremble the only sign of apprehension. "What have you got against my family?"

He raised an eyebrow. So she would confront him head on then? "Nothing. It is the company you keep I dislike."

"Who? The Radclyffes? I do not understand. They are perfectly respectable." Her forehead puckered into a frown. "Does this have something to do with your scandal?"

"Do not forget your pretty beau, Lord Hampton." He relaxed his clenched hands. He didn't like how she seemed to bloom under that man's attentions. But she was a Stockwell, and not for him.

"He's not my—" she began, heated.

Relief jolted through him, but he couldn't stop now. It had to end here. For her sake.

"I suppose you have told him everything? Is he not your knight in shining armor? I saw how you hang upon him." He hung his head, holding his breath, although surely if Hampton knew about his presence, he'd be out on his rear, or dead, by now.

"Everything?" She clasped her hands together as if to plead with him to speak plainly. "If you mean does he know you are here, no, he does not."

He looked up, hopeful. "Then he knows nothing."

She frowned. "I daresay he knows a good deal more than you have cared to tell me, Henry." Their eyes met. He concealed a smile. She had consciously dropped the "Mister."

She blushed and babbled on. "I have not been to London for two years and I have no interest in any gossip from there. The only scandal I can possibly think of involving the Radclyffes happened just before their recent marriage, but that was all kept very quiet. From me at least. All I know was that there was a duel." Her eyes widened. "A duel, a scandal, involving a lady."

"Do you know who the duel was with?" he murmured. He wished he could read her mind. Her reaction could be deadly to him. He prayed she wouldn't overreact—that would bring Hampton and Radclyffe, and they would exact their revenge.

"Yes," she replied, her tone chilly. "You are he?"

"Yes." He couldn't bear to say more.

"Lord Langdon?"

His eyelids lowered, but not before he saw the torrent of mixed emotions in her eyes. "Yes." He saw her hands tremble and clench together. Yes, she hated him for what he had done, this pretty, naive woman. He sensed her regard for him, however slight it must have been, swept away by this newfound knowledge.

"My God," she whispered. She stood, irresolute and took a deep breath. He tensed, certain she would cry out an alarm. Instead, she spoke with effort. "All you did was avoid the wrath of my family's friends. That makes me much relieved."

"It does?" How could she speak so calmly of such a despicable act?

"You see," she confessed, "I thought that despite your talk of scandal you had maybe broken the law."

"Dueling is not exactly legal, Miss Stockwell."

This didn't appear to faze her one whit. "Tell me, Henry," she asked, gazing down at him, "is this particular Stockwell going to continue to be your enemy?"

*Ah, here it comes. The conditions.* His reply was pitched low. "Only if you betray me."

"I will not," she promised. "But you must promise you will not plague my friends when you return to London."

"I promise," he vowed, solemn. "That part of my life is over. I am no longer the 'dreadful' man most mamas labeled me."

"Aren't you?" She sounded hurt beneath her bravado.

"Elisabeth . . ."

The storm broke. "Stop saying my name, sir!"

He couldn't help it. Her name was a beseeching prayer, a balm to soothe her anger, his torment. "I will take the blame, if you wish. I will not mention—"

She raised a hand, warding him off.

He swallowed. "I am not a saint. There is not much I—" He rubbed his hand across his forehead. He hadn't even bedded her. Why was it this difficult? "It is nothing."

"Nothing?" Tears swam in her voice, where he had anticipated fury.

He wanted to reach out, draw her in and comfort her, but he remained motionless. He was not used to comforting. These feelings welling up within him scared him. "The least I can do is be honorable now, from this moment on. No one shall ever know I was here."

The silence between them grew long. He met her searching gaze and held it. He wanted her to believe it when he didn't dare believe in himself. Oh, he would keep their little secret, but honor? It had been so long since he'd held to that principle. That way led to disaster.

"I know." That acknowledgment surprised him as much as it seemed to surprise her.

She turned, missing her look of tenderness mirrored on his face. Her willingness to forgive him for these crimes he had committed against her friends, and above all those against her, touched a part of him he thought had died long ago.

He relaxed. "You are a good soul, Elisabeth."

"I am glad you think so." He watched her bosom heave in agitation. "You must leave now," she told him, in all seriousness.

Certainly he had to leave her boudoir before somebody discovered them together, but he had the strong suspicion she meant more than that.

"I will leave when you have gone to dinner. I shall not trouble you further."

Her pretty mouth opened and closed. So she wanted to protest his departure, did she? "Henry . . ." Her voice threatened to rise from her apparent conflict in how to behave.

Someone rapped on her door. "Elisabeth?" James called through the door. "Who are you talking to?"

"Myself," she called, gesturing at Henry to hide.

*Where?* he mouthed to her.

"Anywhere," she whispered, raising her voice to add, "It helps me decide what to wear!"

"The country has addled your wits, sister," James responded. "See you downstairs."

He watched her agitated silence until her concern broke free.

"You have to leave," she said. "Now. I have to change for dinner."

"I cannot walk out of that door," he reasoned, smiling, although his heart felt heavy. "What if your brother saw me? How would you explain that?"

"Then you must hide in the closet until we have all gone down to dinner." She pinned him with a glare. "I trust you can find your way back?"

He restrained a chuckle, watching her flit across the room and fling open the door leading to the closet. He spied her maid hovering within. "What of your maid? She might talk, having seen me here."

"She won't say anything, provided you keep your hands off her."

He ignored her waspish tone, amused that she had been stung to jealousy so quickly. He stepped into the room, turning as she shut the door. He blocked her. She looked up at him, frightened and angry. "I would not harm a hair on her head," he said, his voice low. "I am a changed man. I have sworn it."

As if to bely his statement, he leaned forward and kissed her. He meant it to be simple, chaste, but she softened beneath him, a silent offering. He took it, teasing her innocence with his experienced mouth.

Her cheeks flushed a pleasing red. He wanted to kiss her again, kiss her senseless . . . but he had promised honor and a gentleman would not take advantage.

He stepped into the spacious closet, allowing her to close the door between them, reflecting on this. If he pressed his ear to the door, he might be fortunate enough to hear the soft susurration of clothing being shed from skin he longed to caress.

Instead, he retreated farther from the door. His fingertips caressed his lips and then rubbed out all traces of her soft mouth. There were broader barriers between them now. He had no chance to win her affections. She had been polite, gentle, even loving, but Miss Stockwell would surely have nothing to do with him in the future.

Elisabeth pleaded a headache and took to her bed soon after dinner. Why hadn't she screamed or called for help? This man who had attacked her dear friends, the Radclyffes, could have done the same to her at any time. Why hadn't she defended herself?

She gripped the end of her pillow. She had done something, she had let him off the hook. She promised not to reveal him if he didn't approach the Radclyffes.

She bit her lip, restraining a sigh. She tried to think of anything else but Mister Henry—Lord Langdon she must now think of him.

It didn't work. Her thoughts returned to him again and again. Mister Henry was Lord Langdon, the irredeemable rake? He'd gone far beyond her initial "slightly roguish" impression. Everything pointed to his rakishness, the ease with which he'd just kissed her. He could destroy her with a single word.

She couldn't deny the truth, she had been closeted with him, frequently alone. The scandal would ruin her forever. How foolish she was! Did she really expect him to keep the whole affair a secret and to keep away from the Radclyffes!

Langdon had not been as she imagined him. Not a horrible person, but unexpectedly gentle and loving. Perhaps gossip distorted the facts, or was it his charm? Perhaps the truth would redeem her error. There was only one person she could ask.

She cornered Lord Hampton the following morning, inviting him out into the garden. She quelled her concerns at his leaping at the opportunity. "My lord, I have been thinking."

Hampton matched his pace with hers. "What problem is filling your pretty head now?"

She tried to keep her tone casual. "I was thinking about that awful scandal that surrounded your sister's wedding. I have discovered the villain's name."

"Have you, by God." Hampton stopped and glared at her. "And what right had you to stick your nose into things better left untouched?"

She prickled. "I was not prying, my lord. My own servants informed me. I do not understand why it was kept from me. Not even my brother would tell and he is the worst gossip I know!"

He gave a short laugh before shaking his head. "It is in

the past, Elisabeth dear. I do not think the Radclyffes would appreciate talk of it surfacing again. I know I do not."

"But my lord," she protested, "you should know that I am not some old gossip who will spread it all over the country! Could you not at least tell me why I had to be protected from even hearing of it?"

"I had thought such London gossip was above you," Hampton remarked. She knew he stalled.

"Usually, yet this involves friends. Perhaps I am not close enough to them to know these things?" She added the last with a touch of peevishness.

He broke into a smile. "It was never talked about, m'dear, because of some scare that occurred before the wedding. Not at all suitable for young ladies' ears."

"What scare?" she pressed. "Was this Langdon so awful?"

"Awful? Surely you've heard of his reputation. He was a cad, a rogue, and a drunken lecher to boot!" Hampton's fair skin darkened with rage. "He cheated at the duel—turned and fired before it was time. When he missed, they fell to using swords."

This was her Henry? Hard and brutal? She went cold, struggling to maintain her composure. "James said that they fought over a point of honor. This was Odette?"

"Yes, they fought over my sister, but Radclyffe was fighting for her honor."

"Her honor?" She discreetly massaged her temple. She'd been in the company of a man who regularly, and most recently, compromised a woman's honor.

"See," Hampton had not missed the signs of her distress, "I have shocked you." He leaned toward her, his voice urgent. "I do not wish anything further said, for continued talk will exaggerate matters and utterly ruin my dear sister's reputation."

Her thoughts swirled. Poor Odette! "Did he . . . did he . . ."

"No, he did not," Hampton replied, understanding her unspoken question. "Odette has always hated him, for he seduced one of her friends when she was younger. She will never forgive him for that. But here I am rattling on. You must not say anything about the scandal to anyone, d'you hear?"

"Of course not, my lord." She hid the blow of this news behind pretended gaiety. Hampton could not know his enemy had slept under the same roof. Nobody could! "You can trust me not to tell anyone you have been gossiping."

"Elisabeth! You are a minx!"

She laughed at his discomfort and changed the subject, not trusting herself to speak further of the duplicitous and desirable Lord Langdon. She had grown fond of him, but his true identity changed everything. He was the worst of all rakes— but hadn't he declared that was all in the past? It remained to be seen if he would revert to form and destroy her in the process. In the meantime, she would have to guard herself carefully against him.

# CHAPTER FIVE

Her footsteps drew her to Mister Henry's room. She wondered if he'd taken her hint and left.

The bed appeared unslept in. Pulling open the bedside table drawer, she saw his pistol was gone. In its place lay a pouch and a folded paper.

With trembling fingers, she unfolded the note and read it. *I do not expect to fulfill my penance with coin,* the note began without preamble, *but the risk grows too great to enjoy your hospitality further. I wish you happiness, Miss Elisabeth. Do with this gift as you wish, but I hope you keep these coin safe against a day when you may have need of it.*

She dropped the note back into the drawer and slammed it shut. Raising a hand to her forehead, she inhaled a shaky breath.

Gone. She should feel relieved. Yet she wished they'd made a truce between them at the last, rather than a kiss that challenged her soul. She could do nothing about that now. Her fingertips brushed her lips.

She left the west wing and headed to the breakfast room. "My lord!" She barely kept the surprise out of her voice. Hampton sat alone at the table. She hesitated in the doorway. It would not do to breakfast alone with him.

"You look much refreshed, Miss Stockwell," Hampton remarked, carelessly waving her to a seat with a greasy fork.

She took an uneasy step forward. "Where is everyone?"

"My sister and Radclyffe have already breakfasted. Your lackadaisical brother has not yet come downstairs."

"I am sorry I am so late." She headed for the sideboard. Hampton had almost finished. Surely there would be no harm in being together for such a short period. "However, I am glad I am not as late as my brother!"

"He still keeps London hours. Although what there is to do here in the small hours of the morning, I cannot even begin to think." He resumed eating.

She directed him a queer look. She knew very well what he and her brother did after everyone retired. Whether they succeeded in catching a village girl was quite another thing.

Hampton lingered after he had finished eating, chatting about his stay at Stockwell House. He made it easy for her to respond in the same way. When she rose from the table, Hampton rose too, reaching for a walking stick of dark mahogany.

She raised a curious eyebrow. "That looks familiar."

"I believe it was your father's. Stockwell loaned it to me last night. Said it gave my limp some character."

"Did it?" She flung the question over her shoulder as she walked toward the door.

"Tell me what you think." His request made her turn and observe him. He hobbled toward her, leaning heavily upon the stick.

She allowed a small smile to escape. "Have you been in the wars then?"

Hampton gave a somber nod, a mischievous glint in his eye. "Saved my commander, don't you know." He slapped his thigh. "Took a bullet for him."

"A little dishonorable, is it not?" She frowned. "The men who fought at Waterloo . . ."

"Now, Elisabeth." Hampton extended a placating hand. "I was just making it up on the spur of the moment."

"I should hope so, my lord." She turned, dismissing him, finding his familiar use of her name disturbing. "What did happen?"

"I, ah, cracked my knee on the corner of a table last night." Hampton flushed. "Your brother and I had a bit to drink before we left, I fear. It will be well enough in a few days."

"You should be more careful, my lord." She headed for what she still thought of as her father's study.

"Elisabeth?" Hampton called after her. "Miss Stockwell?" he persisted. She turned to face him, finding him in the doorway. "You promised me a game of chess."

"It is not polite to remind a lady of her promises," she replied, frowning. "I need to see the estate's books."

"Your brother has been here, I am sure he has—"

She interrupted him. "I am sure that Mr. Dean attempted to focus my brother's interest, but it will have been in vain." She smoothed a vagrant curl of hair, abandoning her bitterness. "It will take me but an hour. Where shall I find you?"

Hampton beamed. "I will be in the library."

"Why not the solarium? It has a much sunnier aspect—and it will give you something to look at."

She dawdled over the books for as long as she dared before going in search of Hampton.

She found him in the solarium. He rested at ease in a wicker chair, one leg extended, his stick in hand. She paused on the threshold, watching him gaze out at the gardens beyond the house. Although he faced three-quarters away from her, she saw his down-turned mouth.

"Penny for your thoughts?" She took a tentative step forward. "Musing on how I am going to thrash you at chess?"

A smile transformed Hampton's face. Affable once more, he returned, "As I recall, you were unable to win a single match against me at Christmas."

"I was being kind." The corner of her mouth twitched from hiding a smile. Here was a man she did not need to be afraid of. He felt—safe. "You were so down, I had to let you win to cheer you up!"

He faced away to the gardens. "I was thinking of her."

She sat in the white wicker chair opposite him. "Lady Sophie?" she asked in a quiet voice, unwilling to intrude.

He straightened his shoulders. "When I think of what a fool I was over her, the time I wasted pursuing her . . ."

"You were not to know your interest would not be returned," she murmured.

"True." Hampton gave a slight nod in acknowledgment. He leaned forward, his legs shifting to accommodate the change in position. "Miss Stockwell—Elisabeth—those few short weeks we spent together last Christmas were the happiest since I was a little boy."

"That is because we played like children," she reminded him with a jaunty air. "Those snow fights for instance!"

"I recall your brother trying to stuff snow down your back—"

"Most impolite of him." She bit back another grin.

"Even though it was in retaliation," Hampton continued, his green eyes glinting with the memory, "I came to your rescue."

Her eyes narrowed. "You carried me off over your shoulder and dumped me into the nearest snowbank. You and James were in cahoots!"

Hampton chuckled. "That is what I let you think. Shall I tell you now my true motivation?" She nodded, chewing the corner of her lip. "You had teased me like you would a brother; you flirted—" At her peremptory head-shaking, he continued, "You flirted, even if you did not realize it, you made my heart light again. I carried you off because I wanted to, because it was the only excuse I could find to hold you in my arms."

She thought back. "When you helped me out of the snow . . ."

"You were cursing and carrying on in a most unladylike way, until you looked up and saw my face."

She nodded, recalling that tender look. She'd thought it only concern. It seemed impossible Hampton desired her, then and now. Reflecting, she realized she hadn't wanted to see it.

"I held you perhaps a moment too long than would be conventionally required."

"I believe I was getting my breath back." Her gaze dropped to her lap. Her knuckles were white. With effort, she relaxed her grip. She didn't dare look up.

"Nothing more was said then. I could see you were confused and uncertain."

"I thought I had imagined things, my lord," she murmured.

Hampton rose and knelt by her side, ignoring the fact he rested on his bad knee. He took her hands in his. "My dear Elisabeth, I have thought of you as a sister, but I cannot think of you as that any longer."

She extricated her hands. "My lord, this is too sudden. You cannot, must not, make any declarations yet. It is too soon."

"If I wait?"

She gave a small, rueful smile. "I cannot answer to that. You must be patient with me."

"After that disastrous near-engagement, I cannot say I blame you." Hampton returned to his chair, unaware of her stiffening with disliked memories. "You do not love me? Just a little?"

"I am fond of you, Hampton, but I have never allowed myself to think of love." *Liar,* a little voice in her brain declared. *Why were you blushing when that rake Langdon kissed you?*

Leaning forward, Hampton pursued his topic. "Elisabeth, you are too young to consider yourself an old maid. You must come to London. Burying yourself in the country has not been good for your state of mind."

"Move from one marriage market to another?" Her lip curled. "Hampton, I am tired of being looked over as someone who, perhaps, might do as a wife."

He shook his head. "You would more than do for anyone. The Radclyffes and I are leaving on the morrow. How can I woo you from such a distance? If my sister asks, as I am sure she will, you must come. There will be no setting you up for the highest bidder, I promise you. Come to London and enjoy yourself."

She must go, if she were to give Hampton a fair chance at her heart. "Very well. If your sister asks, I will accept." She smiled brightly. "How about that game of chess?"

Hampton grinned back, victorious for the moment. "As long as you do not let me win."

She chuckled. "Never question a lady's strategy, my lord," she admonished, setting out the ivory pieces.

That evening after dinner, Mrs. Radclyffe and Elisabeth progressed to the drawing room, while the men remained in the dining room. Mrs. Radclyffe opened the conversation with caution. "I noticed you and my brother were much together today."

Elisabeth looked up from her needlework. *I didn't have a patient to tend to.* "Oh, Odette, it was not my intention to slight you!" she protested, aware that she and Odette had picked flowers together in the garden that afternoon. It could also not be denied that Hampton had also been in constant attendance.

"Never mind about that, my dear," Odette soothed, her blue eyes twinkling. "I was hoping you would accept my invitation to come stay with us in London. That way I get to see you more often, and besides," she leaned forward to confide, "you cannot hide yourself in the country any longer."

"I should very much like to visit," Elisabeth replied, choosing to ignore the echo of Hampton's words.

The door opened, the men entering with a burst of laughter. She noted the meaningful expression on Odette's face as Hampton came to sit by her. Careful not to let the exchange affect her own friendly countenance, she teased Hampton to discover his joke.

Radclyffe swiftly followed up his wife's invitation to Elisabeth to come stay with them in London and her brother magnanimously gave his approval.

There seemed little choice. She accepted the invitation, her heart leaping at a sudden thought. What if Langdon dared show his face in London? What if they met? If he showed up in London, well, she'd just have to make sure he had kept his promise to change, otherwise her stay would be most unpleasant!

Elisabeth spent her second night in London attending Fanny Syndersham's debut ball, a rousing success. She rediscovered an old acquaintance, Mr. Bradshaw, the only gentleman thus far who deigned to dance with her that night. When the dance ended, he led her toward Mrs. Radclyffe, making slow progress through the crowd.

To stop the conversation from stalling, she remarked, "It has been so long since I have seen any of my friends from London. Do you suppose I shall see any here?"

"A few of them, I should think. They would all be wed by now. We shall have to discover their new cognomens," came Bradshaw's unthinking reply. "If they are not, this would be their fourth Season out. Their mamas must be getting frantic over their little darlings unmarried state."

"I daresay," she replied, stung by the reminder.

"Oh, Miss Stockwell!" Bradshaw realized his error. "I did not mean you! After all, you have been away in the country. How could you be included in that?"

"Please, Mr. Bradshaw, do not apologize. If I still had a mother, she would be fretting over me as well."

Without warning, Bradshaw walked faster, even to the extent of using his elbows to push through the crowd.

"What is it, Mr. Bradshaw? Why do we go so fast?" She caught up her skirt before she tripped.

Lord Langdon appeared at her escort's side, answering her question. Bradshaw did not pause, but she slipped her arm free of his, bringing their flight to a halt. She would not run from him like a coward.

Seeing Lord Langdon here in full evening dress dispelled a vision of a sweaty, shirtless Mister Henry. He looked cool, immaculate, and in control. She ignored Bradshaw's prodding and her own qualms. This Lord Langdon seemed nothing like her Mister Henry. Would his promises hold?

Bradshaw turned back to her in consternation. "Miss Stockwell," he insisted, "I am sure the Radclyffes are waiting."

Langdon sketched a short bow. "Miss Stockwell, may I have the pleasure of being your partner in the next dance?"

"Miss Stockwell is with me, my lord," interceded Bradshaw, a stubborn cast on his pleasant face.

"Lord Langdon, I am surprised to see you here," she said, refusing to cut the man. Not yet. Not until she knew for sure. "Are you not the dreadful man all the ladies of London whisper so fearfully about?"

"As it happens, I am a friend of Miss Syndersham's uncle," Langdon replied, his coolness indicative that he remained unperturbed at her insult. "Do I take it you do not wish to dance with me?"

If she did not accept this dance she would have to sit out the remainder of the evening. "I am not afraid of you, Lord Langdon." She extended her gloved hand to be accepted into his.

He raised her gloved hand to his lips. "You should be," he murmured.

Her heart pounding, she stood her ground. She bearded the lion in his own den, it seemed, but in such a public venue it would be a small risk.

"Pray excuse us, sir," Langdon said to Bradshaw as he swept Elisabeth away and onto the dance floor.

"Have you ever danced the waltz, Miss Stockwell?" he asked, a warm kindness in his voice, offering her a last chance to escape his clutches.

Too late, she recognized the introductory music. A waltz? How fortunate she was not some naive miss who needed permission to dance it! "Of course, my lord," she replied, smoothing down the pale blue silk of her high-waisted gown, adding, "as long as the tempo is not too fast."

Langdon guided her toward the center of the ballroom floor where they could dance at a slower pace. "You are beautiful tonight, Elisabeth." His arm slid about her waist, drawing her close to him, indeed so close their bodies touched. His hand slid lower.

Indignant, she reached behind her and pried his arm loose. "Do not even think of putting it back," she warned, glaring at him.

"As if I would dare to, Miss Stockwell," he replied, "having been most firmly put in my place!"

She caught the amused twitch of his lips, a hint of the Mister Henry she knew. She couldn't help but echo it. "It is about time somebody did."

"Somebody has, my dear," returned Langdon dryly. "Our good friend, Mr. Radclyffe."

"Yes, I have heard all about it." He remained silent. "Indeed," she continued, seeing he wasn't about to tell his side of the scandal, "I begin to wonder why I am dancing with you at all, considering not only your reputation, but your heinous conduct toward my friends."

"I wonder the same thing myself," he said, all warmth gone.

She gazed at him, examining his features. "You do not deny these things I have heard of you?" she asked, incredulous, wanting to stir some reaction from him. "You abused Mrs. Radclyffe, almost killed her husband! You are a criminal, sir!"

"And yet you dance with me." His eyes glittered with anger. "I was not aware, Miss Stockwell, that you were one of those creatures who relish flirting with dangerous men."

Incensed, she rose to his bait. "This is no flirtation, my lord! I merely wish to discover the truth!"

His grasp loosened and their bodies drifted farther apart. "I see we are no longer friends. You condemn me for my past, for which I am unable to make amends. I can only strive to become a better man."

"How can I know this to be true?" she murmured, avoiding his gaze.

"You will have to find that out for yourself," he replied gravely. "Trust to your own heart."

She would not dare do that. She must find a way to reveal his duplicity. She forced a brighter note into her next words as they twirled around. "It must be wonderful to be back in England after all this time."

"What the deuce do you mean?" he asked, missing a step. "I have been in England for weeks and you know it!"

"You have? I thought you returned only this week," she said, all innocence.

"You have kept my secret?" He shook his head in disbelief.

She responded with honesty. It was the only way she knew. "My lord, I cannot call you my friend, at this instant, but neither can I call you my enemy. There is no reason to let your secret be known." She blinked up at him. They both knew the damage to her own reputation if their rustic adventure were discovered.

"I see." He gazed over the top of her head, the brief warmth of their connection broken. "It is as much your secret as it is mine. It would not do for it to be known that you are little more than an adventuress."

"How dare you, sir!" Her heart palpitated. Was he threatening to reveal everything? "You would not!"

He disengaged himself entirely and bowed before her. "No, Miss Stockwell, I would not. The sad thing is you believe I will."

He walked away, leaving her standing alone in the middle of the ballroom. Her hands clenched into fists, she headed back toward the Radclyffes, awkwardly sidestepping the waltzing figures, aware of her humiliation at being so abandoned.

Hampton intercepted her, tucking her arm into his and

guiding her from the floor. "What were you doing with that man Langdon?" he demanded, glaring at her.

"Dancing," she replied, knowing it infuriated him. "Let us discuss this later, my lord, please."

"We shall do no such thing." Hampton returned her to the disapproving Radclyffes seated against the wall.

"Elisabeth, I hope you can explain yourself." Radclyffe's quiet voice declared, his visage grim.

"Oh, Elisabeth! How could you dance with that horrid man!" Odette twisted an almost shredded handkerchief.

She kept her voice calm. "He asked me to dance."

"You should have refused." Odette dabbed at her eyes. "Mr. Bradshaw gave you the opportunity. Why did you not take it?"

She lowered her gaze. "Mr. Bradshaw has spoken with you?"

"He felt it was his duty to speak to us," Radclyffe informed her. "Please answer my wife's question."

"I agreed to dance with him because I refuse to show I have any fear of him." She sensed her friends would never be ready to discover the truth of her connection with him, or that she even dared to carry out an independent investigation into the man to see if her reputation would remain secure.

"You should have cut him!" Odette declared, her voice harsh with fear. "The *ton* of London society may welcome back Langdon but we shall not!"

"I do not wish to make him my enemy." She didn't know how she remained so calm with her friends' hysterics, the memory of Henry's jeering words, and the warmth of his touch.

"Good God!" Hampton's face flushed dark red, his fair coloring making it more prominent. "He is your enemy already! Have I not told you that the man is a fiend?"

Radclyffe sputtered. "He could easily take revenge against us. It cannot be discounted."

"Revenge?" Startled, she stared at Radclyffe, her stomach twisting in fear, someone else confirming her gravest terrors.

"Why would he? What could he do that would not bring condemnation upon himself?"

"Our marriage thwarted Langdon's dark plans. It is natural he would want revenge."

"My husband is right." Odette's fingertips quivered against his arm. "We cannot be too careful as far as that wicked man is concerned. You must promise you will be wary of him."

"I will be wary," she assured them, surrounded by their anger and fear, "but I will not so hurriedly condemn him." She didn't dare.

"You know of his atrocities, yet you do not condemn him?" Hampton choked.

"As I said before, what could he do?" Seeing Hampton's angry eyebrows snap together, she added, "I am not saying I will openly embrace him either." In Langdon's embrace? She concealed a shiver. "You have been good to us. I daresay I shall discover your estimation of Langdon is correct."

Radclyffe's arms folded. "And yet we see you in his arms! You shall do no more discovering, Miss Stockwell."

She wished she could remind him that he was no longer her guardian.

"You must beware the Langdon charm," Hampton added, "for it can be your downfall. Remember what he tried to do to my sister."

She hoped her paling face was read by her companions as fear, not guilt.

"You cannot blame us for worrying about you," Radclyffe said. "You have shown yourself to be quite grown, yet accept our wisdom in this matter. We do not wish you to be hurt."

She felt her temper rise. All it needed was her brother wagging his finger at her and the set would be complete. "Do you all think me incapable of looking after myself? I assure you that is not the case! If you will excuse me, I think I shall go into the garden for some air. It is stifling in here." She turned on her heel and made her way through the crowd to the garden at the rear of the house.

A number of ladies had retreated outside to catch a breath of air away from the ball's crowded confines. Her fan beating the air, she failed to note her arrival among them caused a slight disturbance. Word had already begun to travel about her daring to waltz with the heartless Langdon.

She stood apart from the other guests, quite furious. She had to stop thinking of the dreaded Langdon as the nice, ill stranger, who left behind a hefty payment for her nursing services. Of course, his generosity with money did not necessarily make him a good man. All the other evidence pointed against it.

"Elisabeth?" Hampton's gentle voice stopped her pacing.

"Yes, my lord?" She snapped her fan shut in one sharp movement.

"I came out to see if you wished to dance."

She saw his apologetic smile and turned away. "I am not in the mood for dancing." She needed to be alone with her thoughts, without justifying them to anyone.

Hampton tucked his hand under her elbow and steered her farther away from the fluttering fans of the overheated company. "If you do not want to dance, I hope you do not object to my remaining by your side."

She glanced at his sincere face. "Keeping me safe from harm, is that it, my lord?" She glared. "I cannot be trusted any longer?"

Hampton clasped both her gloved hands in his. "Of course I trust you. It is Langdon I am worried about. I only want to keep you safe from him. I tell you he is after revenge and he will not stop until he gets it! Something should be done about him!"

Alarmed by the force of his ire, she rested her hand on his arm. Truly, she wanted to faint and needed to grip something real to anchor her. Hampton's angry features relaxed. Softer, he began, "Perhaps this is the wrong time to—"

She cut across his words, already knowing that look, that tone of voice. She did not want him to broach the subject tonight. "I do not want to argue with you any more, my lord." She gave a coquettish smile, hoping he would be distracted.

"I do not want to argue either." Hampton leaned closer.

She guessed Hampton would make another declaration anyway and she didn't want to hear it. "I am glad you do not want to argue, my lord. Does your offer to dance still stand?"

"Of course. I have told you I would dance every dance with you." With great formality, he took her hand and escorted her back into the ballroom. Once there, they joined in the end of a quadrille.

Hampton kept his promise, fending off any other man who wished to dance with her. Laughing, and flattered at his attentions in spite of herself, she begged him to let her sit out a dance after they had danced twice together. He acquiesced, sitting beside her and engaging in inconsequential conversation.

She kept on the lookout for Langdon, fearing that at that very moment he destroyed her reputation, but his presence did not grace the ballroom again. She should be relieved she hadn't yet been pointedly snubbed, but her fear gnawed at her, waiting for the final blow.

A couple drew close. Her heart seized up, recognizing them. Hampton noticed no change in her at all, and continued to flatter her with his compliments.

Leading Miss Fanny Syndersham to dance was the Honorable Jasper Kerr! Elisabeth bit her lip. Mr. Kerr, the younger son of a younger son, who had wooed her over two years ago.

His pedigree alone should have warned her of his need for her inheritance and a comfortable future for himself. He had been so charming and considerate toward her that it wasn't until she overheard a dreadful conversation between Jasper and another fellow, how he—

She swallowed, abandoning the old "what ifs" about their past. He couldn't be after Miss Syndersham's money, could he?

Hampton asked her a question and she nodded. To her surprise, he took her by the hand and gestured her to rise. "You agreed to dance, my dear?" he asked, nonplussed at her confusion.

*Oh Lord!* she thought as he led her out onto the floor. *Three dances!* She drifted through the movements, preoccupied with Mr. Kerr's reappearance. She would have to warn Miss Syndersham.

She refused to dance any more after that, professing herself too tired. Hampton stayed by her side the rest of the evening, rendering private conversation with Miss Syndersham impossible. Perhaps, she mused, it would be impossible anyway, for Miss Syndersham was the darling of her coming out ball, swamped by admirers.

Elisabeth grew painfully aware that Hampton's attentions made them a topic of conversation by the other guests. Still, in the back of her mind lingered her fears—her concern for Miss Syndersham and the secret she shared with the debonair Langdon. What kind of man was he?

# CHAPTER SIX

Their carriage rumbled through the dark streets of London. "You make a handsome couple." Odette bloomed with pleasure. Had there been any other occupants in the carriage, even the most casual observer would see their joy at Elisabeth making such a match. "I think it is wonderful how our families will become bound in ties stronger than friendship."

"Marriage? It is too soon to say!" Her cheeks flushed. Her foolish third dance had probably sealed the contract.

"Dear Lamby has not exactly said anything to us yet, but he is my brother after all." Odette beamed. "You did enjoy yourself, did you not?"

"He is a superb dancer and a great friend." She struggled to maintain her composure, wanting to flee.

"No more than a friend?" Radclyffe raised an eyebrow.

She looked down at her clasped hands, feeling the heat of her cheeks deepen. How could she explain the lack of romantic feeling she had for Hampton?

"Now, my dear," Odette chastised her husband, "do not tease the poor child." She leaned forward and patted Elisabeth's tightly clasped hands. "Do not fret, Elisabeth. We shall not ask you any more questions to make you blush."

"Not tonight, anyway," Radclyffe added.

"Thank you." She exhaled and sank back into the leather seat of the carriage. Escaping thoughts of Hampton, she thought of the single waltz she had shared with Langdon. Her shoulders tensed. What was she to do?

Her mind frequently returned to Langdon that evening and the following day. These thoughts were broken by darker musings surrounding Miss Fanny Syndersham and Mr. Jasper Kerr. Society's mores would insist she do nothing and let Fanny's parents take care of the matter, but she simply couldn't let it go.

That afternoon, she and Odette drove in their carriage toward Hyde Park. Odette chattered without pause about the previous evening, extolling her brother's virtues. Elisabeth said little, reluctant to speak of Hampton.

"Oh, if only you had not danced with Langdon!" Odette cried, finally catching her attention. They had at last entered Hyde Park. "The evening would have been quite perfect otherwise."

Elisabeth colored, remembering their almost intimate waltz. "No harm was done."

Yet.

"Yes, I must be thankful for that." Odette took her proffered handkerchief and dabbed at her eyes. "It is just . . . it is just whenever . . ."

"The very thought of him terrifies you." Her friend nodded. "I do not think you need to fear any revenge or reprisal from him. He will not harm you."

"How do you know?" Odette endeavored to restore order to her tearful face.

She took Odette's hand in hers, pressing it. "He told me. Nearly dying has changed his attitude. We can but hope we can trust him."

"Trust him? Ha!" Odette echoed her own feelings, but she had to believe it or she was lost.

The depth of Odette's revulsion prompted further questioning. How far had Langdon fallen? "Radclyffe was not badly injured in the duel, was he?"

Odette shook her head. "Not at all." She spoke in a rush, as if eager to get the dreadful words out. "When I was engaged, Langdon tried to . . . to . . ." She took a deep breath. "I managed to escape him. He fled the country, but when he returned, Mr. Radclyffe challenged him. Afterward, Langdon's seconds carried him away. We were all certain he was dead. That is why it was such a shock to hear he is alive and back in London!"

Elisabeth held her tongue. Odette would have a fit of the vapors if she knew she'd shared the same roof as Langdon.

"Goodness!" she exclaimed, in an effort to distract Odette from her bad memories. "I do believe the Syndersham carriage is approaching. I fear I may have put Miss Syndersham out of the limelight last night when dancing with your brother."

"Nonsense, child," Odette scolded. "You were not the sole topic of conversation at her coming out."

"It felt like it," she replied with feeling.

"Good day to you, Lady Syndersham, Miss Syndersham," Odette called as their carriage drew opposite. Further greetings were exchanged. "How did you enjoy your coming out?"

"It was beautiful, ma'am." Fanny Syndersham beamed with remembered pleasure. Her pale red curls bobbed.

Elisabeth frowned. She wished Fanny wasn't on the far side of the carriage. Their relative positions made it impossible to privately converse with her about Mr. Kerr.

"Forgive me for asking," Odette continued, directing her attention to Fanny's mother, "but may I ask why Lord Langdon appeared at your ball? As you know, we hold a great dislike for the man. If we had learned earlier he would be there, we simply would not have gone."

"I see." Lady Syndersham's lowered eyelids spoke of disapproval at being thus questioned. She was a stouter, faded version of her daughter's beauty.

"I fear you do not." Remarkably, Odette remained calm. "The hatred is mutual. The only reason we did not leave immediately is that we felt it might cause a scene. We could not dare risk spoiling the ball for your dear daughter."

"I am sure your husband would not have caused a scene," replied Lady Syndersham coolly.

"Can you be so sure about Lord Langdon?" Odette's voice rose in agitation. "I consider his behavior toward my young friend"—she indicated Elisabeth—"last night to be quite scandalous. Asking her to stand up in a waltz with him!"

"Odette," Elisabeth murmured in gentle warning.

"Miss Stockwell seemed to be enjoying his company when I saw them." Lady Syndersham's countenance remained icy.

"Would you dare admit you are afraid of a man?" Odette challenged.

"Of course not. They should be afraid of me!" Elisabeth saw that with a riding whip in Lady Syndersham's hand, no man frightened her. "I invited Lord Langdon to our ball," Lady Syndersham continued, seemingly pleased by Odette's shocked expression. "Have you not heard of his great donation to the Leicester Laborers Fund? The Langdon I once knew would never have given those poor fellows a second thought. He's not even frequenting the clubs, I hear." She turned to her daughter. "My dear, make your farewells."

Fanny did so. "Will you be at the charity ball at the end of the week?" she asked Elisabeth, who nodded in reply. "Then we must find a moment together so you can tell me all about you and Lord Hampton."

Her excited appeal made Elisabeth chuckle. "There is not much to tell," she said as the carriages separated. "But we must talk!"

A week until she could speak privately with Miss Syndersham. She bit the inside of her lip. Perhaps she could find the opportunity during a morning visit in the meantime.

"Donations to the poor?" Odette had recovered her facility of speech. "Impossible."

"There is no reason for Lady Syndersham to lie," Elisabeth reminded her.

"She must be mistaken," Odette declared. "Either that or it

is some nonsense Langdon is spreading to appear respectable!"

Elisabeth couldn't believe the *ton* could be so easily deuced. This news of Langdon's unexpected altruism disturbed her, reminding her of Mister Henry's kindness. Were his actions part of his self-proclaimed penance, or was it all a sham to lull her into a false sense of security?

The remainder of their afternoon drive was pleasant, although conversations unerringly drew to the Syndersham ball. Many made a sly query to Elisabeth about Hampton's health. Thankful that while a few alluded to her dance with Langdon, none had referred to her adventure with him. She stayed noncommittal about her feelings for Hampton. So far it appeared Langdon had kept the secret too.

On returning to the Radclyffe house, Elisabeth confessed, "I do not think I can take another day of this gossip. Would you mind if I did not go to the park tomorrow?"

"You do not intend to remain indoors all day, do you?"

"Of course not. I shall take an early morning ride instead. I should do it more often," she added, gazing out at the street. "It makes for good exercise."

"I will not let you ride alone," Odette insisted. "London is not like the country, you know."

"I should hope not. One of the grooms should do for an escort."

From where she stood in the hallway, Odette checked the tall clock in the drawing room. "We should change for dinner, my dear. I believe my husband is taking us to the opera tonight."


The Radclyffes included Lord Hampton in their party. He shared their carriage to the Royal Opera House. She felt his gaze settle often upon her but only responded with a polite smile.

"When was the last time you saw an opera?" Hampton

helped seat her in the small box Radclyffe had rented for the evening.

She turned from her eager survey of the opera's audience, flicking him a curious look. "Two years ago, as you know."

"Have you missed it?"

Glancing over her shoulder, she noticed the Radclyffes talk with quiet determination between themselves, giving the young couple some measure of privacy. "Somewhat. I play a little Mozart. Not that I could play it for anyone else."

"Not even for me?"

"My lord, your ears would be unable to stand it," she advised with a dry smile.

He settled in the chair behind her. Leaning forward, he whispered to her the latest gossip involving the Cyprians across the way. Diluted for ladies' ears, Elisabeth felt, turning her attention to the first act of *Don Giovanni*.

Hampton resumed whispering gossip when the curtain fell, criticizing the dandies who paraded in the pit below. "None of them could hold even a match to the Beau."

"Brummel had better things to do for a start," she remarked, her attention on the stage. "I wonder what became of him."

"Living on credit on the Continent, I heard."

After the final curtain dropped, the Radclyffe party joined the crush of people heading for their carriages. "I will go on ahead and get us the coach." Hampton pushed his way down the stairs before anyone objected.

Elisabeth concentrated on keeping her footing in the press of people. Beside her, Odette made a sound of annoyance. Following her friend's gaze down to the lobby, Elisabeth glimpsed Hampton making a constricted bow to a beautiful blond woman.

"Who is that?" she asked Odette, raising her voice over the cacophony of the chattering crowd.

"The Lady Sophie Cunningham." Odette frowned. "I thought he'd finished with her."

Watching the conversation, she felt her small reticule snag

on something and tugged on it. She met resistance. Turning, she found herself face to face with a young man holding a knife.

The knife slashed toward her. Stunned, Elisabeth drew breath to scream. A man's white gloved hand grabbed the thief's wrist, twisting it away. The knife clattered to the floor. Her purse relinquished, the thief pushed off through the oblivious crowd.

"My lord." She trembled, gazing up at her rescuer.

A step higher, Langdon towered over her. She felt caged by his presence, more helpless than when confronted by the thief. She thought she saw a light of concern in his eyes. "You should be more careful, Miss Stockwell."

Hearing his voice, Radclyffe shot a murderous look at him, tucked his wife's arm under his and pushed through the crowd.

"I will," she replied, breathless still with the shock of the attack. "Excuse me." Not wanting to become separated from the Radclyffes, Elisabeth followed them, not even sure if he heard her word of thanks.

Hampton waited at their carriage. "What a crush!" he exclaimed, no doubt thinking their peaked looks came from being hemmed in.

"Indeed." Radclyffe helped his wife into the carriage. He said nothing of their encounter with Langdon on the way home. Hampton struggled to keep some form of conversation going, clearly baffled by the terseness of his fellow company. In the end, he managed to engage Radclyffe on the topic of boxing.

Early next morning, with the night mists still wrapped around the city streets, Elisabeth rode alone in Hyde Park.

Even with the memory of the attack last night, she dispensed with the groom. It would not have been solitary enough, and she had plenty to think about. Another soul present would have distracted her too much from her dilemma.

She saw a few early risers dedicated to exercising their

horses. She urged her horse into a canter, enjoying the refreshing mist against her face.

Her thoughts kept circling back to Langdon. Had she imagined that tender look at the opera? Had he been following her? Had it all been planned?

The mist grew thicker. Trees stood tall and ghostly in the otherwise featureless fog. She slowed her horse to a walk. The last thing she desired was a collision with another. Uncertain of her whereabouts, she peered over her shoulder, squinting into the mist to see the way she had come.

"Good morning, Miss Stockwell," drawled a familiar voice.

She started and faced forward. Langdon sat astride a fine bay gelding. How had she not heard him approach? In his simple brown tweed riding suit, he reminded her more of Mister Henry—a little bit dangerous, a lot mysterious, but nobody to fear.

Somebody to love.

She banished the thought at once.

He bowed from his saddle. "My apologies for startling you."

"Apology accepted," she responded with feigned indifference, leaning forward to soothe her fidgety mare with a gentle hand. She banked down the rush of energy that always encompassed her when she saw him.

"Miss Stockwell, may I ask why you are unchaperoned?" He edged his horse nearer. "On such a gloomy morning, it is dangerous for a pretty young woman to be out on her own."

"I have no need for a chaperone," she told him, ignoring his flattery. Her mare shifted away from his. "I can take sufficient care of myself." She could outride any who dared to accost her. There was no crowd to hem her in here.

"This is not the country, Miss Stockwell. Your folly may be your undoing," he reproved. "The opera last night should have made you aware of that."

He felt concern for her? Truly? She concealed her surprise, afraid he might somehow take advantage. "You are here now, my lord, as you were last night, to protect me from any harm." Her gaze met his and held. "I did not have a chance to properly thank you for that service."

He delivered a short bow from horseback. "I had thought you had given me the same thanks as your friends."

She glanced down at the reins, feeling shame stain her cheeks. "Please, that was inexcusable. I wished to, but I did not want to get separated from them." She begged him with earnest eyes. "I must ask you to excuse them. They fear you."

"Do you?"

She regarded him for a long moment. She didn't know if she wanted to run to him, or from him. She feared many things, but she refused to show sign of it. "No, I do not. You have had opportunity to reveal our secret and yet you have not. Last night you came to my aid." Those were the reasons she did not run now.

He dismissed her reasons with an abrupt wave. "I would have done that for anyone." The gruffness of his voice suggested otherwise.

"I know you consider it your duty to protect a friend." She spoke with confidence, but she only guessed at his true nature.

"You call me friend?" he challenged, disbelief rampant in his voice. "Do you change sides whenever it best suits your company?"

What was it about him that made her want to reach out to him? He confronted and challenged her at every turn. She murmured, "I do not want to be your enemy."

"You have friends who are my enemies," he reminded her with an undeniable chill.

Her shiver didn't come from the brisk morning air. "You made a promise to me not to harm the Radclyffes."

"And what of your beloved Lord Hampton?" His voice held a dangerous edge.

"I do not love him!" Her cheeks warmed and she struggled to regain her calm demeanor. "Lord Hampton is a good friend."

"So many friends, Miss Stockwell," he drawled. "You need

not be so shy before a friend, such as myself, and hide your true feelings about your young man. You made quite a lovely couple, dancing together at the ball."

Her horse skittered, sensing her anger. "Will people never stop?" He opened his mouth to reply, but she cut him off. "Dare to say how in love Hampton is with me and I swear I will whip you for it!" That was what she had wanted to say yesterday to all the gossips who had quizzed her. How odd that she should feel comfortable enough to say it to Langdon now.

He chuckled. Leaning back in his saddle, he rested his hands before him. "So you do not love him? I take it you do not know how to discourage the man without hurting his feelings?"

"Short of running away," she admitted. "The other reasons I do not wish to discuss."

"Even with a friend?"

She refused to give in to that crooked smile. "Even with a friend." And especially not him. She didn't dare give him that advantage over her. The less leverage he had over her, the better—although she feared he held too much in his hands already.

"By any slim chance," he sidled nearer, "would I be numbered among those reasons?"

His soft cajolery sparked warnings.

She drew herself upright in the saddle. "My lord, you assume too much!"

"Alas, I am heartbroken." He placed a hand over his heart, bowing his head.

Was he really? She bit her lower lip.

He glanced at her and smiled. "I speak but in jest, Miss Stockwell."

Her mouth curved in a tiny, uncertain smile. His returning warm gaze inexplicably lightened her spirits. "Your heart is not broken, even by the merest fraction?" she teased, the words springing from her lips with little thought.

"How can it be broken when I know I remain your friend?"

His eyes danced with mischief as they settled into their old ways of teasing.

"It is not the easiest of tasks being your friend, my lord." Her smile faded at the problems that confronted such a friendship as theirs. What had begun in frank curiosity and warmth seemed steeped in ambiguity and innuendo. Friendships required trust—and she didn't dare trust Langdon.

"How so?" His mischief diminished into a wary kindness.

"I have thought ill of you from what my friends report." After all, she wasn't deaf. Any maid would question his motives.

"What they say is most likely true," he murmured.

She met his quiet gaze. She would tell him the truth. "Yes, but you promised me you had changed—and I want to trust in that." Even she heard her uncertainty. "It is . . . it is very difficult."

"Your confidence in me is overwhelming," he remarked dryly.

"I am not a saint, my lord." His remark stung. He asked too much of her, too soon.

He shifted in his saddle. "I am trying to make a new life for myself. It's not easy when all the old temptations beckon and there is no sight of a reward."

Reward? What kind of reward did he expect? She headed for safer ground. "I have heard you have become quite the philanthropist."

"I am no saint either." He grimaced at her fearful reaction, quickly hidden. "You need not fear, Miss Stockwell. I shall avoid Mrs. Radclyffe and all your friends like the very plague." His grim look convinced her of his sincerity. "It is how they treat me and I shall do the same."

"I should trust your promise, my lord, and not doubt you." She thought she sounded more certain this time.

"Yet the things you hear scare you just a little," he finished for her. He smiled in his most charming manner.

"Miss Stockwell, will you dismount and walk with me a little way?"

She hesitated. To dismount meant losing her advantage of a swift escape. To refuse would end the conversation and be an opportunity missed in plumbing Langdon's depths, and gaining some measure of security about her future.

She slid from her saddle. Gathering up the reins to lead her mare, she turned to find he had done the same.

Side by side, they strolled along the gray lane. Trees lining the path loomed like stately giants out of a mist melting from the morning sun.

She sensed him watching her, waiting for her to relax. She refused to give up her vigilance. Yet she would discover very little unless she engaged him in conversation. "I must thank you."

"Thank me? Have I done another good deed without knowing it?" Amazed, he struck a pose, a hand against his chest.

She grinned at his foolishness. "I think not. It is crass of me to mention it, but you left something behind . . ." She saw his wary smile. "You do remember."

"I hope you are not going to insist on returning it."

"No. I put it to good use as you requested. It has gone toward reroofing a few of the cottages on the estate."

He raised a sandy eyebrow. "None for yourself."

"I have no need of it, my lord. The estate did however. Had I thought to meet you here in London, I would have returned it."

He bristled. "Miss Stockwell—"

She hurried to continue, "Please do not take offense, but you see how improper it is for me to have accepted such a gift." Appearances were all, but her cheeks stung with the hypocrisy of her words.

"I am not offended," he replied, his tone crisp.

She ventured another question. "How is the scar?"

"I have been taking care of it. It has healed."

"I am glad to hear it." She clasped her hands in front of her, the reins trailing over her shoulder. Some barrier had risen between them.

Langdon muttered, more to himself than to her, "I was a fool to come back so soon."

"Then why did you come back?"

Langdon grimaced. "Which time? The time I came back from the Continent to get myself half-killed over your little friend, or this most recent time in London?"

"Either. Both."

"The first time, I left . . . well, it seemed advisable under the circumstances." He shrugged. "I then made a drunken dare in Dieppe and was all too pleased to remain in that state while recrossing the Channel." He rubbed his jaw. "No, that is untrue. A fellow expatriate called me a coward for having fled the field. Having dealt with him, I returned to claim her and face Radclyffe." He pulled a face. "The bit about being drunk is true. For some reason that state serves me best when crossing the sea."

"You fled the field?"

His mouth twisted. "That expatriate was right. I am a coward."

The agony in his voice pricked her sympathy and she sought to find some honorable ground for him. "But you fought him, the expatriate."

"Yes." His clipped tone suggested the ground she had chosen was shaky at best.

"And returned to fight Radclyffe."

"Hmm."

"So why did you come back?" she persisted.

He stopped and faced her, taking her hand. "Elisabeth, my dear, sometimes you ask too many questions."

Even with leather riding gloves, his clasp felt deliciously intimate. She struggled to maintain control. "But, my lord . . ." She didn't know whether she protested the familiar use of her name or that he hadn't answered her question. The latter, for she quite liked the sound of her name on his lips.

"Very well," he snapped, reddening. "A duel would have brought the scandal out for all to hear of it, and honor demanded it. I wished to avoid that, for her sake."

"For Odette?" Her mind raced. Honor? But hadn't he attacked Odette? Where was the honor in that?

"Yes." Only the abruptness of his response indicated any emotion in his reply. His features remained impassive. Did he still want Odette Radclyffe? Did he love her? Was that why he came back?

"Yet her reputation survived it."

"Yes, well . . . I did not foresee that."

"Thought you would win?"

Again, that off-putting "Hmm."

The tension eased. His disarming honesty reminded her of when he was Mister Henry. Now, she doubted she knew him at all.

"You are beautiful when you smile like that." She almost missed his soft-spoken words.

"My lord," she said, as soft as he, all her defenses close to crumbling. "Please do not complicate matters and presume upon our friendship."

"Friends speak only the truth to each other." A wrinkle deepened in his brow. He found it difficult to regret his words? He slipped a hand under her elbow.

"Then it is very kind of you," she said, at a loss. Had she rebuffed him for no cause?

He stopped and frowned. "It is not kind of me at all," he said, his voice gruff. He made her face him. Behind them, their restless horses pawed at the ground. "You should listen to your friends and not associate yourself with me any longer. Go and marry Lord Hampton; that is my advice to you." She couldn't read the real meaning behind his unfathomable expression.

Why did he twist and turn on her? One moment she thought she understood him and the next he behaved like a heartless rake, or a prim preacher. She dropped the reins, reaching for him. "My lord, I do not understand . . ." Her fingertips brushed his coat.

"You do not need to understand," he told her brutally, backing away. "Elisabeth, can you not see that by remaining friends, I am dividing your loyalties? I cannot ask that of you."

Her arms dropped to her sides. "I confess it is difficult, but it is nothing to concern you. I am sure their anger and hatred will diminish in time, as long as you do not do anything to provoke them." She strained with her senses, trying to discover the underlying problem. "I have had friends they have not liked before."

Langdon gave a dry, short laugh. "Not like me." He let her go. "I do not deserve your friendship, Miss Stockwell."

She laid a hand on his sleeve, an odd pang in her heart. "A moment ago, you called me Elisabeth."

"I had no right to do that. There is a deeper danger in our friendship. You know it as well as I." His eyes regained that world-weary look she'd seen earlier. She let her hand drop from his sleeve and walked on. Langdon followed. Her whip tapped lightly against her skirts as they walked.

"Miss Stockwell?" He broke the strained silence.

"Yes, my lord?" Would the ice between them thaw again? It was better this way, but she liked it little.

"I must be sure you understand we cannot be friends." The apologetic words were wrung from his lips.

She uttered a low cry of annoyance. "Have we not gone through this already? You made your promise to me. It does not matter now what you did before we met. That is past. If you want a second chance, I will give it to you." *I will give it to you,* she silently amended, *so long as you keep our secret safe.*

He noted her pleading look, the lines of his face hardening.

Her breath caught. She'd offended him. She continued with fervor, "You are a friend and no other person, not even my maid, is going to change that."

He smiled, appearing to relax. "Not even your servants?"

"Mainly my personal maid, Maggie. If she knew I was speaking with you . . . You see," she continued, answering his unasked question, "Maggie does not approve of you either. She would not say anything to anyone, but she would give me an earful at every opportunity." She exhaled. "She is so like her mother."

"Her mother?" he echoed, a puzzled furrow in his brow.

"Mrs. Peters, my childhood nurse. Maggie has been working for the Radclyffes and when I came up to London, she became my maid." She drew breath.

"Ah, the secrets of domestic woes," he drawled, "revealed in all their splendor."

"You asked," she pointed out, realizing with horror that she had been babbling on. Infuriating man to make her so lose control. "Do not be facetious." She prepared to remount her mare, lifting the reins over the mare's head.

"Miss Stockwell!"

She ignored him. She'd tried to be nice, to be encouraging. Let him reveal the secret. She never expected to marry and preferred living alone in the country anyway. Losing her friendships would be tough, but she'd manage somehow. She placed her foot in a stirrup and prepared to swing up.

"Friends cannot part like this," he protested. His hand touched her boot. "Elisabeth! Please!"

Hearing the unexpected desperation in his voice, she stopped in midswing. Had she misunderstood?

His large hands at her waist steadied her descent. She turned to face him, her arms resting along the length of his, conscious of his hands still about her waist. She could feel the heat of him.

Her heart thumped against her ribs. "Henry . . ." she whispered, her breaths shallow. She stepped closer into his embrace, her face turned up to his. The naked emotion she read in his eyes startled and warmed her. She knew he saw the same reaction in hers.

"I am sorry, Elisabeth," he murmured.

She knew he apologized for more than a few discourteous words. "Do not be," she said, scarcely audible. *Kiss me anyway.*

His head lowered.

# CHAPTER SEVEN

The clattering of approaching hooves pulled them apart.

Blushing, Elisabeth allowed Langdon to help her back into the saddle. In the time it took for him to spring upon the back of his own horse, she almost had herself back under control.

Almost. She couldn't believe she had come so close to doing such a foolish thing. Kissing him? Her lips flamed as if he had already done so.

"My lord," she called, "wait a moment." He looked back at her, awaiting her word. Yet she didn't know what to say. They couldn't part with so much askew between them. "My lord, there is one favor I would ask you."

He frowned. "A favor?"

She nodded. "There is a man, a Mr. Jasper Kerr. I fear he has designs on a young friend of mine. In my experience, he seeks money, not a wife."

His frown deepened.

"He may have changed, as you have done. I will warn my friend, but I would be greatly eased to know there is no need for it."

"I will do what I can." He bowed to her from the saddle before galloping away through the mist.

The strange rider appeared out of this mist and tipped his hat in her direction. She nodded in acknowledgment, abstracted.

What had she done? Her investigation of Langdon's true

self had turned into shameless flirting. She could not deny her heated emotions when held in his arms. She thought never to love again after Jasper Kerr's deception. Hadn't her lack of response to Hampton proved this?

And her response to Langdon? Did it matter? Did it matter that her heart beat faster in his presence, or when she thought of him? She'd given him a second chance, but what if he reverted to his old ways? What if this was a ploy to make her fall even farther?

Her doubts and forebodings about him faded beneath his charm and she struggled to regain them. They had met when she was a mere companion and he a complete stranger, but that didn't change their current circumstances. She was not that green. She promised herself a little caution where he was concerned. Even he had warned her of his ways. Recalling their conversation, a little smile lurked about the corners of her mouth.

"Elisabeth!"

Odette's sharp exclamation roused Elisabeth from her musing. She'd been unable to find a private moment in which to speak with Fanny Syndersham about Mr. Kerr. She'd also been unable to speak to Langdon on the subject. It had been a week of evenings at the opera and the theater, with Hampton dancing constant attendance.

Elisabeth stood in the middle of her room, her new evening gown undergoing a final fitting. "I am sorry, Odette. What did you say?"

Odette chattered on about that evening's charity ball, while Elisabeth changed into a white sprigged muslin gown.

Butterflies leaped in her belly. Would she see Langdon? "Will our beloved Prince Regent be there?" She brushed her hair into some semblance of order, twisting it into a simple knot.

"Perhaps," Odette replied. "I do not know. The Queen will be there, for it is her ball."

Elisabeth dreaded having to ask the question, but she had to know. She turned to face her hostess from her dressing table. "Odette, do you suppose Lord Langdon will be there?"

"Langdon?" Odette pursed her lips. "I hope not. It would quite ruin the evening for us if he did."

"I doubt it. He has enough sense, I think, not to cause an uproar tonight." She hoped so.

She saw Odette's worried expression and admired her courage in facing her fear of Langdon. "Do not worry about it." Odette managed a smile. "I promise we will not leave if that despicable man is there. Besides, there will be such a crush of people, I am sure we would not see him even if he were present." Odette smoothed away a few stray hairs around Elisabeth's ears. "With Lamby there, you need not have any concerns that Langdon will steal another dance with you."

No more dancing with Langdon? Hampton's words came back to her: "I will dance every dance with you." With him constantly by her side she'd have no chance to slip away and find Langdon, if he was there, or indeed find a moment to speak with Miss Syndersham in private. Maybe fate would be kind and Hampton would be late.

Odette snapped her fingers in front of her young friend. She giggled at Elisabeth's disconcerted blink. "Dreaming about Lamby?"

Guilt made her blush. She hadn't been thinking about Hampton at all, at least, not in the way Odette suggested. "What makes you think I was thinking of him?" she asked, defensive.

"I know that look. You are in love with my brother, are you not?" Odette didn't wait for the answer but swept to the doorway. "I will leave you to your dreaming." She winked.

"But Odette—" Elisabeth called after her, dismayed.

How could she explain she didn't love Hampton but was instead attracted to Langdon? It couldn't be done. She found it hard to understand herself. How could she even want Langdon? He was wrong for her in so many ways.

Her head ached with repressed emotion. She lay upon her bed and covered her eyes.

Was losing Odette's friendship worth pursuing her attraction to Langdon? She might have to forsake all her family and friends. Could she make that kind of sacrifice? Lose the people dearest to her for a love that might only be imagined?

Maggie woke her some hours later. Elisabeth dispelled memories of a dream featuring Langdon. She saw her new gown over Maggie's arm and scrambled up. Maggie laid it out on the bed.

"Oh," she breathed. "Is it not the most beautiful thing you have ever seen?" She lifted the hem of the gown between her fingers. It was of the palest cream silk. Mauve velvet ribbons were appliquéd upon the short poufed sleeves and along the hem of the skirt in a flowing classical pattern. Lace trimmed the skirt's edge and around the low neckline. A mauve silk sash around the high waist, matching mauve satin slippers, and a simple string of pearls would complete the charming effect.

An effect not lost on those nearest the entrance at the Queen's charity ball. Even a few young men pushed their way through the crush to request future dances from Elisabeth.

"Do not forget to leave one or two for Lord Hampton," Odette reminded her.

"Lud, if the deuced fellow is not here—" A tall fellow plucked at his coat lapels. He aimed to emulate the famous Beau Brummel in his attire but had fallen far short of the mark.

"Remember your manners, young man," Odette rebuked.

Elisabeth's attention wandered. Idly waving her fan, she took in the visual feast of the large ballroom. Women dressed in all their finery, some with feathers in their headdress, others like Elisabeth with their hair decorated with tiny silk flowers, danced a stately quadrille with their lords. Dress uniforms of officers dotted the crowd. Glittering chandeliers hung from the ceiling, reflecting light from the ladies' jewels.

The entire spectacle dazzled her eyes. On the point of being overwhelmed, she saw the person she had been searching for.

With a slight nod, Langdon acknowledged her smiling recognition of him. He stood in an alcove, impeccably dressed in the conventional evening garb of black and white. The white stovepipe trousers fitted finely over his well-formed thighs and calves without straining the weave of the material. Similarly, the black coat fitted well over his shoulders, tapering to his waist. She longed to touch the fine embroidery on his embossed white satin waistcoat, feel the warmth of him piercing it.

She damped down that heated feeling, becoming aware she too was minutely observed in turn. His unmistakable approval warmed her cheeks, and she fanned herself.

"Elisabeth, I do believe you are blushing!" Odette had rid them of the dandy. She looked in the general direction Elisabeth faced. "Can you see my brother?"

As if Hampton could make her blush so. "I think I saw him over there." She pointed in a different direction. Odette craned her neck to find Hampton, while Elisabeth glanced at the alcove. Her eyes widened with surprise. The little alcove was empty.

"I cannot see him anywhere." Odette complained.

"No doubt he will show up soon." Her voice held little enthusiasm. She followed the Radclyffes down the few steps into the ballroom.

During the evening, Elisabeth retired to the room set aside for the ladies. The heat and press of the guests had given her a slightly disheveled appearance and needed some repair.

A woman, well advanced in years and dressed in a wine-red satin gown accosted her. "Would you please come and lend weight to my argument?" she demanded, dragging her to a woman of similar age before Elisabeth could protest. An imperious gesture instructed her to sit.

"What would this girl know?" the seated woman asked in a manner matching her sharp aquiline features.

The first lady turned to Elisabeth. "I saw you dancing with Lord Langdon at the Syndersham Ball, did I not?"

"Yes, ma'am." Elisabeth felt the blood drain from her head. Had he spoken of their secret?

"Lady Westbrooke seems to think that Lord Langdon is a changed man," declared the second woman, her eyebrows raised in utter disbelief. "Although how a few weeks of refraining from gambling and . . . and other matters," she hastily improvised, stumbling to an embarrassed stop.

"'Tis not only his habits that have changed," argued Lady Westbrooke, "but now he is only seen in the most respectable haunts and behaves most charmingly. Do you not agree, child?" The last she directed to Elisabeth.

"Lord Langdon is a charming man," she agreed. How had she ended up in such a conversation? "I am certain he is not the reprobate he was over a year ago." It was a risk, but championing him might get her fresh news on his true activities in London.

"Oh, really?" Lady Westbrooke's companion examined her through her lorgnette. "You are closely acquainted with Lord Langdon, young lady? I would have thought the company you keep is more honorable by far."

"Lord Langdon was once honorable and he will be again," interceded Lady Westbrooke. Noting Elisabeth's mute amazement, Lady Westbrooke explained. "You see, child, Henry Langdon was not always the gambling lecher for which he has become renowned."

"Lady Westbrooke, you are not going to spout that fairy tale again, are you?"

"Mrs. Adams, it is only our lifelong friendship which prevents me from answering that most unkind question!" Lady

Westbrooke sent a sly wink in Elisabeth's direction. "Harriet, you should know better than anyone that it is the truth."

*Harriet?* Elisabeth's startled eyes opened wide. Was this the woman whose name Lord Langdon had called out in his fevered dreams?

"Even after all these years, I still think you are suffering from a queer, romantic delusion about that man." The feathers agitated in Mrs. Adams's turban.

" 'Tis no delusion." To Elisabeth, Lady Westbrooke said, "Pay no heed to Mrs. Adams. 'Tis a story that brings back unhappy memories for her."

"If that is the case, perhaps you ought not to tell it," she said, although she burned to hear it.

"Now, m'dear." Lady Westbrooke rested her hand on Elisabeth's arm. "I feel certain you should know of it and so not make the same mistakes as my friend here once did. You can see the good in Lord Langdon?"

Baffled, she replied honestly. "Yes, ma'am. His faults are not hidden from me either."

"Good!" approved Lady Westbrooke. "It is encouraging to see wisdom in one so young."

She went on to tell her how some years ago, Langdon had fallen in love with a widow, much older than he but still youthful in appearance. The widow had encouraged his attentions to the point of proposal. Then to everybody's surprise, she ran off with an admiral of the Royal Navy. "From that moment on," concluded Lady Westbrooke, "Lord Langdon plunged into his dissolute ways right up until his recent return to London."

"He actually did propose to me," said Mrs. Adams, her sharp features softening at the memory.

"Lord Langdon was in love with you?" Elisabeth failed to keep the surprise out of her voice. *It must be her. She must be his Harriet.*

"Do not sound so shocked. I was still quite beautiful when we met. You'll get old like me one day too."

"My pardon, ma'am. I did not mean to be rude."

"Your apology is accepted." Mrs. Adams's gaze traveled about the room, avoiding Elisabeth and Lady Westbrooke.

Eager for more information, Elisabeth turned to Lady Westbrooke. "Why do you suppose he has changed?"

"I think he has found love again." Lady Westbrooke gave a dreamy sigh.

"Isabel, you are getting too old for these nonsensical notions." Mrs. Adams's attention snapped back to their conversation. "Why, there could be any of a dozen reasons why the fellow has suddenly changed his ways."

"Name one, Harriet," was Lady Westbrooke's hurt response.

"He needs an heir for his estate," Mrs. Adams pointed out.

Elisabeth's fan fluttered. Was that Langdon's plan? Dare she wish it were so?

She spotted Miss Syndersham across the room. Although she wanted to hear more, she did not wish to miss her chance in speaking with Fanny. Her muttered begging of leave went unnoticed by the two ladies in the thick of their dispute. She rose from the low settee.

Lady Westbrooke nodded her dismissal before returning her attention to the argument. "Rubbish! He has his nephews! 'Tis not as if the Langdon name is going to die out."

Mrs. Adams's reply came faint to Elisabeth's ears as she moved away from them and toward Miss Syndersham. "'Tis not the same as leaving your own son at the helm, is it?"

Could it be true that Langdon was once as decent and honorable as Radclyffe? Her heart found new hope in that thought. She put the information aside to go over in private later.

"What is going on between you and Lord Hampton?" Miss Syndersham clasped Elisabeth's hands to draw her closer. "Everyone says you will be the Season's first wedding!"

"They are saying this on the basis of one evening? It is hardly enough evidence for such gossip!" With annoyance, Elisabeth realized things had gone too far with Hampton.

"Not just one evening. Why, I have heard he has been of

your party for the entire week." Fanny bubbled with enthusiasm. In the past couple of years, she truly hadn't changed.

"Mrs. Radclyffe *is* his sister," she reminded Fanny.

"He has not proposed to you yet?"

Tidying her hair in the mirror, Elisabeth studiously ignored Fanny's pitiful expression. "No, he has not." Elisabeth faced her, untroubled by this lack.

"Well, perhaps you are right about it being too early for a proposal," Miss Syndersham consoled.

"Hampton and I have known each other for a long time. We have become friends. But if he proposes, I will refuse."

"What?" Fanny's mouth gaped. Turn down a marriage proposal? All eligible women wanted respectable and wealthy husbands. Hampton was an excellent catch for a girl on the shelf. Elisabeth could hardly do better. She knew all the arguments. "Why?"

Elisabeth heard in her protest the unspoken criticism that she was not of an age to be choosy. She didn't care about that. "I do not love him," she explained. "There is . . . someone else." She spared herself the mockery of being in love with a rake by biting back his name in time.

She scarcely heard Miss Syndersham's thrilled response, stunned that she had reached this conclusion. In love with Langdon, and he yet unproven? What an absurd notion! She banished it firmly.

"Who is he?" Fanny brought her back to the present. The girl smirked.

Elisabeth laughed, uneasy, realizing that she'd had a dreamy expression on her face. If only Fanny knew the half of it. "That is a secret."

"He is not . . . unsuitable, is he?"

*Yes.* She rallied her thoughts. "If you mean, 'is he penniless?', the answer is no." She couldn't lie to Fanny. Avoiding the truth was far easier. "My friends would much rather see me married to Lord Hampton. That is why his name is a secret, at least until I can smooth things over and allow them to see other choices. You will not tell anybody, will you?"

"Of course not!" Miss Syndersham bounced. "Imagine! I wish I could be involved in such a romantic adventure!"

"It is scarcely that!" she replied with a smile. Perhaps it was a better story than saying she simply did not wish for marriage. She turned the topic to her second concern. "Miss Syndersham, speaking of adventure, how well acquainted are you with Mr. Jasper Kerr?"

Fanny grew somber, her gray eyes turning to iron. "He thought you might ask me that."

She raised an eyebrow. "Did he now?"

"He told me what passed between you." The words rushed from Miss Syndersham's mouth. "How you jilted him. He says that you do not ever want him to be happy. He said you would try and dissuade me from seeing him."

"It was not quite like that. I had good reason." Elisabeth rubbed her clammy arms. "You are seeing him?"

"I have met with him every evening since my coming out. He always seems to know where to find me." Her eyes lit up with happiness. "We dance and talk. He is very charming."

Elisabeth nodded, her lips twisting. "Yes, I remember that. Miss Syndersham, please do not take this unkindly. I ask you only to be careful with your heart regarding him. He may have changed since I knew him, but if he has not . . ."

"Do not be unkind, Miss Stockwell."

"That was not my intention." She gnawed the inside of her lip. "If you would take my advice, don't accept the first fellow that comes along. There are others . . ."

The room seemed quieter. "Is that another dance starting?" Miss Syndersham listened to the muffled music. Elisabeth nodded, sensing the girl had heard enough. "You must excuse me," Fanny continued coolly. "I have a partner for this dance."

Elisabeth trailed after her young friend. As she suspected, Kerr claimed Miss Syndersham's hand for the dance. He smiled down, adoring, at her and then glared over his shoulder at Elisabeth.

Her fan setting an idle beat, she concealed her churning emotions, dismissing him and looking elsewhere about the room. She had promised this dance to Hampton but he had yet to appear. She stood in the ballroom's arched entranceway, searching for both Langdon and Hampton, unsure who she dreaded to see most.

"You are sitting out this dance, Miss Stockwell?"

She gasped and spun, the hem of her gown swirling around her ankles. The sound of Langdon's voice sent an unaccountable thrill through her. She rested her chin on her white silk fan. "My lord, you gave me a fright."

Langdon stepped around the tall white column, one of a pair that framed the archway. He gave a slight bow. "My pardon if I startled you," he murmured, taking her gloved hand and kissing it. "I fear I seem to be making a habit of that."

Her face suffused with warmth. "This dance is for Lord Hampton." Langdon frowned at the name. "But I cannot see him anywhere. In fact, I have not seen him all evening."

"You long to be in his arms again?" he asked, a sardonic eyebrow raised.

"You know I do not!" she snapped. If only he knew the whole of it. "Now if you will excuse me, my lord. . . ." She turned.

He took her by the elbow and forced her to face him. "Miss Stockwell, you say you do not love the man and yet you speak of him with such fondness." His low voice held a touch of menace.

"Of course I am fond of Lord Hampton," she murmured. "I have known him for a long time but I have no wish to wed him." She avoided Langdon's eye, half afraid that he would see the truth.

"Then who shall you marry?" he bantered.

"Who says I shall marry?" It occurred to her that Langdon might also consider her past her marriageable prime and not worthy of serious pursuit. A younger woman would bear more children.

She sighed. What was she thinking? *Stop daydreaming, Elisabeth and wake up!* She swallowed, fluttering her fan.

His eyebrows rose. "You are the first girl I know who is not a bluestocking and does not wish to be wed. What notion is this?"

"A very sensible notion." She rapped him lightly on the arm with her fan.

Chuckling, he took her hand, guiding her away from the ballroom and along the corridor. Her hand settled into the secure crook of his elbow.

"Where are we going?" He hadn't disagreed with her. What did he plan to do?

"Here." They entered a large salon filled with people perusing the contents of long tables containing all kinds of trinkets. Directly opposite the couple stood a set of wide doors, through which the dancers in the ballroom were visible.

Langdon's outflung arm took in the entire room. "All the money made here goes to the Queen's chosen charity." He led her to a table containing small ornaments and pieces of jewelry. "I came here just after you arrived and by luck I found a bracelet that would go perfectly with your gown."

"Why, I did not know you knew so much about ladies' fashion!" she replied with a forced note of gaiety. He wanted to give her a gift? What did he mean by that? She trembled, afraid that it might mean the worst. That he would make her his mistress.

He ignored her flippant comment and leaned over the table to speak to the hovering attendant. He retrieved a black velvet bag from under the table and opened it, revealing its contents.

She gasped with delight. A slim bracelet of small amethysts and moonstones glittered in the flickering candlelight.

"Do you like it?" Langdon asked, taking the piece from the attendant.

"It is beautiful, my lord," she breathed. She couldn't insult him, nor lie about the comeliness of the piece.

He handed over a number of gold sovereigns. Too many, by the pleased look on the attendant's face. He guided her to another room, tipping a footman to guard their door for privacy.

She had to stop this before she succumbed. "I cannot accept this." She bit her lip. She shouldn't even be alone with him.

"I am not putting you under any obligations." It didn't matter—etiquette demanded young ladies should not receive presents from gentlemen who were neither relatives nor their betrothed. Which left them where precisely?

"Yet it will also provoke a lot of unanswerable questions," she hedged, hoping for a hint of his reasoning. What did he want from her if she accepted them?

"Does this have something to do with your determination to become a dried-up old spinster?" he teased. The bracelet lay in his palm, unclaimed, between the two of them.

"My lord, friendship is all I have asked of you."

"It is yours." His voice lowered. "My dear, I know you have been burned, but believe me, it is possible to fall in love again." For a moment, he appeared uncertain. He surveyed the shimmering bracelet in his hand. "It was unforgivable to tempt you so. You are, of course, a respectable woman. I shall return it so that it can be sold again."

She swallowed, gnawing the inside of her lip. She wanted it, and what it would give her. Him. It was wrong, terribly wrong.

He took her left hand in his. She let it lie limply, her breath coming quick. He bent over, pressing his lips against the inside of her wrist through the small gap left between her pearl glove buttons. That kiss, that intimate kiss, was hers and hers alone.

She watched him fasten the bracelet about her wrist. He met her wide-eyed gaze with a smoldering expression. "Do you accept?"

"What am I accepting?" She trod on dangerous ground. The almost inaudible sounds from the charity ball, the music

and conversation, reminded her just how alone they were—
and how close to discovery and ruin.

Yet, she had taken that chance. Why? For a kiss? For more?

He smiled, with that heartbreaking, crooked twist of his
lips. "The bracelet, of course." He paused. "And me."

# CHAPTER EIGHT

"I am accepting you?" Confused, Elisabeth echoed him. He wanted far more than friendship, but what exactly?

He kissed her hand and released her. She swayed toward him, trembling, and then righted herself. "Yes," he said, "as your husband, lover, friend, whatever you wish."

"And . . . and what do you wish for?" she asked, delaying her answer.

"I wish for you." He closed the space between them and brought his mouth down on hers.

She responded at once to his sudden, yet gentle kiss, arching toward him. Not until he'd kissed her again had she realized how desperately she needed this—needed him. Lost in him, she moaned at his gentle caresses. She molded herself against him, wanting more, feeling his need for her.

At last, the kiss ended. They parted, their breathing ragged. She affected him as much as he affected her, she realized, her eyes widening.

"Husband? You really mean you wish me as your wife, not your mistress?" She winced, wanting to take back the M word.

His eyes sparked dangerously. "As close as I am to ravishing you right here on the floor, I am a new man—I would be true to you, Elisabeth." He must have seen the doubt in her eyes.

"If you would be true . . ." Her fingertip played around the edge of his lips, her heart pounding with this fresh danger and his delicious kissing. "Friend, husband, lover. I wish for all three, yet I dare not."

His brows knit together. "What happened to my brave, beautiful Elisabeth? I offer you an honorable path."

"Ask my brother, then I shall take it." Her heart pounded.

He growled. "You set a difficult task, my dear, but one I shall accomplish." The noises from outside their temporary sanctuary grew louder. "Come." He led her from the room.

In the hallway, he looked beyond her and bowed to her in some haste. "Elisabeth, will you dance with me?"

She accepted his arm and they headed for the ballroom. They danced the cotillion in contented silence, joining at the bottom of a set. They shared a warm, intimate look. The small matters of family and reputation were, for the moment, forgotten.

She felt the weight of her new bracelet upon her wrist, a constant reminder of her mysterious partner and their new pact. What would it mean if there was no marriage? How far did she dare let him take her in the meantime?

James would surely send her home, perhaps even farther. She had heard of ruined women being sent into obscurity, with a new name and a meager annuity from which to survive. In many ways, it would not be much different to her expected lonely future.

She directed many shy glances toward him, wondering at the depth of his regard.

His dazed expression found words. "Elisabeth, when can we meet again? We need to discuss wedding arrangements. I want to do this properly, no elopements." He paused with a wolfish, endearing grin. "Once I receive your brother's permission . . ."

His intensity made her molten with an answering need. She swallowed, remembering the thin line on which her virtue trod. "Have a care," she warned, her cheeks hot. "He may see the need to rescue me from a marriage he sees as a fate worse than death."

They exchanged a look heated with desire. "I would kiss you at this moment to ease your fears." He grinned, dispelling any hint of grimness. "Alas, I must be an honorable gentleman and not shock Society by doing so." He bent closer to her. "But soon, Elisabeth, soon."

Her breath caught. "When?"

"Meet me in the park," he murmured, "very early. We'd have hours before you need to return to your hosts."

Hours to make a few wedding arrangements? She frowned at him, suspicious.

He looked abashed, clearing his throat. "I have some information regarding Mr. Kerr and Miss Syndersham."

Her gaze narrowed. "What has she to do with Mr. Kerr?"

He shook his head at her. "Come now, Elisabeth. You did not think I would not find out? Not that I required further impetus, but as a friend of her uncle's, I was obliged to investigate."

"What did you find out?" Shivering, she recalled Kerr's hateful glare.

"If he is after her money, I would be much surprised."

She shot him a startled look. "How so?"

"He has come into an inheritance from an unexpected quarter. An uncle, I believe. Clothes appear to be his only vice and he pays off the tailor's bill every now and then." He smiled at her. "You see, my dear, I am most thorough."

"Indeed," she murmured, wondering how thorough he could be.

"You do not seem pleased with my news," he observed.

She tried to marshal her thoughts, hide her vulnerability. Yet Kerr had damaged her, heart and soul. Could change be so simple? She wanted to confide in Henry. "It is just that he—"

"I know your history with him," he interposed, sparing her. "I do not blame you for your fears, as I do not blame Mrs.

Radclyffe for hers. But those fears are groundless. You must see that."

She managed a shaky smile. He looked so earnest, so needed to be understood, and in more than the matter of Kerr's metamorphosis. "Yes, so I see," she managed at last. "I am very relieved to know Miss Syndersham is in no danger."

"She is a particular friend?"

"Not at the moment," she admitted, her lips twisting ruefully. "She is not pleased with my warning her to be careful. I shall have to make it up with her."

"Quite."

She met his hooded gaze. "Have I disappointed you, my lord?"

"You could never disappoint me, my dear Elisabeth. It is your impetuosity in warning Miss Syndersham before you received all the facts that surprises me. Although . . ." His gaze slid to her wrist where the bracelet sparkled. "Perhaps, I should not be surprised at all."

His regard was so warm, it dissolved all her fears of disappointment. The dance drew to an end. They remained standing in their places, their hands still linked. Neither of them wanted to part. He drew her closer and they strolled to the floor's edge, watching the dancers line up for the next reel.

"Now, I shall escort you back to the Radclyffes. Unless . . . this dance is also free?"

"I believe it is, my lord." She paused, seeing Hampton and Radclyffe approach. "However, I think those two may have something to say on the matter. Shall we retreat?"

He saw the men's angry faces. "I think it would be advisable. We do not want to give the guests a melodrama, do we?"

"Definitely not."

They escaped from the ballroom and hurried along the corridor, heading for the charity auction room, her hand in his. She dreaded the furor hot on their heels.

"Langdon!" Hampton bellowed. Elisabeth and Langdon

stopped, a safe distance from the ballroom where the altercation could not be overheard. They turned in the same movement. "Take your hands off Miss Stockwell!"

Langdon's hand slipped from hers, but not before giving her hand an encouraging squeeze. "Good evening, Hampton, Radclyffe. Perhaps we could find a quiet room to discuss this in private? I am sure none of us wish for a scandal to brew."

"I know well that you do, my lord." Hampton pointed an accusing finger at him, his contempt for the man ill-concealed.

"A few words are all that are needed, " Radclyffe snapped. "You will stay away from Miss Stockwell. I will not have you ruining her reputation as you nearly ruined my wife's."

"I have no intention of ruining Miss Stockwell's reputation," Langdon drawled. "I would not dare dream of such a horror." His eyes darkened. "Neither shall I keep my distance from her."

Elisabeth clasped her hands together. He did want her—and honorably too. Her heart sang with it, quashing her mind's rational protests.

"You will stay away from her," said Hampton hoarsely, "or you shall pay dearly for not heeding us."

Her lips pursed, the thrill fading from Henry's public claiming of her. They talked of her like they owned her. She gritted her teeth, hoping for a quick end to the interview.

Langdon's eyebrows rose in a mixture of amusement and scorn. "By what right do you dare to threaten me? You are no kin to Miss Stockwell."

"I am her chaperone, in lieu of her brother. She is my responsibility." Radclyffe folded his arms, immovable.

"For goodness sake!" she burst out, unable to hold her temper in check. "Stop treating me like a mere possession! Has it occurred to anyone that I have a mind and feelings of my own?"

"Elisabeth, please calm yourself," Radclyffe reprimanded, gesturing with his palm facing the floor. "We only care for your best interests."

She glowered at them, getting her breathing under control. Langdon, his own anger masked by nonchalance, remarked, "Her best interests or yours?"

"What the devil do you mean?" demanded Hampton. "Our personal interests account for nothing where this is concerned."

"Oh, really?" Langdon's sardonic mouth twisted.

"You are a regular out-and-outer, Langdon," Hampton snarled. "You will not have your lecherous ways with Elisabeth. You are not worthy of her and never shall be!"

She winced, seeing the insult hit its mark. Too late she moved in front of Langdon, screening him from further sallies. "No, do not say such things!"

Hampton ignored her protests. "You can be sure that you shall never have her, for she will never have any part of you!"

"I should hit you for that, you insolent pup," Langdon growled.

She felt quite prepared to do so for him. Tears of humiliation slipped from her eyes.

"Hampton, go and fetch my wife and tell her that we are leaving at once." Radclyffe handed Elisabeth his handkerchief just as Langdon was in the act of doing the same.

She dried her eyes. Wretched waterworks! She liked it better when her heart had been left in peace.

Langdon returned the handkerchief to his pocket. Hampton stalked off.

Radclyffe's anger reduced to a simmer. "My lord, I am sure you are able to ignore my brother-in-law's remarks?"

"I am sure I shall be able to find some small morsel of honor in my black heart." Langdon ignored the implied insult of cowardice. To her, he said in a gentler tone, "I am sorry your night had to end like this."

Her moist eyes met his sorrowed ones. "He should not have said those cruel things to you, my lord." She tried to say more but the words would not come. Besides, she did not want Radclyffe to witness it.

"Come away now, Elisabeth." Radclyffe took her arm.

She let him lead her away, frequently glancing to see Langdon standing there alone and staring at their retreating forms.

Elisabeth refused to speak during the drive home, staring out the darkened window, remaining lost in her thoughts. For a brief moment, she had allowed herself to love and be loved, but that moment was gone. To be replaced by what? She shot a displeased glance at Hampton who had chosen to drive back with them.

The chastisement started in the hallway of the Radclyffe home. "Elisabeth, we must talk," Radclyffe declared.

"Talk? What is there to talk about?" Speechless with fury and resentment, she turned away, heading for the stairs.

"Where did you get that bracelet?" Odette asked, her voice sharp. "I do not recall seeing it when we left the house."

Elisabeth halted, pivoting to face Odette. She glanced down at her wrist, hating to lie, but she'd had enough recriminations tonight. "It is mine. I forgot about it until the last minute, so I tucked it away to put on later." Her shoulders straightened. "Now, if you will excuse me, I am tired."

"Elisabeth!" Radclyffe bellowed. "You shall come into the drawing room and we shall discuss your disobedience." He led the way.

She stood irresolute in the hallway. Must he make it worse? "I am your guest, Mr. Radclyffe, not your ward."

Radclyffe glared. "You are under my roof, and in the absence of your brother, you are my responsibility."

She trailed into the drawing room behind him. Before anyone could speak, she said, "I know none of you approve of or even like Lord Langdon. You detest him for what he tried to do to Odette and rightly so. But there comes a time for forgiveness. I have forgiven him for his transgressions, why cannot any of you?"

"Elisabeth, you cannot forgive a man you hardly know,"

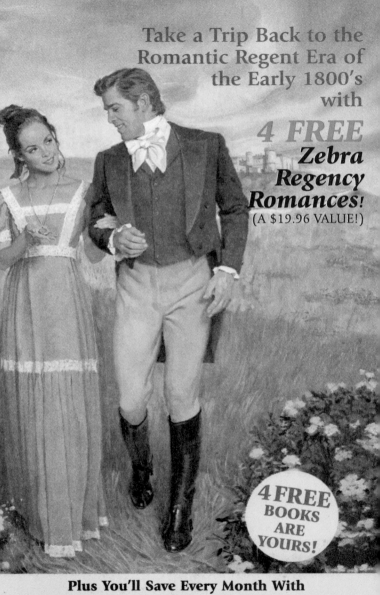

Take a Trip Back to the Romantic Regent Era of the Early 1800's with

# 4 FREE Zebra Regency Romances!
(A $19.96 VALUE!)

4 FREE BOOKS ARE YOURS!

**Plus You'll Save Every Month With Convenient Home Delivery!**

# We'd Like to Invite You to Subscribe to Zebra's Regency Romance Book Club and Send You 4 Free Books as Your Introduction! (Worth $19.96!)

If you're a Regency lover, imagine the joy of getting 4 FREE Zebra Regency Romances and then the chance to have these lovely stories delivered to your home each month at the lowest price available! Well, that's our offer to you and here's how you benefit by becoming a Regency Romance subscriber:

- *4 FREE Introductory Regency Romances are delivered to your doorstep (you only pay for shipping & handling)*

- *4 BRAND NEW Regencies are then delivered each month (usually before they're available in bookstores)*

- *Subscribers save almost $4.00 off the cover price every month*

- *You also receive a FREE monthly newsletter, which features author profiles, discounts, subscriber benefits, book previews and more*

- *There's no risks or obligations…in other words, you can cancel whenever you wish with no questions asked*

Join the thousands of readers who enjoy the savings and convenience offered to Regency Romance subscribers. After your initial introductory shipment, you'll receive 4 brand-new Zebra Regency Romances each month to examine for 10 days. Then, if you decide to keep the books, you pay the preferred subscriber's price, plus shipping and handling.

## It's a no-lose proposition, so return the FREE BOOK CERTIFICATE today!

Odette protested. "You see our dislike for Langdon as unreasoning hatred but truly, we are only being wary of him as you must be."

She sat, staring ahead, preparing for a mental siege. Over her head rained the warnings and accusations against the man to whom she'd given her heart.

Langdon had tried to kill Radclyffe and attempted dreadful, unspeakable things upon Odette's person. He used his charm to take advantage of women and cruelly discarded them when he had used them. He was a drunken lecher! Dishonorable!

Elisabeth kept her thoughts private. Had he not once been as decent and respectable as Radclyffe or Hampton? Did not Lady Westbrooke say that he had changed his ways since returning to London? Here were the two faces of Langdon: the good philanthropist and the lecherous rake. Which was the mask and which was the true Langdon? She doubted it was that simple. Even loving him was complicated.

She looked up at Radclyffe, and he paused in his harangue. "Enough, please." She glanced at Odette, who reclined upon a sofa, smelling salts to her nose. "Odette, I know you think I am being cruel and do not understand, but I do. Do you not remember Mr. Jasper Kerr?" Odette nodded. The men's visages turned grimmer.

"What is your point?" snapped an impatient Radclyffe.

"What do you know of Kerr now?" She watched them.

Hampton said with reluctance, "I heard there was something of an inheritance . . ."

"Quite. Do you not see? He is no longer a money-hungry knave, but a man honorably seeking a wife. Did you know I warned Miss Syndersham about him? How right she is to despise me as I now despise you!"

She stormed from the room.

Hampton followed. "Elisabeth, you have quite lost your mind." He strode to the foot of the stairs where she had stopped.

She stared up at him, registering the depth of his anger. "My lord, I think—"

He grabbed her by the arms and kissed her. His mouth mashed against hers, unforgiving.

The kiss lasted but a moment. He released her. Her fingertips brushed her bruised lips, shocked and dazed by what he had done. Her stomach threatened to review its contents.

"I will not hear another word in favor of this man, nor will his name pass between those lips again. Is that understood?"

"You do not own me, my lord," she snarled. "Do not think you can so control me." She fled upstairs before Hampton could make another assault.

Elisabeth rode out to Hyde Park in a defiant mood, still seething from last night's lecture. The heavy morning mist soon calmed her. At any time, her Henry could ride up to her. She assumed they would meet where they had last time and urged her horse toward that tree-lined boulevard.

A rider waited for her, his mount tramping the ground impatiently. She drew near and he doffed his hat. Henry.

"I wondered if you would come," he said, his smile crooked and endearing.

"I am here." She returned his smile. "How could I not come? We have much to discuss."

"Will you dismount and walk with me a little way?"

She slid from her saddle, keeping the reins in her gloved hands. "Is there something wrong?"

He joined her on the ground and they strolled along the edge of the path. "Elisabeth, last night was a giddy dream. I want to be sure that this is what you want to do."

She squeezed his hand, laughing. "Is this the dangerous rake? You who are so uncertain?"

He made a face, drawing them both to a standstill. "Do not tease, Elisabeth. You are my saving grace. If I know that I have you beside me, I can do anything."

His words touched her more deeply than she expected. Could she be such a force in someone's life? What kind of future would she have, married to a rake? What if he didn't plan to reform at all? At some point, she would have to trust him. She loved his touch, his kisses, the way he made her laugh. She was not green. She could handle this.

"I want to be your wife," she said, clasping his hand. "How long do you think, then, before we are wed?"

"A little time yet, if you truly want your brother's approval."

"It is important to me." She examined the dusty road and met his level gaze.

"Then it shall be done." He drew her into his arms. "You are mine, Elisabeth."

Her lips brushed his. "I did not know it then," she whispered against his mouth. Truly, she did not know it now, but the hazards remained the same. His mouth covered hers and she subsided against him, his kiss filling her with a languorous need. Her arms twined around his neck.

He broke the kiss, his lips brushing her nose. "If we do not talk now, my dear, I fear we never will."

She crinkled her nose at him. "Wedding arrangements? What man is interested in that?"

"I will leave the fripperies of your gown and other womanly mysteries with you." He kissed the tip of her nose again. "We need to set a date. Where do you wish to be married? Your parish or mine?"

"I want us married as soon as possible." She kissed the corner of his mouth. Marriage would be safer than these dangerous meetings. "I do not care to wait until June, nor is it important where we are married, so long as it is in a church." She grinned up at him. "There, have we discussed everything?"

She watched him choke back a laugh. "Then I will find us a church before we meet again. Can you meet me tomorrow?"

"Yes, of course," she murmured, feeling her cheeks flame. She had just turned her world inside out with her agreement. She took her leave, hugging the special moment to herself.

Henry tipped his hat in farewell, silently cautioning himself to be more careful. The temptation to keep her and keep kissing her led down a dangerous path for them both. He liked to think she looked brighter since his proposal. No more gray Miss Elisabeth Stockwell, despite her somber riding habit.

He watched her go, making sure she made at least part of the journey safely. As much as he wanted to, he couldn't follow her. That might arouse suspicion and he couldn't afford that. He didn't need a fresh scandal in the midst of trying to change his ways.

He did want to change. He was sick of the old life. He wanted to prove to the world that the man who could outdrink, out-wench, out-gamble any other in London had had enough of dissipation and would rather spend every moment with the woman he loved.

He swallowed. Loved? He desired her, wanted her, but love her? He wanted a respectable wife, a woman who would give herself unreservedly, was there room for love in there? Henry Langdon had to concede that it was very possible.

Two evenings later, Elisabeth settled to reread Fanny Burney's *Evelina*, ignoring Odette's reproachful glances from across the room. Nearby, seated at a small cherry writing table, Radclyffe dealt with correspondence.

She'd said nothing to either of them about what Hampton had done to her. Odette had suggested there might soon be a match announced between the two of them, but Elisabeth had quashed it in silent remembrance of her promise to Henry.

Her brother and Hampton entered. She looked up. "I see the cavalry have arrived," she dryly remarked, returning her attention to her book. Glancing over the top of it, she noticed they joined Radclyffe in a whispered conversation.

"Lamby dear," Odette called. "What are you conspiring at?"

"Conspiring, madam?" Hampton forced a smile. "I am merely making arrangements."

Elisabeth lowered her book, curious now. "What kind of arrangements?"

Hampton met her gaze with a meaningful one of his own. "It is an affair of honor."

"Of honor!" Odette's hand fluttered at her throat. "Explain yourself."

Elisabeth's eyes closed, feeling dread surround her.

Hampton fidgeted. James stepped in. "He is to meet Langdon tomorrow morning."

"Langdon!" Elisabeth joined in Odette's cry of dismay. She felt ill. Henry had only just survived the last duel. She didn't know Hampton's skills, but this was insanity.

"You cannot!" declared Odette.

"You must not fight him." Elisabeth schooled her features to hide her dismay. "Can you not cry off?"

"My honor and yours is at stake here," Hampton responded, calm once more.

"Honor!" She spoke with scorn. "No honor has been damaged except in your feeble imagining. Langdon has done nothing wrong!"

Hampton barked a cry of disbelief.

"Nothing wrong?" James pursued. "That bracelet you always wear does not belong to the family. It is a gift from him."

The blood drained from her face. She shot a frightened look at Odette.

She found no sympathy there. "You should have known better. Now look at what you have done."

She rose. "You cannot fight Langdon. Who is your second? May there not be some other resolution?"

James laid a hand on her shoulder, his blunt fingers massaging her, coaxing her to relax. "I am his second. There is nothing to be done."

She shrugged off his hand. "Only because you do not wish

anything to be done! This is absurd! How could you agree to this? He has not done anyone any harm!" How could the way for their nuptials be smoothed if her brother participated in a duel against him?

"I will fight him," Hampton said. "He has corrupted you."

"No!" She turned to her brother.

James spoke in a soft, kind voice. "There is no getting out of it now, Elisabeth. Please calm yourself."

Shaking, she resumed her seat. "Tell me everything," she said. "Where is this to take place?"

"You do not need to know," Hampton interceded. "Such details are not for such refined ears as yours."

She wanted to give Hampton's refined ears even more of a shock, but took a deep, controlling breath instead. "I will not rest until I know."

"We would not have you upset," Hampton said. "This is for your own good, my dear."

She turned away, tears rising. What could she do to stop this disaster?

Her brother abandoned the planning and came to console her. "It will all go well, sister dear, Do not fear."

"Go well for who?" Elisabeth retorted, swallowing her tears. "What is it you plan, James? You must tell me."

"You are upset enough already." He patted her shoulder, awkward at this fatherly task.

"I will be less upset if I knew . . ." she trailed off, tears threatening to overwhelm her again.

James cleared his throat before speaking. "We meet Langdon at Hampstead Heath by sunrise."

"Stockwell," began Hampton, "there was no need—"

The makings of a plan sprang into her mind. "You must be early to bed then," she interrupted, smiling upon Hampton. "If I cannot dissuade you from this impossible course, you must at least survive it. I would not like to see you killed."

"See, Odette?" Hampton turned to his sister, smiling. "She does care for me."

Elisabeth's stomach churned. "Not enough to marry you." She rose, and dipped a brief curtsey. "I am tired. I believe I will retire." Getting a nod of permission from Radclyffe, she exited, her motion unhurried.

Out of sight, she bolted upstairs. She couldn't stand being in the same room as Hampton another moment. She needed peace and quiet to think, to plan. Would a note reach Henry in time?

Judging from Hampton's and her brother's mulish faces, it could not be stopped. Yet, she knew she had to try. She would slip from the house a few hours before dawn and hide somewhere by Hampstead Heath. Perhaps her mere presence would be enough.

With these thoughts, she lay awake, trying to plan how to stop them, not having enough facts to think of anything coherent. Someone tapped at her door. "Come in."

Odette entered, carrying a candle. "I thought you might still be awake."

She sat up. "What is it? Is there something wrong?"

"My brother is to duel with Langdon and you ask that?" Odette managed to contain her hysteria, the edges leaking through.

"I will try and stop it," she promised. She reached out to Odette and their hands clasped.

"It can be done," Odette agreed. "Although I fear it will but delay their confrontation."

Elisabeth knew enough to hazard a guess. "As with Jeremy?"

Odette blinked, startled. "How did— A note seemed to be sufficient for Langdon to leave London then. Perhaps a note from you now?"

"I thought of that. Even if Radclyffe allowed such a note to leave this house, I fear it would not be in time." She inhaled deeply. "If I have to stand between them to stop it, I will."

Odette gripped her hand tighter before releasing it. "Godspeed to you," she murmured. "I knew you would not let Lamby come to any harm."

# CHAPTER NINE

After Odette left, sleep eluded Elisabeth. She managed to doze for a few hours before rising, dressing by the light of a single candle. Through the quiet, dark house she crept downstairs. Unlatching the back door, she slipped out to the stables, saddling her mare by feel alone.

She led her horse out to the street, glancing over her shoulder to see if she had disturbed the household. Not a soul stirred. Once out on the street, she swung onto the back of her mare and urged it toward Hampstead Heath.

There would be a point, she knew, where she'd have to allow Hampton and her brother to lead the way. The Heath was a large, wooded area, its size part of the reason why it was popular with duelists. By the time searchers found the particular dueling spot in use, the duelists were long gone, either eating breakfast or being tended by the doctor. She didn't have such time to waste.

She waited within the first clump of trees that marked the borders of Hampstead Heath, hiding in the predawn shadows, waiting for Hampton, or even Langdon to pass. She shivered within her cloak, sniffling as the dew settled on her, wetting her face.

The sound of hooves brought her to attention. She leaned forward, trying to read the coach door's insignia as it passed.

She identified it as Hampton's, letting it pass and waiting so she would not to be noticed. She nudged her horse out into the road behind the coach. Keeping the hood of her cloak pulled up high over her head, she hoped to escape detection if spotted.

Neither the driver nor the coach's occupants spotted her. She fell back in order to keep distance between them. She gripped the reins tighter. She really had no idea how to stop this madness—short of throwing herself into the line of fire. Reason would not work with Hampton. Langdon was her only hope.

The coach disappeared into the woods. She hastened to catch up. The paths within the Heath were many and she didn't want to lose them now.

Ahead, the rattling of coach wheels ceased. She paused, waiting half-breathless to see if they'd reached their destination. The wind brought back to her the sound of the carriage door squeaking and low voices. The occupants had disembarked from the coach.

Dismounting, she led her horse through the woody undergrowth until they were out of sight from the road. She tethered it to a tree, returning to the dirt track and following it until the coach came into sight.

She ducked out of view. She tried to move through the woods silently, wincing at each snapping branch. Discovered too soon, she knew she would be bundled into the coach, destroying her chance to stop this. She dared to glance through the trees to a small clearing.

She stopped. Her slow progress through the woods had rendered her too late! In the small clearing, Hampton and Langdon were back to back, already pacing out the steps between them. At any moment, they would turn and fire.

She pushed her way through the undergrowth, breaking free of the woods as the men spun and fired. She registered that her brother had seen her, but the duelists wholly had her attention.

Dirt and grass flew up at Hampton's feet, marking the accuracy of Langdon's intentional missed shot. Hampton's own shot must have been wide, for Langdon showed no sign of being hit.

Thank God. She could still stop this.

"The other!" Hampton called to James, who wrenched his gaze away from her to proffer the pistol case to Hampton. Langdon left the field, heading toward his own carriage.

Hampton raised his pistol to fire, taking careful aim.

"No!" She sprinted across the final distance between them. She saw Langdon stop and turn at her cry. Hampton's pistol fired, the noise horrifyingly loud.

Langdon staggered and collapsed to the ground.

"Henry!" She raced to him, hearing thudding footsteps coming after her. *Do not be dead, please do not be dead!*

She threw herself to the ground beside him, spotting blood blossoming on his shirtsleeve. Without further ado, she began ripping at her petticoats.

"I am not badly hurt." His blue eyes regarded her with a hint of amusement. A hand from behind her tugged at her arm, but she twisted out of its grasp.

"Elisabeth, leave him!" Hampton commanded.

She gazed up at Hampton, her vision blurred. "You will leave me alone, sir!" she declared, hating the sob in her voice. "He needs my assistance."

Langdon sat up, examining the wound through the bloody rent of his sleeve. "A mere scratch, that is all." He regarded Hampton, who stood at his feet, the smoking pistol in his hand. "Hampton wanted first blood, not to kill me."

Her hopes he spoke true were soon dashed. "By God," snarled Hampton, "I would have killed you if I had not feared hitting Miss Stockwell."

Langdon snorted, wincing as she bound his wound.

"Hampton," she said, her voice steadier now she knew Henry was out of immediate danger, "I think you should leave."

"I will not leave you alone with that rascal!"

"For a man who has just illegally fired upon another . . ."

She controlled her anger. "Wait by the coach then. I will be but a moment."

Hampton remained where he was.

"I suggest you take heed of my second's firearm and retreat," Langdon said with a casual air.

His second stepped forward, pistol raised. Hampton staggered back, before turning and striding toward the coach where her brother waited.

Henry smiled at her. "I take it, my dear, you wished private converse with me?"

She did not return his smile "Indeed, sir. How could you have allowed this to happen?"

"Ah. I thought it might be that." He took her hand in his. "Help me up, I can feel the dew soaking through my breeches."

They rose, Elisabeth needing to do little but steady him. "Well, sir?"

Their embrace grew tender, more intimate. She didn't care who saw, too thankful that Henry lived. She couldn't help it. She reached up and kissed him, dragging his head down between her hands. She kissed him hungrily, aware she might have never been able to kiss him like this again.

He drew back, pulling a dead leaf from her curls. "Believe me, Elisabeth. I tried to get out of it every way possible."

"You could not have appeared here today," she suggested.

He wryly shook his head. "With that insolent pup having already publicly called me a white-feathered coward—yes, my dear, those were his exact words—there was little else I could do."

"You did not fire to wound," she remembered.

"Quite. If I had fired in the air, I would have accepted responsibility for his accusation."

"Which was?"

"Now that you will have to ask him." His masked features revealed nothing, but from the dangerous glint in his eye, he had been deeply angered by it.

"He accused you of more than being a coward?"

Henry's shoulders stiffened. He ended their loose embrace and turned away.

"Henry!"

He looked back over his shoulder. "Elisabeth, if I told you, you would not believe me."

"When will you trust me?"

He swallowed, but did not reply, gripping his wounded arm.

She glared at him. "Then answer me this. Am I defending you in vain?" At that he faced her. "I need to know the truth about all of it, Henry. No more alluding to it, no more delicacy. Tell me the truth of what happened between you and Odette."

"Jealous?" His mouth twisted.

"You know I am not."

He regarded her for a long moment. "Yes," he said. "I am being unfair. You have been nothing but loyal. Will you keep that friendship even after I tell you this?"

Her heart pounded. "What did you do to her?"

He winced at the sudden trepidation in her voice. "I had been given to understand she was available to me, not knowing about Radclyffe. You remember her before she married—she flirted." His brows drew together. "But this is not her fault. Somewhat intoxicated, I rather overestimated her attraction to me and acted on it. Radclyffe appeared on the scene. I . . . I panicked and forced her with me. I let her go but—" He shrugged. "The damage was done. She tried everything to prevent a duel between us, but Radclyffe was too hotheaded and I . . . I did not care."

It sounded like a misunderstanding with a solid dose of bad behavior. Could she forgive him for it? Was that why Hampton took advantage, because he had regarded her actions as inducement? *This is how Odette felt,* she thought, for the first time getting a true inkling of how completely Odette reviled Henry.

He broke the silence. "I regret my actions utterly."

She saw, and believed, his sincerity. "Yes." She touched his cheek with her fingertip. "I know. Yet, therefore, you understand Lord Hampton's position."

He made a noncommittal noise. "Are we still friends?"

"Of course." He had given her much to think about.

"Betrothed?"

"Yes." She darted a look over her shoulder. "Now is not a good time to speak with James regarding that matter."

He inclined his head in agreement. "Soon, though. I must go. Your brother—and fiancé—are waiting for you."

"Is that what he said?" Her mouth worked in outrage. "He is not my fiancé, Henry, you know that. You know it!"

He cradled his wounded arm. "I believe, my dear, it is only a matter of time before he and Society claim you. Not I." He managed a smile. She had never heard him so downcast. "I am glad you came. You saved my life." He strode away, leaving her staring after him.

She wanted to run after him, but she had already declared she was free of Hampton. What more could she say?

Kicking at a grassy tussock, she wasted no time in discovering the cause of the duel. She hastened across the wet grass, accosting Hampton. "You challenged him?"

Hampton nodded. "How was your sweet tête-à-tête?"

She ignored his question, folding her arms. "Why?"

Gazing upon her with infuriating indulgence, Hampton tugged at his shirt cuffs. "Why? Is that not obvious? He is in the process of seducing and ruining you."

She stared at him, her skin feeling clammy. "I am not ruined, my lord. And . . . and he is far better than your most unwelcome attentions!" She spun, striding along the dirt path.

"Elisabeth!" called her brother. "Where are you going?"

"Home." She kept walking.

"We have a carriage!"

She heard the plaintiveness in his cry. "I have a perfectly suitable horse. Good morning, gentlemen."

All the way back to the Radclyffe residence, she pondered everything she knew about the scandal surrounding Langdon. With the information pieced together, she at last acknowledged a certain truth—Henry had behaved as a rake, but apart from frightening Odette he had not harmed her.

By the same token, she wished she could say the same thing of Hampton. He hadn't harmed her—his kiss, while unwelcome, had been brief. She couldn't believe he had broken the dueler's code. His reputation would be sadly tarnished by this, and yet he seemed unrepentant. Was he so sure of her? Could things escalate any higher between Hampton and Langdon? She hoped not.

The Radclyffes said nothing about her unchaperoned adventure. She had either managed to return without them being aware of it, or Odette had smoothed the way for her. In spite of their persistence in her marrying Hampton, they were good people who had treated her with great kindness in allowing her to stay with them in London. Without them, she would never have renewed her acquaintance with Langdon.

Odette entered the sitting room, waving an invitation. "The Bradshaws have invited us to a dinner party tomorrow night. How odd of them to schedule one so quickly."

Elisabeth managed a smile. "Perhaps she has heard of the duel and wishes to be among the first to reflect in its celebrity."

Odette regarded the envelope with sudden distaste. "Perhaps we should not go."

"Nonsense. The duel came to naught in the end. I am sure if we had been 'at home' today, her curiosity would be satisfied."

"I shall see if her invitation includes Lamby," she said. "If so, then we shall all go."

Not relishing the prospect of another evening with Lord Hampton, Elisabeth wondered if Henry had also received an invitation.

* * *

The next morning, Elisabeth met Henry at their accustomed spot in Hyde Park. The mist had just started to rise. She cantered alongside him easily. "How is your shoulder?"

He flexed it to show her it was fine. He winced. "It's a little sore, but it's naught more than a gash."

She smirked. "So I will not need to play nursemaid to you this morning?"

He laughed. "That brings pleasant memories . . . Mmm, indeed, the idea appeals." He brought his horse nearer and leaned over to kiss her.

Snorting, the horses pulled them apart before he reached her. "I have news," he said. She looked at him, curiously. "I have spoken with the curate at my home parish. He will call the banns whenever we wish. It only remains to speak with your brother."

"Will he listen to you after yesterday?" She frowned.

Henry shrugged. "I have to try. I'll talk to him and get him into a civilized frame of mind before I ask for your hand. That is what I plan to do anyway." He chucked her chin. "Cheer up. It is not as bad as all that."

She gave him a wry smile but didn't answer.

"When shall I see you again?"

She bit her lip. "I do not know. The Radclyffes are starting to wonder my early morning rides. Mrs. Radclyffe has hinted at it. We have received a great many invitations but have only accepted one for tonight."

"The Bradshaw soiree?" Langdon smiled. "I shall see you there, my dear. Until then . . ." He kissed her gloved hand. "Pray for my success. Perhaps we will be able to announce our engagement there. Do you not think it would be a good time to announce it?"

She couldn't help but smile at his eagerness, but her smile was tinged with sadness. "If my brother agrees."

He glowered. "We should announce it anyway. In such a public venue, he can hardly turn his back on you. It is forcing his hand, true, but it will gain his permission." His gaze softened. "If it gets you what you want, Elisabeth, I will try any means."

"I would rather not ambush my brother in such a way." She bit her lip.

"Elisabeth . . ."

"I want to marry you, my lord, but if it can be done without a cloud of scandal over our heads, then we shall continue to be received in Town." She offered a conciliatory smile. "I would rather we were tagged with the epithet that I have tamed a rake, rather than you have absconded with me."

"Very well. But I cannot wait much longer, Elisabeth. It is devilishly difficult fighting the old temptations alone." His smile was strained, stiff.

"I know."

They parted for the second time. She turned in her seat as she rode away and saw him watching her. She felt her insides quiver and melt at his regard.

When Elisabeth arrived at the Bradshaws' evening festivities, Mr. Bradshaw drew her aside. "Miss Stockwell, I am glad you came." He took her gloved hand and kissed the air above it.

"We could not refuse an invitation from such an old friend." Elisabeth's cheeks tinged pink.

"I must compliment you on your pluck, Miss Stockwell. I do not know any woman who would have dared what you have done."

Her smile snapped. "Has there been gossip?"

"No, no!" Bradshaw hastily reassured her. "Your brother told me in the strictest confidence and I have kept it. I merely have not had the opportunity to tell you in person." He took her by the elbow, leading her to the rest of the assembled company. "I do hope you will not be too angry when you discover who else is our guest? It was Mother's idea."

"Lord Langdon, by any chance?" At Bradshaw's confirming nod, she smiled. "Mrs. Bradshaw has planned an interesting evening!"

"I am much relieved." His voice dropped. "Mother thinks he is much changed." Bradshaw grimaced. "I can scarcely believe it myself. Certainly he has been reclusive since his return but that means nothing, since the one time he was not—" He halted.

"How has he been reclusive?" She'd seen him so often, she found it difficult to comprehend. When they had not been together, had he stayed by his fireside? Had his latest dueling wound turned septic? Yet, if that were so, he would not be here.

"It almost shames me to say it, but he and I share the same clubs. He has not been seen at any of them. I will wager he is lying low like the scoundrel he is."

"Indeed." She kept her reply noncommittal. Hampton was the scoundrel, not Henry.

"May I have the honor of the first dance?"

"It would be a pleasure, Mr. Bradshaw."

Bradshaw bowed. "If you will excuse me, Miss Stockwell, I must attend to the rest of my guests."

The design of the sumptuous dining hall was left over from a previous era: dark paneling creating murky shadows between the huge candelabras. Oil paintings darkened with age hung in gilt frames, their subjects indistinct.

"It is positively Elizabethan," Hampton murmured, seated to her right.

She turned to tell him that she hoped he meant that as a compliment—and saw a beautiful blonde enter the dining room on Henry's arm. Who was she?

She saw Hampton look toward the dining room door, glancing down at his empty plate before looking back again. His face grew as pale as hers.

*Interesting,* she thought, jolted from her fit of the greens. Hampton knew her.

She leaned toward him and whispered. "Who is she?" Who

was this ravishing beauty with diamonds sparkling in her luxuriant blond hair?

Hampton didn't respond, so rapt was he in gazing upon Langdon's dinner partner. "My lord," she whispered, nudging him. "Who is that?"

He answered without moving. "Lady Sophie," he breathed.

So this is what Lady Sophie looked like up close: absolutely stunning. Elisabeth elbowed him a little harder. "You are staring."

"My pardon," he said, forcing a smile. "I have not seen her for a long time. What the devil is she doing with Langdon?"

"You will have to ask her yourself," she responded. "Perhaps she was also late." She guessed she hoped for that in vain. Lady Sophie's carefree attitude suggested a high comfort level with Langdon. Too comfortable in Elisabeth's estimation. As a young widow, Lady Sophie could afford to be so bold.

Elisabeth picked at her food. She toyed with the contents of her plate listening to Hampton's incessant chatter, each new thread of conversation an attempt to keep her attention from the far end of the table, where Langdon sat eating with gusto.

More than once, Hampton's hand found its way to meet hers where it rested on the table. Every time he did so, she moved away. How dare he publicly claim her? She tried not to grimace at the Radclyffes' approving smiles. Worse, other dinner guests had noticed and discreetly observed his game.

Hampton recaptured her hand with his own. In her ear, he murmured, "If you do not wish me to hold your hand then you must otherwise occupy it." His lips brushed her earlobe and the very touch of them made her shiver.

She cast an imploring gaze down the length of the table. Who else would rescue her but Henry?

Langdon had noticed Hampton's possessive and ardent behavior toward Elisabeth. His upper lip curled into a sneer of frustrated anger, the furrows on his forehead deepening.

His sneer turned into a polite smile when he encountered

her gaze. She rolled her eyes in the direction of Hampton, snatching her hand away from his grasp. *See?* she suggested. *I am not his.*

Langdon's smile widened. She smiled back—he did understand her predicament, even if dinner etiquette currently prevented him from helping her escape Hampton's clutches.

His look grew tender as he raised his glass to her in a silent toast. She returned the toast, feeling his charm work its magic on her. She rolled the mouthful of wine on her tongue, savoring the honeyed yet tangy taste before swallowing. In that brief moment, nobody else in the room existed for her except him.

The rim of her glass still touched her lips. A small shy smile played about her mouth. She felt as if the moment could last forever.

"What the devil do you think you are doing?" Hampton growled.

Startled, she returned the glass to the table before she spilled its contents. "What do you mean?" She didn't know if her voice trembled from Hampton's anger or Langdon's regard.

"I think you know what I mean. What are you playing at with that damned Langdon?"

He couldn't know. One duel between them was more than enough and she suspected Hampton would not be so careless the next time he met Henry on the field.

Placing her hand over his where it lay clenched on the white tablecloth, she was all sweetness, although she hated dissembling. "My lord, I like you, but you are awful when you are mad at me." The slightest suggestion of a pout made Hampton blink once or twice at this sudden change. She relaxed, satisfied another altercation between he and Langdon had been avoided.

Seeing Hampton preparing to pursue the brief romantic moment, she turned and spoke to her brother James on her other side.

"Nothing more than a common actress," James said to his

dinner partner, "and she thinks that just because she is Prinny's mistress she can be accepted into society! Word has it she is the most vulgar creature—and the worst actress ever seen in the West End."

"Surely you exaggerate, James," Elisabeth interrupted. "I have heard that the woman is the most interesting conversationalist."

"It ain't her conversation Prinny is after," James observed. *Rather crudely,* Elisabeth thought, considering the company.

"James . . ." Elisabeth reproved in an undertone.

"Bah!" her brother responded.

The dancing began shortly after dinner, with more guests arriving. Bradshaw quickly came forward to claim his dance with Elisabeth. They had the honor of opening the first set, a cotillion.

Some time passed before the opportunity to talk arose. "Lord Hampton did not look pleased to see you leave him," Bradshaw said.

"He has become impossibly protective. Mr. Bradshaw, I scarcely know what to do with him without causing offense!"

He thought about this for a moment. "I do not think it helps him to see you making eyes at Langdon across the room."

"I was not making—"

"That is what it looked like. I hardly blame Hampton. There is not a soul in London who wants you in Langdon's lair."

She curtseyed to her opposite partner. She had to remember she spoke to an ally of her brother and thus of Hampton. She met his reproachful gaze evenly. "It is kind of you to show such concern, but you need not be."

"I hope not." They made a turn. "One pities Lady Sophie—she deserves better company than he."

"Did they arrive together?"

"Really, Miss Stockwell, I thought you would be the last to carry on Lord Hampton's intrigues."

Of course she wouldn't be interested for herself. Her mouth quirked. "Intrigues? I merely enquired . . ."

The dance parted them. When they rejoined hands, Bradshaw picked up the conversation. "My mother engineered the dinner pairing, but no, they did not arrive together."

She exhaled, relieved. She hated the thought of sharing Henry with anyone. He was hers, even if Lady Sophie outshone her.

At the end of the cotillion, Bradshaw escorted her to the Radclyffes. Hampton paced, waiting for her. Before he had a chance to escort her to the floor for the next set, Elisabeth spotted Miss Syndersham in the company of her mother and Mr. Kerr.

"Excuse me, my lord," she said to Hampton, relieved to find an excuse. "I must go pay my respects to Mrs. Syndersham."

"Can it not wait?" Hampton demanded, his lower lip petulant.

Shaking her head, she pulled away, hastening across to the Syndershams. Hampton caught up, tucking her hand under his arm. Plainly, he did not want to lose sight of her again.

Seeing her approach, Miss Syndersham turned her back. Elisabeth saw Mr. Kerr touch the young woman's arm, glaring over her head at them. Ignoring him, she curtsied to Mrs. Syndersham, who gave a stiff nod in reply.

"Miss Syndersham, I have come to—" Elisabeth began.

"Come, Mama." The young woman took her parent's arm. "Let us see if there is anyone worth seeing here." Miss Syndersham, ignoring her mother's displeasure, took Mr. Kerr's arm as well, leaving her on the outside.

Dismayed by the cut, Elisabeth hovered, uncertain of what to do next. She only wished to apologize.

Kerr gently released himself from Miss Syndersham's grasp. "I think I may stay for a few words with Miss Stockwell." He winced at Fanny's angry look. "I will explain all, by and by." Miss Syndersham nodded, eyeing Elisabeth warily, but moved away with her mother. Kerr bowed to Elisabeth. "May I have this dance, Miss Stockwell?"

She turned to Hampton. "My lord, you will excuse me?"

Hampton frowned. "Elisabeth, my dear, I do not see why you wish to dance with an old flame when it is promised to me!"

"To make amends." She hoped he heard the sincerity in her voice and would allow it. "Besides, you have not yet asked me to dance." She nodded her acceptance to Kerr. He led her out to the floor, forming up part of a quadrille.

# CHAPTER TEN

"Amends?" Kerr asked while they waited for the music to begin in earnest.

"I have wronged you, Mr. Kerr."

"Indeed?" He raised a bushy black eyebrow. She saw he would not make this easy for her.

They stepped through the lively dance. "When I saw you building an acquaintance with Miss Syndersham, I thought you may be . . ." She tried to think of a way to put it delicately. She noted with a spurt of annoyance Kerr did not come to her aid. ". . . angling for her money. I warned her about you before I discovered your circumstances had changed." They turned and bowed to each other. "Congratulations, by the way."

Kerr added an extra flourish to his bow. "You may congratulate me again," he said, taking her hand as they stepped through the dance.

"I may?"

"Miss Syndersham has agreed to become my wife." Kerr held his head high.

"Then I hope I may congratulate you *both* on that happy event," she said. Kerr gazed at her in an arch manner. "Please, Mr. Kerr, will you extend my apologies to Miss Syndersham? She is a friend. I would dislike very much to lose her."

Kerr nodded his acquiescence. They danced in silence for a while, each adjusting to the change in their relationship, altering old opinions to mesh with modern facts. "Tell me, Miss Stockwell," Kerr asked eventually, "who are you to wed? Which lord will it be?"

"At least you offer me a choice!" she blurted. Realizing what she said, she pinked.

His question was a good one but not one she was ready to discuss. She snatched her hand from his grasp but remained within the pose required for the quadrille. "That, sir, is none of your business."

"May I offer you some advice?" Kerr said, undeterred.

She stared ahead, not sure she wanted to hear.

"Marry the richest. After all, then you can be sure he will not be after your precious money."

She twisted to look at him as they paraded. "Mr. Kerr, any man is welcome to my money provided he also gives me his heart."

"*Touché,* Miss Stockwell." The dance drew to a close and Hampton approached them through the crowd. "I see one lord is eager to regain your company. Where is the other, I wonder?"

"Where indeed?" Her anticipation deflated on seeing Hampton come toward them. She wished she knew. Why hadn't Langdon found her instead of Hampton? "Who do you think is my other lordly suitor?"

"If I were a betting man, Miss Stockwell, I would wager it was Lord Langdon, the way you batted eyes at him over dinner." His cold voice softened. "Have a care, Elisabeth. People will talk."

"I only wanted to annoy Hampton." Her brow creased with concern. "Are they talking?"

"Not yet, but it is a dangerous game you play."

"As you say," she uttered, dispirited.

Kerr took her hand and kissed it, returning her attention to him. "Rest assured, Miss Stockwell, I shall endeavor to restore good relations between you and my future bride—and perhaps us as well. I was fond of you, in a way, you know."

She managed a small smile. "In a way."

"That is not enough, I now know." Kerr released her hand and smiled. "How well things have worked out for the two of us after all." He bowed. "Good evening, Miss Stockwell."

Elisabeth and Hampton danced their second cotillion together. He remained cordial and polite, even a little distant. She started to relax in his company once more. Whatever bee had been in his bonnet was gone now.

"Elisabeth, I do hope you do not mind sitting out the next dance."

"It sounds as if I do not have a choice in the matter." She remained cool, while within her heart she fiercely rejoiced. Another round of three dances would practically seal an engagement. She wouldn't allow that.

Hampton looked put out. "It is just one dance."

"I do not mind, my lord." Perhaps she could find a moment to meet with Langdon and ask him his opinions on his dinner companion.

Hampton's boyish smile returned.

"To be honest," she continued, "I will be grateful of the rest. I feel quite danced off my feet!"

"I know I would much rather dance all night with you, but you must tell me when you tire. I am your adoring servant, m'dear. I am yours to command." At the dance's end, he bowed low to her.

His unceasing compliments restored her discomfort. Hampton reminded her too much of Kerr in former days. "I will be out on the terrace," she murmured and fled the ballroom. He did not follow.

Moving through the crush of people, she heard a name that gave her pause. "—Langdon. Kitty's been complaining he has not come to visit her since he came back to London."

"Even I have to say Langdon's doing well to get out of that

Cyprian's clutches. Besides, what chance does she have against Lady Sophie?"

"What chance does Langdon have? That girl has no more heart than the blackest of Cyprians!"

Elisabeth moved on. So Langdon had even abandoned the company of the demireps? How often had he made use of them? She wasn't sure she wanted to know.

She glanced back into the ballroom, curious as to why Hampton had not pursued her. It was unlike him to let her go so easily.

She should have known. The couples forming up for a waltz included Hampton and Lady Sophie. Elisabeth took in the scene with a curious uplift of one corner of her mouth before escaping to the fresh air outside.

With luck, this meant Hampton had renewed his suit with Lady Sophie and she would be forgotten. Had it been guilt or an attempt to inspire jealousy that had him fawning over her all evening?

She leaned on her elbows against the terrace wall, gazing into the blackness of the small garden. Mrs. Bradshaw had chosen to hire stables for her horses instead of building one behind the house. The scent of roses wafted in the air.

She turned on hearing someone approach.

"Good evening, Elisabeth," Henry said. He took her breath away in his formal attire, even in this dim light. "It is a beautiful night, is it not?"

She nodded, gazing up at the dark sky. "It would be perfect if the moon was out."

"I find it perfect now with you in it." He stepped close enough for her to feel his warmth. "These past few days have been the loneliest I have ever experienced."

She softened. "I missed you too." She glanced at him. "By the by, has your wound kept you indoors?" She couldn't tell if he favored his shoulder or not.

"It is but a scratch. Annoying but little more than that."

"And has Lady Sophie helped nurse you back to health?"

She flushed, wishing she could call back the question. That was not how she wanted to bring up the subject.

"Lady Sophie was my dinner companion at Mrs. Bradshaw's behest. Nothing more. She's far too vain for my liking." He grinned. "I am not nearly handsome enough for her scheming."

She smiled, feeling relieved. Mrs. Bradshaw's orchestrations this evening could not have been finer!

"What of you and Hampton?"

Did his lighthearted voice have a touch of the greens as well? "His Lordship's constant companionship is driving me utterly mad!" She remembered him dancing with Lady Sophie and fell silent. Perhaps he'd stopped pursuing her already.

"I thought the match between you and Hampton was made. I had heard talk."

She smiled at him, letting her fingers explore the covered buttons of his waistcoat. "Of course not. Whatever made you think so?"

He was too close. In this proximity, she could do something very rash. She reached up to smooth the frowning lines from the edges of his mouth. "You should not listen to talk."

He tilted his head, kissing her gloved fingertips. "You are right, of course."

She leaned forward, replacing her fingertips with her mouth, all thoughts of discovery and ruin forgotten. His arms slid around her and he pulled her close, trapping her hand between them. She abandoned herself to his kiss, a kiss that was all the more sweeter now that they'd stopped arguing, stopped their jealousy.

He pulled away and cupping her face in his, he gazed at her for a long time. For Elisabeth, nobody else existed in the world but him, gazing at her with such compassion and love. Her eyes filled with unshed tears. "Elisabeth," he murmured. "I have loved you from the first minute I saw you in your dusty riding habit. Even in all my agony, I knew it." He smiled and took her hands in his.

She freed one of her hands and pressed it to his mouth. He kissed her fingertips. "Do not say another word," she whispered, her breath coming ragged as she tried hard to withhold her anguished tears. "Henry, you were right. What I feel for you, it—"

"What do you feel?" he murmured huskily, leaning closer. "Tell me."

"Oh, Henry, I do not think I could put a word to the emotion." She struggled not to repeat the words, but he had to know what she truly felt. It was only fair. "My heart is filled with it and yet my head wonders if it is all a cruel illusion."

"Do not say that," he begged, his voice hoarse.

"I am sorry." She examined the toes of her pale blue slippers.

He raised her chin with a fingertip. Their gazes met. His expression, naked with longing, with emotion, with something deeper but undefinable roused her. "Do not be sorry, my dear. I will wait for your heart and mind to be of one accord. I will not ask your brother for your hand until you are certain of me."

"You will wait?" She shook her head. "No, Henry, I could not ask this of you. After Mrs. Adams strung you along with no reward . . ."

His nostrils flared. "Elisabeth, how do you know about Harriet Adams?"

"When you were delirious, you spoke her name and I—" She gulped, seeing his displeasure. "And I happened to meet her. Her friend, Lady Westbrooke, told me what had happened. That is why I cannot ask you to wait."

He relaxed. "Do not ask me then. I will wait for you anyway." He squeezed her hands. "Elisabeth, you have given me a glimpse, a real glimpse, of what it is to be loved. If you can find your trust in me, it is worth waiting for."

"I do not want to wait." She felt a tear spill onto her cheek and hastily brushed it away before he saw.

"Then there is a chance . . ."

She hated talking in gambling terms, but she nodded. "I ache for you, Henry. I do not want us ever to be parted."

They kissed again, a sweeter communion this time. A delicious warmth suffused her veins. She wanted them to stay joined like that forever.

"Then I will speak to your brother."

"But he—"

"If he refuses, then we will find another way, an honorable one. I have promised you that."

Her fingertips lightly brushed his cheek and lingered at the edge of his mouth. She wanted him to kiss her again, but already she feared they had been too indiscreet. "I have been out here too long, I must go." She hastened back into the house, her heart rubbed raw.

Inside the deserted dining room, she wiped away another unbidden tear as the last refrain of the waltz came to an end. Smoothing the folds of her sky blue silk gown, she slipped through the hallway and into the ballroom, making her way to Hampton, who stood alone at the edge of the dance floor. It would not do for him to become suspicious of her whereabouts.

"Let us take a walk in the garden," he suggested without enthusiasm.

She resisted, unwilling to take the night air with him. "What is wrong, my lord?"

"Nothing."

Oh Lord, it looked like he would cry. *Damn that Lady Sophie!* Taking his arm, she steered him from the ballroom, crossing the terrace and entering the small garden. Here, he would have some measure of privacy.

"How was your dance with Lady Sophie?" she asked in a soft voice, not wanting to tear at his heart. Just because she didn't love Hampton didn't mean she should not be kind to him.

Discomfited, he twisted a shadowy rose from its stem. "Lady Sophie does not care two pins for me," he replied, "and I do not care about her either! It is you who I care for, Elisabeth."

He dropped the rose and grabbed her arms where they were bare above her long white gloves. His gloved fingers dug into her, but he ignored her shocked struggles. "I love you to distraction. Elisabeth, will you put a poor fellow out of his misery and marry me?"

She could only think of the misery such a marriage would bring. Twisting out of his grasp, she walked further into the garden, trying to get away, to think, to breathe. Hampton followed. "My lord," she began, trying to find the right words.

"Just tell me—yes or no," he demanded in an agonized whisper.

"I cannot give you a one-word answer," she cried, impatient. "My lord, you are sweet, but I do not love you enough to make you a good wife. You deserve someone who will adore you without questioning."

"You love me a little," Hampton persisted.

She backed away from him. "I am fond of you, my lord, but as a friend."

"Elisabeth, my darling, the best marriages are based on friendship." He wrung his hands. "My love for you is strong enough for us both. It is so very difficult to wait for you to say yes."

She batted away his hands. "I am not asking you to wait."

He pulled her into a gap in the bushes lining the path.

A breathless cry escaped her lips.

"I knew you loved me." His mouth pressed to hers in a brutal, passionate kiss, his arms clamping her to him.

With all her strength, she pushed a little distance between them, gasping for breath. "What the devil—"

Hampton kissed her again with the same intensity, one arm firmly around her waist, his other hand behind her head, clawing into her curls in his ferocious embrace.

Panic welled. This couldn't be happening. How could she

have been so foolish? Hampton had lost all control. If he took her . . .

She fought harder to be free of him. His mouth slid from hers to nuzzle at her neck. His hands pawed all over her, tearing fabric. "Hampton!" she protested. "Stop! Please!"

"You want it." His hand scooped below her neckline. "You know you do."

"You heard what Miss Stockwell said."

Hampton released her, springing around to defend himself.

Falling free of Hampton's loosened embrace, she staggered, wiping her mouth with the back of her hand. She shook with relief at the sight of her rescuer.

An irate Langdon stood with a firm grip on Hampton's collar, twisting his arm up behind his back. "Keep your hands off her!"

Hampton shook himself free of Henry's grasp. "You are one to talk!" he snarled.

Seeing Henry's fists close and rise to strike, she hung onto his arm. "No, Henry! Do not hurt him!"

"Very well." With painful slowness, Langdon lowered his fists until they remained clenched at his sides.

She clung to him, drawing in a shuddering breath. "I am going to get my cloak and go home."

Henry gave her a tender look. "You cannot go back inside looking like that," he murmured.

Her hair falling about her shoulders, she started to tug her gown back into some semblance of order.

"I will fetch your cloak and take you home if you wish."

She didn't want to stay a moment longer in Hampton's presence. She clutched at Henry's coat sleeve. "I will come with you. Do not leave me alone with him."

"Heavens, no. I will see you to my coach first." Coolly polite, he turned to Hampton, who sagged against the bushes, his face white with shock. "Good evening, Hampton."

Henry strode down the short path to the house, Elisabeth hastening after him.

Stirred into action, Hampton grabbed her arm, holding her back. "Elisabeth, you are not letting him take you home."

Angrily, she wrenched her arm free. "Oh, yes I am! Do you think I would trust you alone again?" She hurried to catch up with Langdon.

"And you would trust him?" Hampton, keeping pace, gaped in disbelief.

"He deserves my trust," she retorted with a cutting sneer. Why wouldn't he leave her be? "Unlike you."

Langdon turned and glared at him.

"He will ruin you!" Hampton hissed at her before scuttling away.

"Perhaps I want him to." She ran to Langdon, her arm entwining in his, leaving Hampton alone in the garden.


Langdon's coach jolted along the macadamized roadways of London at a slow pace, crowded by revelers hastening to their next destination. Within the coach, its two passengers sat in silence, watching the other opposite in the light of a single coach lamp. He appeared relaxed, his double-breasted redingote unfastened to reveal his fine white shirt and waistcoat.

She clutched her dark blue woolen cloak high around her chin, aware of the disarray of her gown beneath. She spoke in a choked whisper. "I am glad you showed up when—"

"I was following you."

His calm, flat voice startled her. "You were?"

"At a distance." Henry's lazy smile showed his pleasure at her delighted surprise.

He had watched over her! "I am grateful to you for rescuing me. I swear, you are turning into quite a knight in shining armor."

He chuckled. "Hardly." He patted the seat next to him. "Come here."

She slipped from her seat and joined him, still shocked by her latest adventure. "Why . . . why did you do it?"

He twisted to face her. At his loving gaze, she felt a warmth blossom deep within her. "You are mine. Elisabeth"—the way he said her name was like a caress—"you are unlike any woman I have ever met. I have not felt like this about anybody for years." His voice had a kind of bemused wonderment in it.

She leaned closer and murmured, "Truly? Not even Odette?"

"Love and lust are two entirely different things," he reproved without a hint of anger. "As I have long since learned but refused to acknowledge." He changed the subject. "You will, I hope, inform the Radclyffes of Hampton's actions?"

She nodded. "They have great plans to marry me to him, but I am sure once they learn of this, they will abandon them." She shuddered, unable to stop recalling Hampton's attack. She'd dismissed the first unwanted kiss as a moment of frustration, but this . . .

She felt Henry's arm about her shoulders and settled into him. Henry's presence might do complicated things to her heartbeat, but she felt safe with him, reassured.

"I will call him out tomorrow," he declared in a soft, dark voice.

"No!" she cried, sitting up and facing him. "Not again! You must not!"

"He has made free with your honor, as I had with Mrs. Radclyffe's, and has dispensed with his by that act," he growled. She felt his entire body coil and tense, ready to pounce.

Her eyes widened. Here was confirmation of how far Langdon had gone with her friend. She forgot about the duel for the moment. "You went no further?"

He grimaced. "I don't want to talk about it now."

He was right. First, she had to prevent another duel from taking place. She leaned against him as if her slight weight alone could prevent it. "But you cannot fight him!"

His eyes narrowed. "You care for him that deeply?"

She pressed his shoulders back against the bolsters. "I care for you that deeply, you fool."

She felt the repressed anger leach from him. He patted her hand. "My dear, you must not allow the specter of one lost duel disturb you."

"Not one," she interrupted, "but two. That is two too many."

He smiled. "I have won many a duel before and am a crack shot with the pistol. This time I will not miss."

She regarded him with a slight tinge of horror. "Then you will murder him?"

"No. Merely wing the wretch. I have no intentions of exiling myself just yet."

Her hands smoothed across his chest. "He will kill you if you give him the chance."

Henry snorted. "The boy is too angry to shoot straight."

She inhaled the night air, calming herself. She could not let this happen. "Promise me you will not call out Hampton," she beseeched, gripping the front of his waistcoat and drawing herself closer to him. "I could not bear to see you hurt again."

Their faces were so close in the shadowy carriage, she felt his breath hot and fast upon her cheek. "It means that much to you?"

Unable to speak, she nodded, pressing a kiss near his mouth.

"Then I shall not challenge him, my dear. I promise." He guided her to his lips, sealing his vow with a deep kiss. He possessed her with a sure familiarity that made her melt.

Certain in the knowledge that she had kept him safe from harm, she essayed a light flirtation. "And now what do you have planned, my lord? A seduction perhaps?"

His fingers bunched around a handful of her cloak. "You are cruel to tease. In a coach? Elisabeth, someone has been a bad influence on you."

She laughed softly. "Hush, my lord. Forgive my mischief. If you do not wish to ravish me . . ."

"Minx, you are too much temptation for an old rogue," he grated with choked restraint. "I promise you would not find me lacking in that department."

His kiss had a challenging edge to it, but his lips soon softened, drawing her into a series of openmouthed kisses that calmed and yet excited her for the remainder of the journey. She wished they would never end, feeling reassured and loved.

After a time, the coachman tapped on the roof.

She resented the coachman for so speedily bringing them home. Could he not have circled the city for an hour or more? Not inclined to move, she felt Langdon shift as he looked over her head out the window.

"Elisabeth," he whispered huskily, "we have arrived at the Radclyffes'."

Her voice echoed his regret. "I do not want to go in just yet." Yet she sat up as the coachman opened the door.

"You have to go," he said. "No doubt Hampton and the Radclyffes are hotfooting it after us."

"Thank you for being there when I needed you." She kissed him on the cheek with lingering gentleness.

He hemmed and hawed, finally regaining control. He chucked her under the chin. "Elisabeth, I will always be here when you are in need. Come to me if the situation becomes untenable."

She smiled. She wanted to go with him now. "I will, I promise."

The coachman helped her out of the carriage. She ran into the house and upstairs to her room. The rattling of coach wheels faded down the street.

Elisabeth undressed and prepared for bed. Clambering in between the cool white sheets, she wished she didn't have to face the consequences for tonight's actions. She smiled, recalling Langdon extricating her from Hampton's clutches and their carriage ride home. This night had ended with a peaceful joy. She would remember it that way without any recriminations.

She snuggled her head deeper into her plump pillows, her thoughts focusing on Henry. Elisabeth could not recall being happier than when with him. If only the shadow of his reputation did not lie over their love, then surely her family and friends could see his true self.

# CHAPTER ELEVEN

Lost in her thoughts and dreams, Elisabeth cried out at hands shaking her. "Elisabeth!" a voice shouted.

Startled, she batted the hands away before she realized they belonged to Radclyffe. "What is it? Are we on fire?"

"Get out of that bed and come downstairs immediately!"

She pulled on a lacy dressing gown over her modest white nightdress. Radclyffe grabbed her arm and dragged her down the stairs. Never had she seen him so unspeakably furious.

Confronted by a tearful Odette and her angry brother in the drawing room, she clutched her gown tight around her.

"Oh, Elisabeth!" Odette collapsed, sobbing, on the couch. "I was so afraid that Langdon had abducted you! You have no idea how relieved I am to see you safe!" She opened her arms wide, but Elisabeth did not run into them. How could she? Odette of all people should understand how she felt.

"We thought we would return here first to see if Hampton's fears were incorrect," James told her.

"I cannot begin to imagine what kind of stories he has told you," Elisabeth said in quiet anger, her cheeks burning with the memory of their liaison in his carriage. "Langdon behaved with the utmost decorum. Not once did he try to force himself on me. Unlike Lord Hampton."

"At the moment, I would much rather believe Lamby," James told her, his arms folded. "You have behaved most irresponsibly since coming to London. Somehow, you have got it into your head Langdon is a good man. There is not a streak of it anywhere!"

"That is not true!" she protested. "You do not know him as I do. None of you! He stopped Lord Hampton from forcing his kisses on me!" Hysteria crept into her voice. "My hair and dress were in such a mess I had to leave. I could scarcely go searching through the ballroom for somebody to escort me!" She tried to breathe normally. "To avoid scandal, Langdon fetched me my cloak and brought me here."

"I never thought you could come up with such lies," Radclyffe blasted. "Langdon has influenced you more than I thought possible. Well, I will put an end to that. Have done already."

"What do you mean?" His announcement puzzled her.

James spoke, his anger fading. "You are going to marry Lord Hampton. He asked me for my consent and I have given it."

"But . . ." What about Henry? Had he not asked James yet? She faced her brother, who stood firm and unyielding. "But you cannot!" she exclaimed, aghast at this turn of events. "I do not want to marry him!"

"It has all been arranged," Radclyffe told her. "You will be wed before the end of the Season."

"I did not come to London to get married," she declared, her voice cold, all hysteria gone. "Most certainly not to Lord Hampton. I would much prefer to be packed off to Stockwell House than to be forced to marry him."

"And Langdon?" asked her brother in a soft undertone. She shook her head. As sure as she was about Langdon, now was not the time to bring it to their attention. They wouldn't listen to her, being so deep-seated in their prejudices.

Odette rose, putting an arm around Elisabeth's shaking shoulders. Her watery smile almost sent Elisabeth into tears. "There, there, dear. You have always liked my brother. Just now you are mad at him, but when you are calmer you will see this is right." Odette seemed incapable of comprehending her brother's reprehensible actions.

"Never!" Elisabeth shrugged off Odette's arm and for a brief moment regretted it, seeing the hurt in her friend's face. "You will have to drag me down that aisle kicking and screaming, because I am not going to marry him!"

"Elisabeth, you will not leave this house until you do!" declared Radclyffe. He eyed her brother, who nodded his support.

"We will see about that!" she flashed back and stormed off.

The first light of dawn scarcely marked the horizon, when Elisabeth slipped downstairs and out to the stables at the rear of the Radclyffe's London home.

She had to see Henry. She had to know why he hadn't asked James for her hand in marriage. Did he not want to marry her?

She saddled her mare, the stablehands not yet stirring in the loft above. Again, she was grateful for the thoroughness in which her horse master had taught her all aspects of horsemanship.

Leading her mare out into the small, cobbled courtyard, she caught sight of a dark figure near the house.

He stepped out into the dim light. "I thought I told you not to leave this house."

She stood her ground. "I am only going for a morning ride. Surely you would not deny me my daily exercise?"

"I will deny you everything until you come to your senses." Radclyffe crossed the small space and took the reins from her. "I know what Langdon is like, Elisabeth. He will not give up. Only marriage to Hampton will keep you safe."

"I'd rather be sent back to the country," she snapped, wincing as Radclyffe whistled for a stablehand.

"I do not think you would even be safe there."

"You are not my guardian any more."

"So you keep saying." Radclyffe managed a tight smile.

Unresisting, she allowed him to take her back inside. She couldn't make too much of a fuss about missing her morning ride.

She remained under the wary eye of Radclyffe for the rest of the day, forbidden to leave the house. She politely resisted any persuasive attempts to change her mind.


Henry stepped into White's, feeling the smoky interior cloak him like a favorite blanket. He'd stayed away from the place as much as possible, but discreet inquiries had led him here to find James Stockwell, Elisabeth's brother. The man had been avoiding him, he was certain. Yet, his Elisabeth needed protection.

His, preferably.

He found him at the gaming tables. Henry hung back, observing the young man play. He frowned. Stockwell had chosen a table devoted entirely to luck, where little or no skill was required. It all depended on the throw of the dice.

Elisabeth's brother dressed in the highest puff of fashion, with a cravat that billowed in a complicated knot from under his chin, bracketed by jacket points that threatened to stab his clean-shaven chin.

Henry's frown deepened. Elisabeth's attire had remained simple, understated and not nearly as expensive as her brother's outfits, if he knew anything about women's fashion. He wondered at it. Why did Elisabeth spend much of her time in the country, wearing simple gowns most gentlewomen would shriek at in horror, when her brother gallivanted about in Town?

And why, in the face of such neglect, was this wretched fellow's permission so important to her?

He bided his time, waiting until Stockwell had left the table, and sauntered forward, intercepting his path. "Good evening, Stockwell."

The idiot tried to brush past him without acknowledgment, but Henry's arm shot out and caught him. "Stay a moment. I would have a word with you."

Stockwell shook free of his grasp. "I cannot think what you would have to say."

Henry sighed. "I have no quarrel with you, nor your sister either."

"I am sure you have no quarrel with my sister, my lord, but I would ask you not to speak of her."

His temper flashed. He wasn't good enough for her, was that it? He fought to take calming breaths. In that short space of time, Stockwell had moved on. Henry followed. "I know you have a poor opinion of me, but if you would just hear me out."

"I have heard more than enough, my lord." Stockwell's face darkened with fury. Henry smelled alcohol on his breath. How much had he had to drink? "Your charms will not work on me, nor on my sister, no matter how hard you try."

Henry couldn't help it. He smirked. His charms had worked a thousand times over on Elisabeth, and he thanked God every day for it. Without her, his road to respectability would be so much lonelier.

"How does she fare?" She hadn't appeared for their morning rendezvous and it worried him.

"She is resting." Stockwell's frown deepened. "After what you have done to her, I am amazed at your gall—"

"What *I* did to her?" Henry's voice dropped into cool menace. "You mean Lord Hampton."

"So your stories tally?" Stockwell sneered. "How convenient for you. What hold do you have over my sister?"

Henry's cravat felt suddenly too tight about his throat. "I have no hold over her. Rather, it is she who holds me." At Stockwell's astonished expression, he hurried on, needing to get all the words out before Stockwell regained his voice. "You have heard I am reforming? It is in every aspect of my life—I am only here to speak with you—and Elisabeth is to be thanked for my sticking to the course. After that idiotish thing I did with the present Mrs. Radclyffe, I knew I had to change. Elisabeth is my encouragement. My new life revolves around her. All it needs is your permission to take her to wife."

"Wife?" Stockwell blurted. "Even if all you say is true, and that I doubt, it is too late. Last night I gave my approval to Lord Hampton to marry her."

Henry caught his sleeve. "You what? Are you mad?"

Stockwell didn't answer, shaking free of him and returning to watch the game.

Clouds of anger billowed over Henry's sight, his hearing, all his senses. Elisabeth was lost to him? Married to that oaf?

Not if he had anything to do about it.

His teeth bared in a smile, he followed Stockwell.


Later that evening, the abrupt arrival of Mr. Bradshaw halted Hampton's undeterred wooing of Elisabeth in the drawing room. He panted with the exertion of running.

"Mr. Bradshaw, this is an unexpected visit." Radclyffe looked beyond him to the butler.

The butler bowed his way out. "He said it was urgent."

Radclyffe turned to Bradshaw. "What could possibly be so urgent?"

Bradshaw bowed. "I have come to relate some news to Miss Stockwell that cannot wait." He glanced, embarrassed, at her curious face. "In private, if you please, Miss Stockwell."

Noting the anxiety in his voice, she agreed. She hoped it wasn't another proposal. She followed him out into the hallway. "What is it? What has happened?"

"Your brother is at White's," Bradshaw told her. "We have no time to lose. Stockwell is on the verge of losing the entire family fortune if we do not stop him. Langdon's luck is better than his and they are betting huge amounts with each cast of the dice."

"Langdon?!" She paled. Henry? Why did he do this to her

now? She was betrayed—all her trust and hope in Henry's reform had been shattered in one fell blow. His abstention from gambling appeared over. "And you left him there alone?"

"I came to you for assistance. He will not listen to me, but perhaps he will listen to his sister. He has before."

She stepped back, waving him away. How could she face him now? "I cannot go into White's, you know that."

"You could send a message."

"We both know my brother would not heed that."

Bradshaw mangled his gloves in frustration. "Then I must return to do what I can."

She watched him go, her stomach sinking with pain. Why could she not get her brother out of this scrape of all scrapes? Her eyes widened. Perhaps she could. "Wait! I have an idea. Have a carriage ready."

She raced upstairs to her room. How she wished she wasn't the only one who could talk James out of his pigheadedness. With the hatred toward Langdon also clearly rubbing off on him, she knew he would not retreat from any challenge Langdon laid down.

Why had he done it?

Calling out for Maggie, she secured her hair into a tighter knot, cursing her foolish heart. How could she have trusted him? All that remained now was to save her brother from ruin. She removed her jewelry and undressed, changing into a set of James's evening clothes brought to her by an astonished Maggie.

"Maggie, Mr. Stockwell should have a court wig in his room. Go fetch it, will you?"

With the wig in place, she dashed downstairs. Bradshaw waited for her in the foyer. He gaped at her, stunned. No doubt he expected her to have written a note. "Hur . . . hurry up!" he managed to get out. "Hampton's waiting in the coach."

She sighed. She had not wanted to draw Hampton into this, but he seemed determined to accompany them. She hastened out, dragging the astonished Bradshaw behind her and climbing into the horse-drawn coach. Bradshaw gave the order for full speed to White's—London's most prestigious club.

Hampton stared at her, startled beyond belief. "Elisabeth?"

"Mr. Elijah Stockwell, if you please, m'lord," she replied, deepening her voice and using a country accent. "Young James's cousin." She elegantly crossed a trousered leg and patted the white-blond wig that crowned her head.

"Give me one good reason why I should not stop this carriage and take you back," Hampton demanded, his gaze flickering over her now very visible legs.

"Are you mad?" Bradshaw echoed, finding his voice.

She adjusted her cravat before replying in her normal voice. "Listen to me, both of you. I cannot very well expect to gain entrance to White's in my evening gown, now can I?" She glanced at Hampton. She had not wanted him to come but perhaps he could be of use. "Mr. Bradshaw has told you of my brother's stupidity?"

"Yes, that is why I am here. You do not need to do this. I could persuade James to—"

She cut him off. "You could talk your head off all night, but he will not listen." She leaned forward, wanting to communicate her urgency. "My family honor and fortune is at stake, my lord." She held up a hand, silencing any further protests. "Hear me out. You see, I have done this before. James once got involved in a similar scrape and it was I who had to talk him out of it. Admittedly, it was in the country, but I can talk him out of this too, if we get there in time."

"How can I help you?" Hampton's plaintive look wished her elsewhere—and dressed in something else. She wished he would stop looking at her calves.

"You are my passport into White's." She thought for a moment, twiddling with her cravat. "To cover any mistakes I might make . . ."

With a sigh, Hampton leaned over. She froze with sudden fear. With one hand, he untied the bow of her cravat. "And to make sure your cravat is tied properly. It is an utter mess!"

"I am Elijah Stockwell, not Beau Brummel." She pouted while Lord Hampton fixed her cravat. She didn't relish the nearness this task required. To judge from his smirk, he hadn't minded at all. When he was done, she curtly thanked him.

Their coach stopped, jerking its occupants forward. Bradshaw and Hampton stepped down from the carriage. Hampton turned to help her.

"My lord, I am not in skirts," she hissed. He held the door instead and closed it when she had descended. "Practicing to become a coachman, old boy?" she guffawed, adopting her hoarse country accent and earning a hastily hidden grin from White's doorman.

With both gentlemen acting as her sponsors, she gained entrance to the club as a guest. She restrained from staring as they hurried to the salon reserved for serious gamblers. To her knowledge, a woman had never yet breached the doors of White's. From what she could see, it looked like any other elegant household, sumptuously decorated in only the very best of fabrics and in the finest of taste.

They reached the salon, a white-walled room filled with dark tables of all sizes. A large group of gentlemen stood around the dice table, leaving only a few dedicated gamblers hunched over their cards elsewhere. At the center of the crowd stood her brother and Langdon.

"You have won everything," said James, defeated.

Her heart plummeted. Ruined! And by Langdon!

Without her brother's financial support, they were destitute, dependent upon friends, and living a very mean existence indeed. If her alliance with Langdon ever came out, there would be no cottage reprieve. She'd be on the streets with nowhere to go, no way to earn money except on her back. Nobody would take her into their house as a governess or companion.

Hampton tugged at her elbow. "We are too late," he whispered. "You must leave before someone discovers you."

Langdon glanced at the new arrivals before returning to his perusal of James's humiliated figure. His cool disdain chilled her. How could this be the same man? She turned her head away and whispered to Hampton, "No, there is something more to this." Neither man had yet quit the table.

"Was I not right all along then?"

She gave Hampton a withering look and nudged Bradshaw forward, following him to her brother's side. "Look here, James!" Bradshaw exclaimed. "Your cousin Elijah arrived in town this evening."

She sensed Langdon's—not Henry, she could never call him Henry again—penetrating gaze but did not dare look in his direction, waiting for James to face her. He turned slowly, reluctant to meet kin when at his lowest ebb. His eyes widened in recognition. "Cousin Elijah," he said, no life in his voice. "You just missed me lose Stockwell House."

Stockwell House lost? Why did Langdon do this to her family? She couldn't help but shoot a questioning glance at Langdon, desperately hoping for an answer. She gained only the knowledge Langdon recognized her, judging from his raised eyebrow. With a sick feeling in her stomach, she met her fear of exposure head on.

"Sir," she addressed Langdon, "are you so ungallant as to purposely pauperize this poor boy?" She ignored his amusement at her deep accent.

"Good Lord, no!" he declared, once he had regained the power of speech. "My apologies, Stockwell," he said to her brother, "I fear in my love for the game, I lost track of the winnings."

"I'll bet," muttered Hampton and it was a phrase echoed in many variations around the table.

Langdon ignored them all. "Tell you what," he said jovially. "I will give you the chance to win it all back."

"And if I lose?" James revived at this unexpected hope.

"Is there any money locked up in trust?"

Elisabeth mirrored her brother's frown. So, this was his

game. He had done his research well. Did he truly expect to win her this way?

James replied slowly, "There is my sister's dowry. Twenty-five thousand guineas. It is in trust until her wedding."

"Then we shall throw for your sister's hand in marriage against all I have won this evening." He directed his triumphant grin not at James but at Elisabeth.

"For God's sake." Hampton grabbed James by the shoulder. "She is betrothed to me. You cannot!"

"Not officially." James glanced at Hampton before turning to Elisabeth, mutely begging for permission to accept the bet and restore his fortune.

Her guts ached. "I cannot believe the bets in London! Never in my life have I heard such outrageousness!" A few guffawed at the naive comments of this country hick. "Look here, cuz. It seems to me Lady Luck has deserted you for the night. If the gentleman here don't object, why don't I throw for you?"

Muttered disapproval masked Hampton's whispered protest. "Are you mad?" James could only stare at his sister. She knew he recalled her lectures against gambling.

"I would rather do it, as it is my marriage," she whispered back. "If it will get Stockwell House back, I must!" She turned back to the table.

"It is most irregular," said Langdon, smiling, "but I have no objections to your cousin throwing for you, Stockwell."

Before anyone else protested, she picked up the small wooden cup containing the two dice. Holding her steady hand over the opening, she shook it three times before tipping out the contents.

Eleven. She allowed herself a small smile, hiding her palpitating heart. It faded at Langdon's cast. The count tied.

The dice rolled again. The two cubes of ivory tumbled across the green felt of the table. A four and a six landed face up. Langdon picked the dice off the table, placed them in the cup, and flicked them out again with a flip of his wrist. Ten. Again, he matched her throw.

"Best out of three?" she quipped. Her luck would run out sooner, rather than later. Her stomach tied in knots, she exchanged a tense, amused glance with Langdon. James wiped his brow with his white handkerchief. She sensed the nervous tension in her companions. With a slightly unsteady hand, she put the dice in the little cup and began to shake it.

She stopped. "It seems to me that the Fates don't want you to marry my cousin." Her accent wavered dangerously into her natural voice, albeit deeper. "Why don't we lower the stakes, if you and Stockwell agree."

"Lower them?" Langdon gazed at her, propping his chin on his thumb, pretending to be puzzled over this change of direction.

"If you lose, Stockwell wins the house and you keep the money he 'as lost so far." *Maybe now James will take some interest in the running of the estate.*

"And if I win?"

"You win his consent to marry Miss Elisabeth, but she must agree to it. Do you dare take the risk?" She returned his cool gaze, wanting to bite her lip.

If he refused this unorthodox change of bet, he did not truly love her, wanting only to destroy her. If, on the other hand, he agreed, he would be trusting that her love for him would see his goals realized. This would be one last chance for Langdon to redeem himself. It would be for naught, unless he could explain why it had reached this pass, without any consultation with her.

Nobody else around the table found any gain in this new offer for Langdon, except that poor Stockwell may be spared any further loss. James quickly agreed. She had ears only for Langdon's reply, which came reluctantly. "Very well. Throw the dice."

She felt a relieved exhalation from Hampton down her neck. Sensing Langdon played a game within a game with her, she had no recourse but to continue. Was he so sure of her? She unloaded the dice cup.

Nine. She bit her lip, unable to help it. She would much prefer to win Stockwell House for her brother. Why did Langdon choose this less than honorable way to make her his? Had he been goaded into this destructive act? Noting his wolfish grin, her hope flickered out.

"By the God of Chance, you have to win!" muttered James.

"According to the *laws* of Chance," she replied, regaining her composure, "I am equally likely to lose."

Refusing to look at the table surface, she examined Langdon. Where had her Henry gone? In his place, stood this cruel, heartless man. Her life rode on this roll.

He also paid no attention to the dice he flung onto the felt surface, his gaze perusing her disguise.

The release of held breaths drew down their gazes to the table. Twelve. Langdon glared in undisguised triumph at Hampton, Elisabeth apparently forgotten.

She scorned him. "You're a foolish man, sir."

His expression changed to disbelief. "Why?"

"I know my cousin well." She ignored the convulsive upward twitch of Langdon's mouth. "Unless she's changed since I saw her last, she will marry only for love."

"How do you know she does not love me?" he asked, deadpan. He directed a queer little look at her, which spoke volumes. Her hunch had been right. Anger had led him down his old path. But she needed to be sure.

"How can she love a man who has destroyed her family and her honor?" She saw the barb hit home, inwardly wincing in sympathy.

James caught Langdon's quickly veiled expression. Hampton pushed past Elisabeth. "Langdon, I will throw you for Miss Stockwell's hand in marriage."

"This young . . . man," and only those aware of her disguise noticed his slight hesitation, "has shown me that luck can desert even the most worthy cause. I think I will stop for tonight. If I may call on you and your delightful sister tomorrow morning, Stockwell?"

James nodded, grim.

Langdon bowed and left.

For the benefit of the club and the remnants of her own reputation, Elisabeth said to her brother, "I'm sorry I lost, cuz. At least Cousin Elisabeth can bawl me out as well as you."

The Stockwell party made a dignified retreat from the gaming room. The carriage door had barely closed upon the foursome when tempers snapped. "Good grief, James!" she exclaimed, abandoning her country accent. She cast off her blond wig, revealing her tightly pinned-up hair. "What on earth possessed you to come up against Langdon?"

"It is scarcely my fault your hand in marriage is lost to him," he retorted. "You agreed to it—and you threw for it!"

"I would not have had to if you had not gone and lost the entire family fortune! What are you going to do now?"

James rubbed his hands through his hair. Bradshaw came to her brother's defense. "Do not be so hard on him, Miss Stockwell. Langdon was intent on playing and beating James. He was so sly and charming about it, we were in over our heads before we realized his game."

"You could have walked away," she stubbornly insisted. "You men have no sense!"

"I hope you are not including me in that rash generalization, Elisabeth," Hampton interceded, appearing churlish. "It is rather unfair. You yourself were extremely lacking in sense to embark on such a ridiculous charade. What if somebody had found you out? Your reputation would have been sadly tarnished."

"I am certain Lord Langdon pierced your disguise," put in James. "He was giving you the strangest looks."

She blushed. In the semi-darkness of the coach it went unnoticed. "If he had, he chose not to unmask me. And before you say another word, my lord, it would have been his perfect revenge, but he did not take it."

"Of course not," replied Hampton, "he already has it in winning James's consent to marry you."

"But he has not got mine." She felt a small thrill of freedom and relief at that. She didn't have to marry him. "Besides, I scarcely see how marriage is the perfect revenge. Surely exposing me within a men's club would bring greater satisfaction than winning me at a game of dice."

"But think of all the cruelties he could do to you once you are wed!" Hampton sounded more disappointed than repulsed. "He could act out all his revengeful thoughts upon you and you would be helpless."

She had to laugh. "You really have the most torrid imagination!" She dispelled a pang of fear, recalling Langdon's predatory gaze.

"It is of no matter now. Elisabeth has foiled Lord Langdon with that second bet," Bradshaw said with renewed confidence. "He may have won the entire estate but as long as Elisabeth refuses to marry him, he is thwarted."

James gazed gloomily across at her, who had started to untie her cravat. "Perhaps," he said, earning a sharp look from her. "In any case, I shall join the army and see if I can regain some respect."

"The army!" she cried in dismay. "You cannot mean it!"

"What else is there to do? I have no money to offer for a decent bride." James ran a tired hand through his hair. "It will be bad enough you will have to live off our charitable friends until you are married. I cannot support you."

"I could buy your colors for you," Hampton offered.

She managed a shaky smile, knowing that otherwise James would be condemned to the common rank and file. James did not look happier.

Hampton added, "You could consider it a loan if you wish and pay me back when you can."

"I wish I had appreciated such good friends as you, Hampton, before this evening." His shoulders slumped, James looked down at his hands.

There was little more to be said. Upon reaching home, she hastened upstairs, leaving the others to explain what had happened as best they may. She caught sight of her small pile of jewels lying on the dresser.

Lifting the amethyst and moonstone bracelet Langdon had given her, tears started to well. Sinking into a nearby chair, she stared at it. Lying balanced against her splayed fingers, it seemed to mock her. So much had happened in one night. She thought she'd reached some mutual understanding with Langdon, had even impetuously called it love, but he'd betrayed it all, breaking his promise with her brother's ruin. This was not the way to get her brother's permission to marry her. What had happened?

Her fingers closed around the bracelet, the supporting precious metal digging into her flesh.

# CHAPTER TWELVE

Next morning, Elisabeth entered the drawing room. Her head felt muffled by wool, her thoughts centered on her family's fall from grace. Why did it have to be at Langdon's hands? How could she marry a man who caused her family's downfall?

To her great surprise, Hampton was already present, pacing up and down the carpet. He greeted her with enthusiasm, kissing her on the cheek. Accepting his welcome with bemusement, she sat on the sofa next to her brother.

Odette sat across from them. She dabbed at her eyes. "You poor lamb," she sobbed. "You must not be afraid, for we will not let Langdon marry you!"

"Then why are you crying?" she snapped. She turned to Hampton. "Have you come to remove Lord Langdon when he arrives?" she inquired with a bitter smile.

"If necessary," Hampton replied, arms folded.

Radclyffe entered from the adjoining study. "Elisabeth, I would like a few words with you before Langdon arrives."

She turned halfway in her seat to face him, her hands folded in her lap. She was not prepared to listen to another lecture, but would endure it. She had already made her decision.

"I will be brief. You are not going to agree to marry that man. You are not going to marry him for the same reasons you are not to associate with him." He came around the sofa to face her. "He is a rogue and a cruel man who will make you unhappy."

"You have proof enough of that from his actions last night." Hampton glanced up from comforting his sobbing sister. "Why allow him to hurt you further?"

"You are all sure I am going to wed him." She regarded them with mild astonishment. Had they not discussed this in the carriage last night?

"Your recent behavior gives us great concern in this regard," reminded Radclyffe.

*Oh. That.*

"There is another reason why you will refuse Langdon," added Hampton with quiet assurance.

"There is, my lord?" Her curious gaze fixed upon Hampton. Did she not have enough reasons already?

"You are going to marry me."

"Oh, no . . ." Why did he insist upon it? She leaped to her feet and stalked toward the door, trying to ignore Odette's increased distress.

"Elisabeth!?" Hampton called after her. "Where are you going?"

She spun and pointed at him. "You have never asked me to marry you! You take it for granted."

She turned to leave but the Radclyffe butler stood in her way. "M'lord Langdon has arrived," he announced, bowing.

Behind him in the hallway stood a smiling Langdon, removing his hat.

Had he heard her outcry? She beat a hasty retreat. Langdon entered, sketching a slight bow to the assembled company.

"Elisabeth is marrying me," put in Hampton, who did not seem at all thwarted by her outburst.

If Langdon noticed her look of fury flung at Hampton, he made no sign of it, smiling pleasantly. "It is for Miss Stockwell to say." He went down on one knee, gazing up at her. "Elisabeth, would you do me the greatest honor by taking me as your husband?"

He said it with such open loving, her heart swelled. She stood there, speechless. For all that he had done to reach this point, he had asked her and asked her handsomely. It seemed a shame to tell him no.

Her heart thumped. She focused upon Langdon's upturned face, remembering her beguilement by him, the shallowness of his apparent reform. He had ruined her family. He had to understand there were consequences.

He rose, his gaze never leaving her face, but she saw the hope drain away from his features. Her answer must be writ plain in her expression. It took all she had to say it.

"I cannot marry a man who would so willingly destroy my family," she told him, her voice on the verge of breaking. "How can I trust a man who breaks his promise?"

Langdon drew closer to her. "I told you I was no saint." He flicked a frustrated look at the assembled company. "Elisabeth, if I could but explain . . ."

"If you had but *thought,* my lord, there would be no need for explanations. If you had but trusted in my constancy . . ." She dared say no more.

"Your answer," Langdon pressed.

She drew in a steadying breath and stepped back. Creating the physical distance cut her almost as deeply as the pain in her heart. "It pains me to tell you I cannot marry you. I could never marry under these circumstances."

Langdon bowed, every line of his body rigid. "It pains me also to hear it, Miss Stockwell. I bid you all a good day."

He was gone. She collapsed, drained, beside Odette.

"You have done the right thing!" exclaimed her friend, beaming. "We have defeated that odious man!"

"He will not rest until he has her," Hampton reminded, once again alarming his sister. "Elisabeth, you and I should be married at once."

"No, my lord." She held up a hand, keeping him at bay. Weary beyond words, she could scarce believe it was not even noon. "I will not marry merely to be safe from Langdon."

"But you love my brother, do you not?" Odette pressed his cause.

How could she say she could not stand him? "I am fond—"

Hampton interrupted. "Fondness is a luxury in arranged marriages. My dear Elisabeth, you will grow to love me as I love you with time. Your safety now is paramount."

Arranged? When had it become arranged? "If I am at risk, I would much rather withdraw to the country."

"Where?" Hampton asked with brutal candor. "Stockwell House is no longer yours."

She bit her lip and glanced across at her brother. She received no aid from that quarter. "My lord, I have refused you twice already. Do not ask me to refuse you a third time." She drew in a breath. "I need . . . I need to think everything through. I have been safe enough thus far."

Hampton captured her hand in his. "I do understand. I apologize for my precipitate behavior." He kissed her hand, his lips cold against her skin. She managed to refrain from shrinking from him. "Do not worry, matters will take their course and you will come around to my way of thinking."

She caught sight of Odette's surprised stare.

Somehow, Elisabeth managed a smile. "Odette, who would have thought I'd have ever had the opportunity to refuse two proposals in one day!"

Late that evening, Elisabeth sat in the library, her eyes fixed upon a novel. She wasn't even sure of the title, needing some semblance of occupation while she brooded on the subject of marriage proposals.

She turned as James walked in, a belated curt knock announcing his presence. In one hand, he held some old documents.

Startled, she snapped the book shut. "What is that you have there?" she asked, regaining her composure.

He held up the papers. "The deeds to the Stockwell estate."

With a pounding heart, she returned to her book and tried to find her place in it. Another reminder of all she had lost. "You have not sent them off to Langdon yet?"

James's grim face belied something further was wrong. "He sent them back, along with all the money I lost last night."

The book forgotten, she stared at him. "He did? Why? But this is wonderful news! Why are you looking so glum?"

Wordlessly, James handed her a small piece of paper.

She read the note from Langdon, schooling her features under her brother's examination. In fine penmanship, he had written a brief apology, regretting his thoughtless actions: *"To remedy this, I have returned to your brother your family fortune. I have some hope of restoring our friendship, but I know this will take time."*

"Have you read this?" She waved the paper in the air.

"No," he snapped. "I expect it is some little love note."

"It is an apology, brother dear," she reproved. Langdon had realized his error then. What was she supposed to do about it now? She had thrust an impenetrable barrier between them, the coolness of his note suggested it.

She wanted to go home. "James, I am tired of London life. Do they . . . Do they know that I was at White's, you suppose?"

James grinned. "Bradshaw's keeping mum even though he thinks you're plucky and foolish."

"Mum? You mean he is keeping that secret?"

James nodded. "Sorry, sis. Been at the club. The talk tends to rub off." He reclined along an ottoman. "D'you know they even had a bet going on whether you would accept Langdon?"

She forced a laugh. "They would have made better odds

betting on raindrops! I assume very little money was made?"

"I would not go down St. James Street in the near future." He grinned. "You made some of the lads very unhappy."

"What?" She shot him a startled look. She wouldn't dare go down St. James Street and be ogled by all the men in any case! "They expected me to marry him?"

"By all accounts, they were delicious odds."

She raised an eyebrow. "Perhaps I should have said yes." She eyed her brother. "How much would you have won?"

James raised his hands, fending her off. "Never even dreamed of placing a bet!" It was his turn to examine her. "You came pretty close to consenting, I thought."

"Does that matter now?" She rose and paced the library floor, at last vocalizing her inner turmoil. "He has apologized for his actions, James. He gave you back everything you lost. Yet he almost destroyed us." She grimaced at the fire still burning in the grate. "Nothing is black and white any more."

James crossed to her and rested his hands on her shoulders. "Nothing ever is, sister dear, but Lord Langdon is a black one indeed. We have proof enough of that."

This act of generosity left her unsure again. "What about the deeds? Why does he return them?"

Her brother shrugged, his mouth compressed into a thin line. "Whatever his reasons, they cannot be good."

"If I cannot be sure of that, how can you?" Was this another twist in Langdon's cat and mouse game with her?

His fingers tightened. "You ought to be sure, Elisabeth."

She stared into the fire. "I need to find out for myself."

James turned her to face him, looking down at her troubled face. "Like you found out about Kerr?"

Grim, she nodded. To say anything would reveal the fragile state of her heart.

"I do not wish to see you hurt again."

She kissed his cheek. "You are sweet, brother dear. I will be careful. After all, I have you to look out for me, do I not?"

He grimaced, nodding. "Did you know that the fellow had the gall to ask me for your hand in marriage before he won it from me? I should have guessed at his game sooner. I am sorry."

"You refused him?" Truthfully, it came as no surprise.

"Packed him off right quick." James sounded proud of his swift action. Trust James to take a sudden brotherly interest in her doings. "I think you better go to bed before I assert my authority and pack you off to Stockwell House." He grinned. "Now that it is ours again."

Bidding her brother good night, she took the book with her, the note safe within.

Early next morning, Elisabeth rode alone to Hyde Park. She needed to escape the claustrophobic wishes of her hosts and hoped to see Langdon. His note of apology begged much in the way of explanation.

Only the most die-hard riders exercised at the park at this hour. No one in this time of transition concerned themselves about a woman riding alone. The mist washed out the spring green of trees wreathed in low clouds.

She kept to the paths, lost in thought. She knew what she had to do: leave London and Hampton's proposal behind and return to the security of Stockwell House. Yet, she did not want to go. It would be best for her to forget about Langdon, but he remained an intriguing, vexing puzzle. One that held her heart, no matter how painful his acts.

Other riders pounded past her. One pulled up short and turned back, settling his horse into a light trot. A thrill ran through her as she recognized him—Langdon. She tried to quench that feeling; she could not fall for him all over again.

"Miss Stockwell." Langdon gave her a stately nod. "I have not seen you here for quite some time. I thought perhaps you had heeded my warning about riding alone."

So he would pretend there had been nothing between them? Two could play at that game.

"My lord, you were quite right when you said this was not the country." Her skittish mare shifted under her. "The hours I have kept in London have prevented me from riding so early." She gathered the reins together. "Until today."

"Now your hours are not so late?"

Her fists clenched. "I must thank you for returning my brother's property," she began.

"You make it sound like I stole it," Langdon almost growled.

She frowned at him. "You goaded my brother into losing it. Although, he was a fool to heed you."

"I would have returned them whether you had accepted me or not. It was never my intention to permanently hurt your family. I had hoped you would see that. I trusted that you would."

She flinched. "I understood your logic, my lord. I also saw its flaw. The mere act of ruining my brother hurt my family, hurt me. If you had but consulted me . . ." She took a deep breath. She couldn't stand this close proximity to him and continue to remain aloof. "Good day to you, my lord."

A smart crack of her riding crop sent her mare bolting across the green. She clung to its back. The cleansing wind batted against her face, her horse riding out her tumultuous emotions.

"Elisabeth!" she heard Langdon cry out from behind her.

Her mare reared up, screaming as a curricle dashed into her path. The horses collided, hooves lashing. She held on for but a moment, before falling, rolling away from the flashing hooves.

Langdon flung himself off his horse and was at her side in an instant. "Good God!" He grasped her arm as Elisabeth struggled to rise. "Are you hurt?"

"Winded." She pulled her arm free of his grip and got to her feet without his aid, stumbling over to the collision.

Her own mare had disengaged itself and now stood to one side, its head hanging low. "Oh, my," she murmured, seeing the state of the other horses, a beautiful black pair. One had got caught up in its gear. Panicking, it plunged in its braces, setting off the other.

She grabbed for the reins, bringing the horse's head down. "Whoa there, fellow," she soothed the struggling animal. Its blinkered partner settled, stamping its hooves. Elisabeth became aware of someone shouting.

"Why didn't you watch the devil where you were going?! Stupid girl!" She looked up to see a rotund man seated in the curricle, dressed to the nines. "I could have been killed!"

She blinked in astonishment, momentarily lost for words. *He* could have been killed?

"You?!" Langdon approached the driver. "You damn near killed her!"

"Gentlemen!" she called, getting their attention. She held out her hand. "Knife," she commanded.

They stared at her.

"I have to cut the traces. This poor beast is all tangled up." Her voice took on a dangerous edge. "Knife."

Langdon retraced his steps to his mount and pulled something from his pack. He returned, holding a small knife. "Allow me."

She held both horses steady while he hacked away at the leather traces. The driver continued to curse them, bemoaning the damage done to his expensive tack. With the last of the tangle cut free, she eased the animal forward.

Once free of its encumbrances, the horse soon calmed. She kept talking to it in soft, nonsense words, until it let her examine its legs. The reins had tangled below the knees, leaving welts, and a cut in its shoulder where her mare had struck it with a hoof.

"You've ruined them!" shrieked the driver. "My best pair!"

She glared at him with barely concealed irritation. "They are not ruined, sir." She ruffled the wounded horse's mane, finding a small carrot in her pocket for it. Her mare whinnied, attracting her attention. Her own animal needed care.

From her coat pocket, she produced a card, which she gave to the driver. "You may send the bill for their medical care to me. I apologize for causing you such an inconvenience."

She turned away before her sharp tongue escaped her control. She had been at fault for galloping so wildly in a city park. She returned to her mare, finding another carrot for it. While it ate, she ran an experienced hand down its forelegs.

"Will you be able to ride back?" Langdon asked, catching her frown. He stood by her mare, a hand resting on its withers.

"I think I will walk her a little, and see how she manages." She gathered up the reins.

"May I walk with you?"

She nodded, feeling the shock of the accident rush over her in a wave. Her own two feet did not seem so steady. Not waiting for him, she headed back the way they had come. Her hands shook, and she gripped the reins tighter.

It was more than the accident however. She took a deep breath. She had told James that she wanted to find out what kind of man Langdon truly was; now she was afraid to start.

Langdon soon caught up and walked alongside, his horse trailing behind him. "Are you quite sure you are unhurt?"

"Quite sure, my lord." she said, taking refuge in politeness.

His eyes closed briefly, as if concealing pain. He continued in a lighter vein. "I did not know you nursed horses as well as people, Miss Stockwell."

She managed a shaky smile and felt its strength double back from Langdon. "I have had a thorough country education, my lord. When I learned to ride, I was taught every aspect of keeping a horse. If what I had done today occurred then, I would not have been allowed to ride for a month."

He chuckled. In the silence that followed, he asked, "Why did you run?"

Of course he would ask. "Fear. I am afraid I do not know who you are anymore, or if the man I—liked—even existed."

His voice grew hoarse. "Oh yes, Elisabeth, he exists."

"How can I believe you after what you have done?" Her jaw clenching, she tried to marshal her emotions. Believing him came as naturally as breathing. She had to fight it. More to herself, she muttered, "If only I had someone to talk to."

"I am sure you have spoken of me frequently with the Radclyffes."

"I could not even begin to explain that you are—" She broke off, walking faster.

"That I am what?"

She stopped and spun to face him. "That I foolishly believed you are an honorable man." She listed his positive acts on her fingers. "You came to my rescue at the opera, have involved yourself in philanthropy, rescued me from Hampton—" She tried not to see the corner of his mouth twitch. She walked on. "You behaved like the perfect gentleman at all other times. Lady Westbrooke told me that in your youth you were an honorable man."

"What else did she tell you?" he asked, his eyes narrowing.

She forged on. "And then you," her voice trembled. "You give me a taste of what Odette feared by gambling for my hand!"

A cloud passed over his face. "I returned everything."

It wasn't enough. "You told me that part of your life was over. Clearly, it is not."

"It is. I—" The charmer seemed at a loss for words. "Elisabeth, I have done you a great wrong that I know not how to undo. It was not my intention to lose you. I wanted to win you."

"I saw that. But I am not a prize, not a possession."

"I meant to do it honorably, but my reputation has denied me that right. I am sorry, Elisabeth."

She stopped, turning to him. The reins dropped unnoticed

from her fingers. She hadn't expected his apology to resonate so deeply within her.

"I have been trying to change my life and yet been frustrated at every turn—then, to be told you were engaged to another! I thought I could win you back via the only means I knew how."

"Gambling." She shook her head, dispelling the helpless tears. Her hands clasped together, she almost pleaded with him. "My lord, how wrong you were! If you had but persevered . . . We could have purchased a special license."

"I am not to be forgiven?" he asked, his mouth crooked, his eyes bleak.

Could she forgive him? In her wishing for things to be different, she knew she had already forgiven him. His note had sealed it. "I have forgiven you." She wanted to throw herself into his arms and forgive him with abandon but held back. "I would not have allowed you to walk with me if I did not think we could make amends."

"Why do you want to?"

"I do not know." Her heart spoke for her. "No, I do! I believe you are essentially good—just imperfect, as we all are." Her fingertips brushed his cheek.

Langdon covered her hand with his and turned his head to kiss her gloved palm. She closed her eyes in delight at the sensation. "Elisabeth, can your trust be rediscovered so soon?"

She lowered her hand. "I want to trust you, my lord, but it will take time."

His hands held both of hers. "I have learned my lesson well. I will show you I can be trusted again."

"I hope you can, my lord."

They stared at each other, almost back to the path where they had met. "Let me show you." He drew her into his embrace.

How could she resist? "Show me, Henry. Show me in every way."

He kissed her, gentle at first, but growing into impassioned possession. She clung to him, pressed along the length of him. She stayed close after the kiss had ended.

Henry recovered his breath first. "How is your horse? Shall you be able to ride?"

"I think so." She walked her horse in a slow circle, the old doubts swirling. "Henry . . ." She caught his nearing mouth with her fingertips. "It sometimes feels nothing will come of this."

"I am not that foolish. I need you in my life, Elisabeth." His fingers curled into her hair. "I will turn all my persuasive powers and charm onto your brother, but if there is no success by this weekend . . . No more delays."

"Then a special license it shall be." She smiled, her heart lighter. She would do her part and smooth the way with Odette. "I would need a few days to gather my things in any case."

"As long as we are together, reputation will not matter. I have a pleasant country house and acres to explore until Society forgets we caused a fuss."

She blanched. "Will it be terrible?"

"I will protect you from it. We will live exemplary lives. I can do that with you by my side." He kissed her then, a soft, cherished kiss.

If asked, she couldn't explain it, but there was something irresistible about Henry's mouth in close proximity to hers. She returned his kisses with a new fervor, sealing their new promise.

That afternoon, James entered Elisabeth's boudoir carrying the *London Gazette*. "Elisabeth," he murmured. "There is something in here I think you ought to see."

She took the newspaper from him. James had circled a few lines. The words announced her engagement to Hampton. She gasped. Why had they trapped her like this? "I am not going to go through with it," she said, heated. "I would rather become the laughingstock of all England first."

"I wish you would see reason, sis. You will be perfectly happy as Lamby's wife."

*Never in a million years*. "James, would you do me a small favor?"

"If I do, will you agree to marry him without fuss?"

*Impossible*. "I cannot promise that."

James regarded his sister, frowning. "Sometimes I think you are more stubborn than I am." He sighed. "Very well. What is it you want me to do?"

She moved to the small davenport desk. "I want you to give this note to Lord Langdon." At his angry muttering, she added, "You can read it, James. It will not be anything controversial."

"The mere writing of a note . . ." began her brother.

"James," she interrupted wearily. "Please." She scribbled her message on a small piece of paper. Folding it, she handed it to him.

He put it in his coat pocket without even giving it a glance. "It does not matter what it is you write to Langdon, for in the end, it will not make the slightest difference."

He left. A few moments later, a wrathful Hampton flung open her door. He waved her note in the air. "Untenable?!" he bellowed the single word she had written to Langdon. "I will make an honest woman of you!"

She glared. How dare he invade her privacy. She cringed, afraid he would hurt her, use her. "Get out! I never want to see you in here again!"

Hampton recoiled. With effort, he calmed down. "Elisabeth, your recent misfortunes have embittered you. All that will change when we marry. Please remember I do this because I love you."

"Somehow, my lord, I do not think so." She sank onto the stool by the dressing table, her head in her hands. "Just get out, will you?"

Alone, she paced the rug-covered floorboards. She had to

prove to them that Langdon was more than his rakish reputation, much more. But how? Words alone would not convince them.

Drowsily, Elisabeth focused on her brother and the candlestick he held near his face. "James?" she murmured, her eyes blinking at the light. "What is going on? It is the middle of the night."

He lit the lamps around the room. When he faced her again, she saw he was pale and trembling. "I saw Langdon this evening."

She sat up, leaning forward, fear and anticipation running through her. "Had he read the engagement notice? Did you say anything to him? Tell me!"

"You are not going to believe this, but he offered to clear my gambling debts."

She groaned. "Oh, you are not *still* gambling, are you?"

He nodded. "In return, I was to do him a favor." He swallowed. "He wants me to help you elope with him."

"But that is wonderful!" She stopped short at her brother's gloomy face.

"I cannot with all good conscience, allow him to—"

"But your debts!" she interrupted, giving him an excuse.

"This is a point of honor, not money." He sat down with a thump on the edge of her bed.

"Does not the fact that I am in love with—"

"Elisabeth." He covered her mouth, checking her enthusiastic words. "In love with him? You have no idea what he is like. He is a ruthless gambler and a lecher. He is a sinister man."

Shaking her head, she removed his hand from her mouth. "That is where you are wrong. Do you promise to keep a secret?" James nodded. Her eyes narrowed. He had betrayed her once before. "I recall how lightly you promised to pass a message onto Langdon for me. How did it get into Hampton's hands?"

"He wanted to know your reaction. I told him and he wanted to read the note, so I let him. I am sorry, I did not think he would react like that."

She snorted. "How did you expect him to react?"

James shrugged, laying a hand over his heart. "I swear by the Stockwell honor that I will not tell a soul your secret."

It would have to do. "Do you recall my spring cleaning efforts at Stockwell House?" He nodded, motioning for her to hurry. She took a deep breath. "I had an ill stranger there, a man. I knew him only as Henry. He was always polite and kind. He even worked in the stables while he recuperated. That man, I found out later, was Lord Langdon. Now do you see why I continue to defend him?"

"He was in my house?!" James bellowed, forgetting to be quiet. "Sister, you are quite ruined."

"He didn't know who I was. Not until the end. He never harmed me, James."

"Why did he not tell you who he was before?"

"He knew he was on Stockwell lands and he knew our connection with the Radclyffes. It was more than enough to keep him quiet about his identity. Do you not see? There is another side of him that nobody has seen for years. Henry's facade was that of a lecher. That is how he lived his life until . . ." She let James reach her conclusions.

"Even if all you say is true . . ."

"There is the bet. You have given your consent and now I have given mine. It is a point of honor," she persisted.

"That is not fair!"

"It is true. James, please," she begged, "will you not help us? I love him and he loves me. He asked you honorably for my hand once."

"You are wearing out the word 'honor.'" James stared at her a long time before agreeing. "I will send my answer around to Langdon. Can you be ready in an hour?"

She hugged her brother. "Sooner." She leaped out of bed and dragged a large tapestried bag from under her bed. James left.

Within an hour, she had packed a few essentials, including some items she envisaged she'd need on her wedding night. She put what little money and jewelry she had into a small velvet bag. She caressed Langdon's bracelet before packing it.

She could not quite believe it. She and Henry were to be married. She risked everything by doing this, but it was better by far than to be stuck married to Hampton.

By the time James tapped on her door, she had changed into a warm woolen traveling gown with a cloak around her shoulders. The velvet bag disappeared into her voluminous muff.

Hand in hand, the siblings snuck downstairs and out to the waiting carriage with only a single candle to light their way. The interior of the carriage was dark.

"Henry?" she breathed, expectant. James got into the carriage behind her and shut the door. The carriage moved off.

"Sorry to disappoint you," snarled Hampton. James lit the carriage lamps.

She fell back against the bolsters, her instincts screaming she throw herself out of the moving carriage. "Hampton? What is going on?" She had more than a sneaking suspicion.

"My darling Elisabeth, you and I are going on a little trip to Gretna Green. I was not about to give Langdon the chance to take you away from me." He placed a large hand on her trembling knee. "My patience with you has gone, my dearest. I could not bear to live a moment longer without you as my wife."

Doomed. Slumping against the hard leather seat in defeat, she heaved a heavy sigh. "There is no escaping you, Hampton. How did you bring my brother into this?"

James snapped, "He did not ring me into it! We plotted it between ourselves." He spoke with utter loathing. "Langdon humiliates me in front of all my peers by giving back the house and all the money he won from me. He treated me as if I was some boy wet behind the ears!"

She groaned, knowing that was not Langdon's intention. In an emotionless voice, she said to Hampton, "My lord, if you insist on this farce, I swear I will make your life a misery."

Hampton seemed unperturbed. "I will do my best to make you happy," he said with complete devotion.

She swallowed, feeling ill, and not from the carriage motion. There was no escape.

# CHAPTER THIRTEEN

Some time later, the carriage slowed to a complete stop. Hampton thumped on the roof. "What the devil is the delay?"

Elisabeth didn't care. She flung herself against the carriage door, unlatching it. She managed to get halfway out before Hampton dove after her, pulling her back in. He held her against his body while she struggled to free herself.

"Good God!" James exclaimed, horror writ upon his face. "Do you want to get yourself killed?"

"Anything would be better than this!" she shrieked, uncaring of his shocked face. She twisted in Hampton's grasp. "Let me go!"

"I cannot do that, my dearest," Hampton cooed, "until you calm yourself."

She ceased struggling at once. "Very well."

Hampton relaxed his grip, but did not release her. "Stockwell, my good fellow, I suggest you sit closer to the door in case your sister tries something again."

James nodded, sliding over. "I think you can release her, Hampton." Calmer, she discerned he was not happy at how Hampton was handling her. "She is not going anywhere."

Hampton relinquished her. She slid away from him, huddling in the farthest corner, glancing at her brother. He watched her with something akin to chagrin. She remained silent, watching with little interest the busy streets and then the utter blackness once they had left London behind them.

They journeyed north for the remainder of the night and the whole of the following day, stopping only to change horses and pay at the toll houses. Hampton had planned ahead to the extent of bringing a large hamper, making sure she remained in the carriage to eat. He gave her no chance to escape. Even her brief forays to relieve herself were closely guarded.

As they traveled, she considered her options. There seemed little chance of freedom while in the carriage with two strong men. If the worst came to the worst, she'd beg the good priest not to marry her.

James sat opposite them and on occasion, she caught his worried gaze. She ignored him, staring out at the rolling green fields, wood copses, and small villages. He had betrayed her. When he tried to engage her in conversation, she did not deign to reply, staring out the window.

The afternoon drew to a close. "We must decide where to stop for the night," Hampton said.

"From what I understand, there are only a couple of choices," James replied. "Unless you wish to travel further into the night before we stop."

"No, I think we have enough distance between us and London." Hampton glanced at her. "There is nowhere for her to run to now."

James cleared his throat but said nothing.

After further debate, Hampton tapped the carriage roof and gave the coachman his instructions.

A short time later, the carriage drew to a halt. Startled, she gave up her idle reverie about Langdon. She'd fantasized about him riding to her rescue like the knight in shining armor she had once teasingly labeled him. She needed him as that heroic figure.

"I will go in and see if they have rooms for us," said James, stepping out of the carriage.

"Could you see about a bath for me?" she called after her brother, concealing her fear of being left alone with Hampton.

"A bath?" James turned to Hampton, seeking his permission. She felt Hampton's gaze on her. She managed to smile. "One wants to be fresh for her wedding day."

"After we have eaten," Hampton assented. She gave him a brilliant smile and endured the resulting kiss on her cheek without dimming her smile one iota. Even a moment alone could bring the opportunity she needed to escape.

The Red Boar Inn's Tudor architecture of black beams and whitewashed walls didn't detract from its obvious prosperity. Hampton and her brother hustled her through the crowded taproom, taking swift refuge in the room reserved for them above.

Hampton, head tilted, listened to the noisy disturbance in the taproom below them. "Being an innkeeper must be hard work," he commented, ending the meal's long, uncomfortable silence.

"Thirsty work, I imagine." James grinned. A faint echo of it appeared on her lips. Heartened by it, he asked her, "You are not still mad at us for deceiving you?"

"No, not anymore." She turned from her brother and batted her eyes at Hampton. "This ki—" she made a quick recovery, "elopement has made me realize I really do love you, my lord."

"That's a quick change of heart," James remarked.

"Not so, brother dear. I have had some time to think and I realize I have been in denial." She turned to Hampton. "Remember at Stockwell House? How I thought you might carry me off then?"

Hampton laughed. "Indeed I do. Why else would I bring a coach and four to your doorstep in the middle of the night? You see, I remembered everything, Elisabeth."

"I have been quite awful to you, have I not?" she asked, looking downcast. She ignored her brother's questioning glances. She'd have to work harder to fool him. "I know now that whatever it was I felt for Langdon, it was nothing. Especially when measured against your love for me."

"It has taken you long enough to realize it, my darling," Hampton murmured. He reached out and took her hand in his, squeezing it. She willed herself not to jerk her hand away but patiently waited until he released it.

"I do not know how you could keep on loving me," she said, soft and meek. "I was quite infantile and rebellious. Everybody hated him, so I decided that I must fall in love with him. How easy it was with his charming manners to help me."

"But what about all those things you told me in your chamber last night?" James burst out.

She cast her demure gaze downward. "Not a word of it was true. I see now 'twas all childish fancy."

James looked at her, still doubting. However, Hampton accepted her words without question, plainly delighted.

"I assume I shall be sleeping here?" she asked.

Hampton nodded. "Perhaps, in light of your changed feelings you would consider sharing your room with me?"

She swallowed hard, hoping her revulsion didn't show. "No. I would much rather wait until our wedding night, my lord."

Chuckling, Hampton leaned back in his chair. "Come now, what difference does one evening make?"

"Quite a difference in the Lord's eyes." She frowned at him. "I am ashamed of you for suggesting it."

Unexpectedly, James came to her aid. "She's quite right, Lamby. Let's not be hasty. Particularly with my sister."

Hampton agreed, poorly concealing his displeasure. "Very well. Elisabeth, my dear, you shall sleep here, with Stockwell." He smirked at James. "I am sure we can get a camp bed installed in here. The two of you can toss for it."

"James has given up gambling," she interceded primly. "So he shall have to make do with the camp bed."

Someone rapped at the door. At Hampton's behest, a young woman entered, black hair tumbling over her bare shoulders. She dipped a short curtsey. In her strong country accent, she said, "Inkeep sent me up to ask ye if ye're ready for yer bath, ma'am."

Hampton rose. "James, I believe this is our cue to retire downstairs."

"I'll stand you a drink." James pushed back his chair. "That will keep you warm tonight."

Hampton eyed the raven haired servant, speculative. "Perhaps."

Elisabeth stood, finding it even harder to conceal her revulsion for Hampton. "You may bring the bath up now. If you gentlemen will excuse me?"

Hampton turned back at the door, pulling her to him. "Do not be long, my dear." He claimed her lips in a rather mismanaged kiss. She managed to smile until the two men had gone.

The door closed and she wiped her mouth with the back of her hand.

The servant woman bobbed a curtsey. "I will be right back, miss. John will help me bring up the bath."

Elisabeth waited, pacing, until the bath's arrival. John, a burly looking young man, arrived with the first two pails of hot water. When he had gone, she surprised the serving girl by splashing her arms and face with the hot water. She reached out blindly for a towel.

The young woman handed it to her. "Excuse me, ma'am, but I thought you wanted a bath?"

Elisabeth hushed her. "Will you help me?"

"I . . . I don't understand, ma'am," the girl stuttered, folding the towel.

"Those two gentlemen downstairs have abducted me."

The girl gasped.

Encouraged, she continued, "I have lulled them into thinking I will go through with this, but what I really want to do is return to London. I have money enough to hire a horse to take me back." She withdrew the black velvet bag from its hiding place in her muff. The bath attendant's face transformed into animated pleasure. The girl obviously longed for romance and adventure. "Is there a way out that does not go into the taproom downstairs?"

The servant shook her head. "No, ma'am. There isn't."

She crossed to the window. Opening it, she looked out. It was quite a drop. "I can climb out and down," she decided. "The tree is almost close enough."

"You'll break your neck, ma'am!"

"I would rather do that than—"

John's arrival interrupted her. He carried another two pails of water. "Last two, ma'am," he said. "I'll leave ye be now."

"Wait, John!" the servant exclaimed. "She's in a pickle."

John regarded Elisabeth with deep suspicion. "Oh, yes?"

The woman clutched his arm, while Elisabeth remained where she stood, frozen at the thought of losing this opportunity. "You have to help her! She's been abducted!"

Elisabeth filled him in on the details, hoping to win him over. At length, he nodded. "I'll lower you out the window, ma'am, if you'll permit me. The drop won't be as steep."

Nodding, she suggested, "Perhaps we could use some bedding to lower me further?"

John selected the faded red quilt as the strongest. Elisabeth slipped her muff over one arm. She swung onto the windowsill. "What about my bag?"

"I'll toss it down to ye, ma'am," John offered.

"I'll ready the horse," the girl volunteered and left.

The descent seemed to take forever. John's strength held out and Elisabeth made it to solid earth without mishap. She dodged her tapestried bag flung from the window.

The servant met her in the garden. "The horse is waitin', ma'am, and I've brought a cloak for you as it's chilly out. Quickly now, ma'am, before somebody figures what's goin' on."

Elisabeth didn't need to be told twice. The girl led her to the stables and to a strong bay gelding, well-suited to the long ride back to London. Grateful, Elisabeth gave the girl a few half-crowns before mounting the horse and settling into the saddle. "Do you think you can stall those two gentlemen for a while?"

The girl nodded. "You can be sure of a good head start, ma'am."

"Thank you. Watch out for the blond fellow's hands."

The girl curtseyed.

Elisabeth spurred the horse out of the stable yard and away. She headed south along the highway, built by the Roman invaders and recently macadamized. It was not long before she had put a number of miles between them and the Red Boar Inn.

What would Hampton and her brother try to do? Overtake her and kidnap her again, or follow behind in the coach in the hope that another opportunity would arise in London?

Either way, she refused to take any chances. She urged the gelding onward.

Dawn saw her changing horses, and by early evening she'd reached London without any sign of pursuit. Long ago spilling over its fortified walls, the city had engulfed the outlying villages. Her speed slowed, making way for farmers returning home from the markets. She tried to ignore the curious glances of the city pedestrians at her genteel, disheveled appearance.

The thought of him sent a happiness tingling through her body. With a joyful smile, she imagined the look on Henry's face when he found her on his doorstep. From the moment she left the Red Boar Inn behind her, she decided she would not go back to the Radclyffe home or to her own in the country. Either would mean a hasty marriage to Hampton once her brother caught up with her. Here was her chance to be free to choose and she meant to take it.

Why hadn't she yet met him on the road? She wondered at his absence. The news must have spread by now. There were many roads to Gretna Green. Perhaps he was on another.

She frowned. If Langdon was out looking for her, he would not be in London. What would she do until he returned?

She couldn't waste time getting lost in London's twisted streets. With trepidation, for she did not know how great an alarum the Radclyffes had raised, if any, she drew her horse aside a hackney cab. "Excuse me, sir."

The cabby doffed his hat. "What can I do for you, missy?"

"Would you know where Lord Langdon resides?"

"Indeed I do, ma'am." The cab driver winked at her.

She waited for him to tell her. It took a few moments for her to understand but with additional signals, she dipped her hand into her muff, where the velvet bag was concealed. "What is his address?" She slipped him a silver crown.

The cab driver told her. Naturally, it was in the most exclusive part of Town. Elisabeth thanked him and rode on.

With its graceful white, columnar facade, Langdon's house was a welcome sight. It took a considerable amount of willpower to refrain from urging her horse into a gallop down those last few hundred yards. Although a mere riding hack, her horse sensed her growing excitement, obliging her by breaking into a fast trot.

Dismounting, she slung the reins over the tall railings outside his house. She gathered her muddied skirts and hurried up the stairs to the wide oak front door.

Langdon's butler promptly opened the door to her impatient rapping. "May I help you, ma'am?" He gazed disapproving at her dirty face and bedraggled woolen gown.

She clasped her shaking hands before her. "Would you please inform Lord Langdon that Miss Stockwell is here to see him?"

The butler looked at her with surprise. "His lordship is not in at present, miss. He has, in fact, gone off to look for you."

Her spirits rose. At least she knew he cared enough to hunt for her. But in the meantime? What would she do? "Have you any idea when he will return?"

"None at all, miss. He intended to go all the way to Gretna

Green. He knows a fast way of getting there, one that would have beaten Lord Hampton for sure. If you would care to come in and wait for him?"

She backed down a step, the impropriety of such an action. . . Besides, the Radclyffes would look for her here. "I am afraid I cannot do that. If I am found here, there'll be hell to pay. When Lord Langdon returns, will you tell him I am back in London? Oh, and that the situation has become quite untenable."

"Untenable?" the butler echoed, puzzled.

"Lord Langdon will understand," she assured him.

"Of course, Miss Stockwell." The butler resumed his polite expression. "Where will he be able to find you?"

She shrugged. "That is anybody's guess. Not at the Radclyffes, that much is certain." She gestured to the horse, loosely tethered and in danger of wandering off. "Would you be kind enough to return it to a post-house." She wracked her memory for the name. "I am afraid I cannot recall where . . ."

"I'll take care of it, Miss Stockwell."

"Thank you. One more thing. Would it be possible to send for Langdon?"

"I will try, miss, but I make no promises."

She turned and descended the stairs leading to the front door. She unfastened the straps that held her belongings and moved on, dawdling along the streets, keeping well away from that part of Town where the Radclyffes lived. She considered turning to the Bradshaws, but immediately discarded the idea. Bradshaw was too close a friend of her brother's. She would find little sympathy for her plight there.

She paid scant attention to where she walked. She had money enough for maybe a few meals and a few nights in a boarding hotel.

What was she to do? The thought kept turning in her head with no answer. She walked beyond the few well-lit streets of London and into a less than savory part of the city.

With a start, she realized her vulnerability to unscrupulous persons. She was a woman walking alone at night and thus easy prey for thieves and pickpockets. She hastened toward a small hostelry whose warm lights at the windows beckoned her.

Stepping across the threshold, she felt the combined gazes of curious customers upon her and quailed. The room reeked of tobacco fumes and ale. Searching for the hostelier, she was roughly pushed aside as a couple of men entered behind her.

Her hand slipped into her muff. With a furtive feel, she found that her meager wealth was safe. She moved farther into the crowded room, shuffling forward uncertainly as she peered through the smoky haze searching for the hostelier.

A burly man approached, a wide leather apron wrapped around his waist. "May I help you, missy?" His voice, deep and gruff, brooked no mischief in his inn.

"Do you have a room free?" She spoke with authority, yet with a slight tremor.

The hostelier took in her rumpled appearance and asked shrewdly, "You can pay?"

She ignored the guffaws of his customers nearby. "Of course. Do you have a room?"

"Yes, ma'am. If you would follow me." The hostelier bowed.

She followed the hostelier around the tables, clutching her bag and muff close to her chest, ignoring the jibes from the more inebriated. They ascended the narrow rickety stairs to the upper floor. "I've only the one room available." He opened a door to a drab room. "Do you require anything else?"

"Could I have a meal sent up, please?" She had regained her composure away from the leering crowd below.

The hostelier held out his hand. "I expect to be paid in advance, ma'am."

"How much?" The hostelier mentioned an amount that was surprisingly large. "That includes the room for one night?" she queried, skeptical. He mentioned a slightly lower, more reasonable amount. Still suspicious of overcharging, she handed over the coins.

Closing the door behind her, she surveyed the room with distaste. The bare wooden walls and floorboards caused her to shudder. She hated to think what kind of vermin lived in them. She dropped her tapestried bag and muff in the middle of the floor and went to examine the bedding.

The lumpy mattress and the tick was not of the fineness to which she had been accustomed. She shook it out along with the single blanket before gingerly sitting on the end, almost certain she would be infected with lice before the night was out.

The size of the room was such that she could easily reach over and pick up the muff lying in the middle of the floor. She heard heavy footsteps along the hallway. She kept her muff close beside her, not daring to open the velvet bag inside.

The hostelier entered with a brief knock, carrying a small wooden tray in one hand. " 'Tis only stew, ma'am, and a bit of bread. I took it upon myself to bring you a small glass of wine." She gazed at him with narrowed eyes. "On the house," he added.

"You are too kind," she murmured, hiding a smile. The hostelier lingered. "Was there something else?" she asked him.

"Now, ma'am," he began, hesitant, "normally I don't pry into other people's business, but you seem t'be a lady of quality and well, I was wonderin' . . ."

"You are observant," she said, damping down her fear and hiding behind cool civility. She had prepared for this. She tripped out a story she read once in a novel. "I hasten to assure you I have come to the city in search of work. My family were pauperized by my father's debts, you see. I only have a little money. Do you know of a job as a governess, perhaps?"

The hostelier shook his head. He seemed to believe her spur-of-the-moment lie. "The only job I know of is for a stable boy at the White Hart Inn near the city gates. I'll bring up a paper with your breakfast tomorrow morning. Perhaps it'll have something."

"After nine, if that is convenient," she said. The hostelier nodded and left her to eat her supper in peace.

The mostly vegetable stew had one odd stringy lump of meat bobbing in it. It was almost inedible but it filled the hole in her stomach. The bitter wine at least cleared her palate.

Having disposed of the tray outside her door, she locked herself in. She emptied the contents of her black velvet bag onto the bed. There was very little money among the jewelry, enough for breakfast and another night at the hostelry. Paying at the various tollgates on her way back to London had put an unexpected drain on her purse.

She could pawn her jewelry but there was little chance of seeing it again. Looking critically at the pieces, she realized that she wouldn't get a great deal for her few strands of pearls, and she could never part with the bracelet Langdon had given her.

But perhaps it would be enough. She shuddered to think what would become of her in London with no money and the only man she could turn to still far from here.

The next morning saw Elisabeth at the Sydnersham's residence. They were not in, she was informed. She refused to give up. "Please," she begged. "Tell them that it is Miss Stockwell. I am a friend of theirs."

The butler gave her a long look, taking in her bedraggled appearance. He nodded and closed the door.

She waited. At length, the butler returned with a message: "Miss Syndersham does not know you, Miss Stockwell."

Stepping back onto the street, tears threatened to spill. She looked up at the house, hoping to catch someone at a window. A twitch of a curtain in the upper storey revealed a presence.

What would she do now?

# CHAPTER FOURTEEN

Her money had run out. She'd pawned her pearls but didn't have the heart to pawn Langdon's bracelet, not yet. Banished from the hostelry, she lugged her bag back across town, into the fashionable district.

From across the street, she gazed at Langdon's townhouse. The knocker had been removed from the door. He had not returned and it looked like the staff had closed up the house.

What had happened? Had he been in an accident? Had he given up on her? She had been out of her social circle for too long. She had to find out.

Afraid of being recognized, she scurried across the road among the traffic, dodging the passing vehicles.

"Elisabeth! Is that you?"

She turned. A gaping Bradshaw stood in an open carriage.

"Do not let her go, you fool!" she heard Mrs. Bradshaw cry.

Elisabeth pelted into the street.

"Elisabeth!" Bradshaw called. "Look out!"

A coachman screamed another warning, almost on top of her. She stumbled and fell, the cobblestones cutting her cheek.

Dodging the striking hooves of one of the pair, she rolled and struggled to regain her feet. She dashed down the street, the traffic along the popular thoroughfare aiding her escape.

What was she to do? She had no money, nothing. She

found herself in the market district of London, the streets lined with shops and hand-carried stalls.

She felt her precious cargo in her muff. She really ought to pawn them, it meant the difference between survival and death, but she could not bring herself to do it. The bracelet was her only physical reminder of Henry. There had to be another way.

She espied a wig-maker's shop and touched her hair. It was a possibility. She stepped inside.

The attendant bustled forward. "Out! Out! We do not serve the likes of you!" She grabbed her arm, steering her to the door.

"I want to sell my hair," Elisabeth murmured, tears starting.

The attendant gave the crown of her head an assessing look. She led Elisabeth through the curtain to the back of the shop. "Sit."

Taking a deep breath, Elisabeth obeyed. The attendant unpinned her hair. It cascaded in brown waves down Elisabeth's back. The woman brushed the length of it. Elisabeth closed her eyes, enjoying the feel of the bristles against her scalp and through her hair. Who knew when she would be so pampered again? The worst had happened. She had to make her own way in the world now.

The attendant gathered her hair at the nape of her neck. With her other hand, she retrieved her scissors.

In the mirror, Elisabeth watched the dim light reflecting on the blade, briefly pondering the course she was about to take.

The attendant caught sight of her pale expression. "Are you sure you wish to do this?"

Squaring her shoulders, Elisabeth nodded. With a series of snips, the attendant cut her hair. *Alea iacta est,* thought Elisabeth, grim. The die is cast.

"How much?" she asked, watching the attendant hold up the length of hair.

"Good hair," she agreed. "Healthy-looking. Be better when it's washed. I'll give you a half a crown for it."

"One crown." Elisabeth dared to haggle.

The wig maker shook her head, casting an eye at Elisabeth's raggedy hair. "Half a crown it is, lass. Take it or leave it."

Elisabeth took it, in small coins. She ventured into a less salubrious part of Town that was almost becoming familiar to her.

One thing she knew for certain—she could not remain a woman. She'd been spotted once already. She'd also seen women taken up in carriages. She had very little illusion as to what services they provided the men in those carriages. Dressed as a man, she would at least be safer. Perhaps she could get that job at the White Hart Inn that the innkeeper had mentioned.

She would not go back to a miserable life married to Hampton. She might be hungry, but at least she was free.

At a stall, she bought a large white cambric shirt, worn thin with age, and an old secondhand pair of breeches. She moved on to a wandering cobbler who sold secondhand shoes as well as his services. From him, she bought a pair of ill-fitting boots. A battered duffel bag completed her purchases.

Nobody seemed to question her motives for buying such objects. Surveying the miserable, dirty faces of the stall-keepers and customers, Elisabeth realized she moved in a part of the city where questions were never asked.

A momentary flicker of fear shivered through her, for she was on the outskirts of the notorious St. Gile's-in-the-Fields. She straightened. Regarded as an outsider now, soon she would become one of them.

At one of the more respectable-looking hotels nearby, she requested a room for an hour, paying in advance with the last of her money.

She undressed, throwing her clothes in a pile on a chair. With a pair of scissors from her tapestried bag, she cut her petticoat into a long strip. She bandaged her bosom tightly with it. It was the only way she could think of to minimize these particular feminine attributes.

Once changed into her male clothing, she used the remainder of the time to rest. A harsh rapping on the door signaled that her time was up.

With her velvet bag containing her jewelry safe in her duffel, she sold the rest of her things at a clothing stall. Cloak, muff, tapestried bag, dress—all went at a price that made the old crone cackle, no doubt envisioning large profits.

She slung her duffel bag over her shoulder. Having disposed of almost everything that pertained to her feminine identity, she now had money to keep hunger at bay in case her plan fell through.

She hurried through the crowded midday streets, cursing her boots, her feet slipping around in them. It wasn't long before her heels and toes became blistered. By the time she reached the city gates, she was unsure of which foot to favor.

She found the White Hart Inn. Willing herself not to limp, she walked through the arched carriageway to the back of the inn. The inner courtyard was crowded with milling horses and carriages of all descriptions.

" 'Ere, you boy!" shouted a man, bare from the waist up. She tried not to notice the man's wiry, rippling muscles. "Get out of the way!"

She flung herself against the inn wall as a coach and four galloped out into the busy street. The man strode toward her. "What the devil d'you think yer doing lounging about in the middle of the street?" he thundered.

"I . . . I'm lookin' for a job," she stuttered, deepening her voice and accenting her words with the broad country dialect from her neighborhood. "I heard you needed a stable boy."

"That was last week, lad. Be off with you!"

Backing away, she took to the streets. Her plan had failed miserably. If she were careful, she had enough money for food for the next couple of days, but she resigned herself to sleeping on the streets until she found work of some sort.

Night came. She returned to safer London streets and settled down in a dark corner of a mews. She would try these houses in the morning and see if any had work.

She settled into a doze, her head pillowed by her thin duffel bag. She couldn't relax, feeling as if at any moment someone would come and stab her in her sleep just to take her possessions.

Someone shook her awake, and she squealed with fright.

"Easy, lad. What are you doing here?"

She blinked up at him blearily, making him out in the early dawn light. "Lookin' for work."

The man was short as a jockey. A thatch of black hair hung over his Celtic blue eyes. He examined her, taking in her crudely cut hair, the boots that didn't fit, the too large shirt.

"What's yer name, boy?" he asked.

She felt sure the man had pierced her disguise. "M'name's Elijah, sir." A nearby church bell started tolling the hour.

"Elijah what?" demanded the man brusquely.

"Bell. Elijah Bell." She hid her fear and faced the man with defiance. "From West Sussex."

"M'name's Reilly. I'm in need of a stablehand. Can you do that work?"

She gaped and remembered to nod. "The job's mine?"

"That's right and you'll answer only to me and the mistress of the house, who will want to interview you herself soon enough. She takes an interest in all her staff."

"Thank you, sir!" She almost cried with the good news.

"Come inside and the missus can show you where to put your things," Reilly said. He gave her a friendly chuck under the chin. "Fine-looking boy. You'll do very well."

She spent a few moments surveying the small space that was to be her sleeping quarters in the stable loft. The stench of horses below rose through the wooden planks. A pallet of straw lay against one wall. At the end of it stood a small box, in which she placed her duffel bag. The box had a lock and she slipped the key to it on a slim chain around her neck. Both bed and box took up the entire length of the tiny room. A holler from below sent her scrambling down the ladder.

"You better muck out stables faster than you can meander down those stairs," Reilly bellowed.

"Yessir," she said, grabbing a pitchfork and running to the first stall, limping, before her new employer could yell again.

From that day on, her life filled with the hard labor of the stable boy—up before dawn and in bed well after dark. The long days wore on her. The first few nights, she simply fell onto the rough pallet and slept until Reilly's banging woke her the following morning.

By the third night, Elisabeth thought to check on her belongings. She found the box still securely locked. Although deathly tired, she spared a few moments to remove the bracelet from its hiding place.

When would she once again be with him and never have to spend another day slaving as a stablehand? That possibility seemed ever more distant. She'd have to wait for her half day before she could make inquiries about Henry's whereabouts.

On the fourth day of her new employment, Reilly sent for her. "The mistress wishes to see you. Wash up." He indicated the bucket of water in her hands.

"Me?" she squeaked. She cleared her throat, deepening her voice. Splashing water on her face and hands, she rubbed off much of the dirt with the ragged towel Reilly proffered her.

He led the way into the main house and to a small parlor. "Don't touch anything," Reilly growled, before leaving her alone.

She stared at the rich surroundings with longing. The colors were brighter than she would use in her own home, but everything was made of quality materials, and she recognized the influence of the designer Adam in the room.

She was ready to bolt. What if the mistress was someone who knew her? It wasn't a house she had visited but that meant little. If the mistress knew her by sight and saw beyond her grubby exterior, she would be done for. She eyed the exits and wondered if she could outrun her new mistress.

A woman entered in a morning robe. Her raven-black hair tumbled down her back in loose waves, held back by a single pastel green ribbon. "You are the new stable boy."

"Yes, ma'am." Elisabeth almost curtseyed and jerked into a short bow instead. The woman sat on a daybed, reclining and looking utterly at ease. Her robe fell open slightly to reveal a cacophony of expensive lace.

"Such pretty manners." The woman crooked a finger, bidding her closer. "Reilly tells me you have been working very hard."

"Yes, ma'am," she replied, gruff. A sense of relief shook her. She didn't know this woman and she remained unrecognized in turn.

"Your name?"

"Elijah Bell, ma'am." She bowed her head.

"I am Mrs. Davis. Come sit by me, Elijah." The woman patted the small space by her hip.

Shaking, Elisabeth perched on the edge of the divan. "I'm afraid I do not smell pleasant, ma'am."

Mrs. Davis lowered a perfumed handkerchief from her nose and smiled bravely. "Next time, you shall." She gathered Elisabeth's hand in hers. "Such a small hand for a boy."

"My family never did run tall." Elisabeth remembered to speak in her district's dialect.

The woman turned over her hand, examining the red marks, blisters, and newly formed calluses. "Hmm, you are new to hard labor, I see. Is there something you should tell me, my boy? Are you a runaway?"

"No, ma'am!" Elisabeth blurted, wanting to pull her hand back but too afraid to even move. She quailed under Mrs. Davis's examination.

"I think you are," Mrs. Davis continued, her voice smooth as honey. "It's a commendable disguise you have chosen, my dear, although there are easier ways. Did your father beat you?"

"No, ma'am." Elisabeth started to rise, but Mrs. Davis held her with a surprisingly strong grasp.

"Yet, you have chosen to sink so low rather than live in your accustomed station. Why is this?"

"You speak in riddles, ma'am, Mrs. Davis."

"Then let me speak plainly: How long have you been a boy?"

"Ma'am?" Elisabeth gazed at her, terrified.

"Come, come." Mrs. Davis smiled. "I pierced your disguise almost at once. True, you are somewhat flat-chested for a girl, but if I am not mistaken, I see a shadow of bandages beneath that shirt of yours. What are you running from, my dear girl?" She patted her hand in reassurance.

Elisabeth bowed her head, clasping her work-roughened hands in her lap. "Let me work in the stables, ma'am. Do not return me to my home."

"Lord, no. My dear, you are far too valuable to leave in the stables. You have perfect manners the gentlemen will appreciate."

Elisabeth eyed her. "Gentlemen? There is . . . there is no Mr. Davis, is there?"

Mrs. Davis's lips pursed. "You are rather too wise, my girl. I am a courtesan and my way of life would bring you greater riches than scrubbing out the stables. I will teach you, and you will be my assistant until you are ready to find a gentleman of your own."

Biting her tongue, Elisabeth stared at the courtesan. She wanted to say she already had a man of her own, but didn't dare. It might not be true anymore.

The courtesan smiled gently. "But come, what am I to call you now? You may call me Kitty."

"Kitty?" The name sounded familiar. "Are you . . . are you Lord Langdon's Kitty?"

The woman chuckled, amused, but her eyes were wary. "And how would a well-bred miss know of this?"

She flushed, not answering how she knew. "I . . . I need to see him."

An elegantly shaped brow rose. "Again, what would a well-bred miss *want* with Lord Langdon?"

She raised her chin defiantly. "He is mine."

Kitty laughed outright. "So you are the little thing he's been mooning over." She held out her hand. "Follow me."

The two women rose from the daybed, and Elisabeth followed Kitty, hand in hand. She felt rather ashamed that her palms were now so rough. Her insides quivered.

Kitty led her to the dining room. The small room was built for intimate meals, a chandelier glittering above the japanned dining table.

A newspaper concealed a person at the far end of the table, the remains of breakfast before him. "Kitty, is that you?" Henry's voice sounded from behind the newspaper. "There's no news of her in this paper either. I will be out of your hair soon, I promise you."

Kitty cleared her throat. "Langdon, I think I've found your little sparrow."

The newspaper folded with a snap. Elisabeth had eyes only for Henry. He sat in a wing-backed chair, at odds with the black enamel of the dining table. His formal dress had a casual edge. A less-than-perfectly tied cravat completing the general disarray.

"Sparrow?!" Elisabeth squawked.

Kitty laughed and tousled her short hair.

Henry gaped at her. "Elisabeth? Good God, is that you?" He blinked, tossing aside his paper and leaping up in one smooth motion. He strode toward her, his crooked smile breaking forth in wonder. "She calls you that just to annoy me, wretched woman." He shot a dark, yet fond look at Kitty.

Elisabeth glowered, hating to see affection between the two of them. Had her escape been for naught? Did Henry prefer Kitty?

"Do not worry, my chickie." Kitty chucked Elisabeth under

the chin. "I haven't bedded your man since he discovered you, despite my best efforts." She sighed. "He's never been so impervious before." She retreated from the room.

Henry smothered her in a crushing hug. "Elisabeth! I've looked for you everywhere!"

She struggled to free herself. Astonished, he loosened his grip. "Why are you here? With her?"

He stroked her cheek. "Nobody would think of looking for me here. I have been repeatedly accosted as to your whereabouts, my house searched . . . If I was to have any success in finding you, I had to go into hiding myself."

"But I went to your house . . ." She felt tears build behind her eyes. She'd been so lost, so frightened.

"Oh, my girl," he murmured, drawing her in again. "Oh, my darling girl. I am sorry. You are safe now." She stood stiffly in his embrace. "You should also know Kitty has a new gentleman now to whom she devotes her favors."

Elisabeth sighed, relaxing at the news. "I like her," she admitted. She buried her face in the crook of his neck.

He chuckled. "I am glad, but you cannot stay here. As much as I appreciate Kitty's kindness—" He paused. "The hell with what Society thinks. You need a bath and Kitty has the most expensive perfumed oils in all of London."

She clung to him, her hands bunching in the folds of his coat. Safe at last! Tilting her head to see his face, she breathed, "Is it over? Is it really over?"

"You are safe now." He kissed her brow.

Burying her face against his chest, she heard the relief in his voice and felt her heart answer. "Henry, I have missed you."

"And I you." He held her tight for a moment before gently disengaging from their embrace. He held her by the shoulders and gazed deep into her eyes. "Elisabeth, I have been out of my mind about you, since that idiot Hampton lost you on the road. What happened?"

She flinched at his agonized face. She strove to maintain

an even voice. "I came back to London and hid at a hostelry until my money ran out. I had no one to turn to, you were gone—" She took a deep breath. "I did not want to miss the chance of never being free to see you again. When I ran out of money . . ." Her voice miserably trailed away.

He took her newly roughened hands in his. "Go on," he urged.

She told him of her adventure. With a sob, she buried her face in his shirt. "I have never been so frightened in my life!" He let her cry. Eventually, she straightened, sniffling, her eyes downcast. Henry appeared willing to take care of her, but did he still want her?

"Your poor hands," he murmured, turning them over and caressing her reddened palms. He brushed her bruised cheek, his voice becoming hoarse. "What happened?"

"I fell on the street, running away from the Bradshaws."

His hand ruffled her short curls. "Why did you have to cut your hair?"

She managed a glimmer of a smile. It widened as his mouth relaxed into a small smile. "Stable boys do not wear wigs," she replied, practical once more. "It will grow back."

"You stink of horses." He grinned. "You must have a bath." He rang for a servant and delivered his request.

Alone again, he continued, "Do you realize everyone has been absolutely frantic as to your whereabouts?" A hint of anger crept into his voice. "I have searched every inch of London for you, hired the Bow Street runners to help. I began to fear you were . . . you were dead."

She laid a reassuring hand over his.

"I never thought for a moment you would disguise yourself!"

She couldn't help but grin. "Not even after White's?"

He raised an eyebrow. He smoothed back one of her vagrant curls. "You are safe now." He wiped a speck of dirt from the end of her nose. "We shall get you cleaned up and then—" Words failed him. "My dearest," he murmured and enfolded her in his arms. His nose wrinkled as he kissed her hair. He pulled back. "What did you do? Roll in it?"

"Of course not!" She grinned at him, so happy to be found.

# CHAPTER FIFTEEN

After her bath, she slept and woke some time later, alone. She slipped to the cool edge of the cotton sheets and slipped out of bed. This was not the stables. The room was decorated in cream and the palest of blues. She rang for a maid.

In moments, one arrived, with Kitty Davis following close behind with a leather bag. The maid bore clean, feminine garments for her.

"Miss Stockwell, come, let's see how my gown fits you."

It fitted, but only just, hugging Elisabeth's form and proving to be a few inches too short in the skirt.

Kitty's lips pursed. "I like it not, but it will do until you retrieve your own clothing, or Langdon buys you more. Now for your stockings."

Elisabeth sat on the edge of a bed.

Kitty applied a salve to the graze on her cheek. The unguent felt cool and smooth against Elisabeth's hot skin. She extended a leg to pull on a stocking when Kitty uttered a despairing cry. "Oh, sparrow! Your poor feet!"

Elisabeth flushed. "Henry isn't here to annoy with that, you know." She knew of the ugly blisters on the toes and heels from her excessive walking.

"'Henry,' is it?" Kitty smirked, bending to work on applying yet another salve to Elisabeth's feet. "As for 'Sparrow,' I know, but the name suits you."

Her physical ills taken care of, Elisabeth followed Kitty downstairs to a small study.

Kitty hovered outside. "He's waiting for you, my dear. Make him happy."

Elisabeth entered the room. The walls, lined with books, framed Langdon sitting at a wide desk. He appeared to be going over accounts, a large ledger open before him. She decided the scholarly attitude did not sit well on his shoulders, although he seemed totally at ease.

Looking up, he returned her smile. "That is much better," he said approvingly. "Kitty has worked wonders, even though she is a different size."

She looked down at herself. Her neckline plunged low, a diaphanous kerchief concealing much of the view. Her booted feet poked out below the silvery gray silk skirt, which was so short her bootlaces were visible. "Are you sure?" she asked, tilting her head to one side. "At least her feet are the same size."

He chuckled. "You are improved."

"What are you doing?" She wanted to tell him she missed him, but feared she'd been clingy enough for one day.

"These?" He gestured at the books before him. "Kitty likes me to check them for her." He closed the account book and rose from the desk, taking her into his arms.

She sank into the warmth of his embrace, glad that he hadn't had enough of clinging to her, and she to him. In his arms, she was home. Henry had not said anything since her return, but she hoped he felt the same. She gazed into his face.

With a grave look, he caressed her cheek. "Elisabeth, I feel I am the cause of all your troubles."

She blinked. This she had not expected. "No, you are not. I have played a part in this, greater than yours."

"My dear, even now I have compromised your reputation. Surely you see that."

Trust her newly reformed rake to notice the niceties *after* the fact.

He took her hands in his. "I have asked you to marry me once before . . ."

An ache started around her heart. Did he wish to break the engagement now she had so ruined herself with her escapades?

"My dear, your very faith in me has redeemed my own reputation. Will you not give me the chance to return the favor?" He tilted up her chin to meet his gaze. "Elisabeth," he murmured, his voice thick with emotion, "I love you. Allow me to love you with honor."

"Love me?" He meant it, truly? She'd known, hoped, in her heart that he did, for his actions had revealed it, but to hear the words was a priceless treasure.

"Yes, you. I love you." He clutched her hands. "I have wasted my life, my dear Elisabeth." She opened her mouth to protest, but he hushed her. "Do not interrupt, my dearest. I have been foolish to think I could fritter away my time on this earth. There were no lower depths I could go. I thought my life would end at the point of Radclyffe's sword and it nearly did." He grimaced. "It was not entirely pleasant, let me assure you. I wanted to change my ways, but lacked the strength . . . And then I met you." His hands gave hers a little squeeze. "I needed to change."

"You changed because of me?"

"I changed because I had to. I changed because in loving you I found honor. You stole my heart that day in the stables. It raised the stakes considerably." She frowned at this mention of gambling. He smiled, wry. "I cannot become a saint, but I am less of a devil."

"If I had to choose between you and Hampton, you would be the lesser of the two evils." She smothered her smile.

He raised an eyebrow. "I will take that as a compliment. And if there were a third choice?"

She stared up at him. Her third choice? The man of her dreams? He stood in front of her. "To be honest, Henry, for me there is no choice. Just you."

She saw his gaze fill with desire. He lowered his head to kiss her. Suddenly nervous, she said, "Do you know, this is the perfect situation for an elopement."

"I do not think that is wise, Elisabeth, tempting although it is." For some reason, he glanced back at the desk.

With a sad sigh, she agreed. "James would never forgive me if we did. As for the Radclyffes . . ."

"Is their approval still that important to you?" He searched her eyes.

"Even after everything they have done . . ." She took a steadying breath. "We have to come back into this society once we are married. Do not you think it is worth a try?"

He groaned. "If I get any more angelic, I will grow wings!"

She barely restrained her giggles. "It must be hard for such a lecherous reprobate."

"Unbelievably hard." A lascivious expression flickered across his face. "Then you will permit me to marry you?"

"Oh, yes, Henry." She thrilled at the sight of his happiness. "Yes!"

Henry bent his head, covering her lips with his in a sweet kiss that hinted at much before he broke it off. "Elisabeth," he murmured, his voice husky. "Are you sure?"

A little breathless, she replied, "I love you. I love who you are now—neither saint, nor sinner. I always have, from the moment you threatened my life."

They exchanged rueful smiles. Her mouth still curved into a smile, they kissed again. His gentle, insistent kiss easily parted her lips, deepening their kiss. She entwined her arms around his neck. She wanted to hold onto him forever.

His arms tightened around her slim form. At length, he released her. She tilted forward, eager for more kisses. "My pardon, Elisabeth." She blinked, startled by the sorrow in his voice. He stepped back. "You are tired. The sooner I return you to your brother, the better."

"You mean to take me back? Now?"

He nodded. "Please do not think I do not want to keep you

here with me," he said. "I do. I have even prepared everything, including obtaining a special license from the bishop, while you slept." He exhaled, impatient. "You told me that their approval of our marriage is important to you."

"It is—it was," she told him. "But they want me to marry Lord Hampton and as soon as I am back with them . . ." She bit back tears. "Oh, Henry! This is our last chance to be together!"

"I know, my dearest." His voice thickened with emotion. "But we must resist the temptation. All will work out, you will see."

She wished she could be sure. Hope that somehow they would be united had kept her going through those darkest days. She could yet lose everything. Her composure cracked, her body heaving with her heart-wrenching sobs. "Henry," she cried as he enveloped her in a comforting embrace, "you cannot do this."

"Elisabeth, I do love you," he murmured, husky with emotion. He kissed her hair. "It is because I love you that I know how they must feel not knowing whether you are alive or dead."

The awful torment she must have put him, her brother, and her friends through with her sudden disappearance. How could she have been so selfish? "I . . . I did not mean . . . I only wanted to . . ."

He caressed her cheek. "I know, I know. You were frightened of being forced into a marriage you do not want. Once you find love, it is so very hard to let go." He tilted her chin so that she gazed into his face. He wiped away the tears with a gentle caress of his thumbs. "I promise you, I shall never let you go."

Of their own volition, her hands clasped at the back of his neck. "But you are taking me back."

Henry nodded. "It will not be for long." She gazed up at him, searching and finding the truth. She believed in him. Of course, she always had. A tear escaped and trickled down her cheek. He bent to kiss the salty path. He kissed her mouth once more, a sweet, lingering kiss that took her breath away. "We will return together, I promise."

"Wait! There is one more thing." She hurried back upstairs to the blue and white bedroom and dug through the old duffel she'd seen in the corner. Finding the bracelet, she dashed back downstairs to find Henry standing confused in the hallway.

She held the bracelet out to him, the amethysts glinting. "Would you put it on for me?"

He took it from her, looping it around her wrist. "You kept it? Despite the hardship, the money you could get for it?"

"How could I let it go, Henry? It was all I had of you."

She caught a glimpse of his crooked smile as he bent near. "Come," he whispered against her ear. "We must go."


A short drive away, the Radclyffe's London house stood just off Grosvenor Square. Their hands clasped together, Elisabeth took strength from his strong grasp to face a task she dreaded.

As the Radclyffe butler opened the front door, Langdon brushed past. Together, they entered the drawing room.

Odette leaped to her feet with a startled cry. She sank down onto the sofa, her terrified eyes fixed upon Langdon.

"So, Langdon, you had her hidden after all," Radclyffe snarled. He stood by the fireplace, his face full of contempt. "Have you come to show off your bride?"

"No! He did not hide me!" Elisabeth cried out, even knowing she would not be believed. She stood close to Henry, protective.

"Your cruelty has gone too far, Langdon," Odette accused, her voice faint. To Elisabeth, Odette added, "You poor child. I warned you, did I not?" She took in Elisabeth's rough appearance and her too small clothes. She began sobbing anew. "Look at your face and hair! And now you are m-married."

"My dear Mrs. Radclyffe," replied Langdon companionably, "I did nothing of the sort. I found her and had my . . . My housekeeper tidied her up a bit. As promised, I have returned her safely to you."

The Radclyffes looked stunned. "You have not married her?" Odette asked, her eyes bright with hope.

Langdon dolefully shook his head.

"Oh, Elisabeth!" Odette exclaimed, opening her arms. "My poor dear! Come and sit by me!" Elisabeth took a hesitant step forward. "My brother will be so pleased to see you safe and unwed." She returned to the security of Henry's side. "He has been driven to distraction since you ran away from him, as have we all." Odette lowered her arms in some confusion.

"I am truly sorry, for all the worry and hurt I have caused you, but I will not marry Lord Hampton," she said, her voice halting from the emotional strain. "You would not listen to me! What else was I to do?"

"We will discuss your irresponsible behavior later," said Radclyffe.

"*My* irresponsible behavior?" she repeated in disbelief. "What of Lord Hampton's inexcusable behavior to me?" Henry rested his hand on her shoulder. He vibrated with suppressed anger.

Radclyffe ignored her outburst. "My lord," he said, clipped and curt, "it seems we must thank you. However, your presence is not required further. My butler will show you out." Radclyffe tugged the bellpull by the fireplace.

Henry went white. The muscles in Henry's cheek twitched. His hand slipped off Elisabeth's shoulder. "I did not bring Miss Stockwell here to be turned away like a naughty schoolboy!"

"Is that so?" Radclyffe folded his arms. The stubborn cast in his face matched Henry's furious expression.

James Stockwell dashed in through a side door. "Elisabeth!" he exclaimed. "You *are* here!" His grin vanished, glancing at the stern faces in the room. "What has happened?" His eyes fell upon her bruised cheek. "Are you hurt?"

"I will recover," she replied, watching James warily.

"Langdon has found Elisabeth and returned her to us," Radclyffe informed him. "He is about to leave."

Henry stepped toward the Radclyffes. "It is not my intention to leave Elisabeth here to be married off to that imbecilic, half-wit brother-in-law of yours!" Elisabeth nearly choked on her laughter at the apt description. He ran over their inarticulate protests. "Do you blame her for not wanting to marry him after he abducted her without her consent?"

"My brother was only doing what he thought was the right thing to do!" said Odette. "He has explained to us he was afraid of losing her."

"He never had me," Elisabeth pointed out. "Lord Hampton broke all the rules in abducting me, I cannot forgive him yet. Langdon, however, has made mistakes and has made amends for them all. I have forgiven him and I—I love him."

"Impossible!" Radclyffe blurted.

"Why do you think she came to me on her return to London?" Henry demanded. "If she returned here she would have married that dolt."

"What makes you such a paragon of goodness?" James retorted.

"At least I would have asked her consent," Henry snapped.

Odette spoke quietly, "I was never willing."

"I have changed since then." Henry's voice softened. "If I was the same man now as I was then, I would never have brought Elisabeth back."

"It is all part of some plot!" Odette turned to her husband for support. "Jeremy, do something!"

"I have been nothing but honorable in my intentions toward Miss Stockwell from the very moment we met. I have brought her back here because of my promise to you, Radclyffe. Elisabeth also wished I be approved of by you."

"She is mistaken if she thinks we could ever possibly approve of you," Radclyffe hurled at him, defiant. He pointed to the door. "Get out of my sight before I have you forcibly removed!"

"Please," Elisabeth begged. Henry started forward in anger. She grabbed his arm, holding him back. "Will you not change your mind? Has he not shown you he is good and honorable?"

"Ha!" Radclyffe responded.

"He has returned me to you, yet you are so ungrateful as to toss him out onto the streets! You make me ashamed to know you!" She turned away, her sides heaving with suppressed anger.

Henry held her close, her face buried against his shoulder. He smoothed back her hair. She found consolation in his touch, in his very nearness. "Elisabeth," he said. She looked up at him. "Will you stay or come with me?"

She gazed up into his eyes, losing herself in the depth of his hidden emotion. They had tried, now she must see to her own future. "I will come with you," she murmured.

"Damn you, Langdon, I shall not allow this!" Radclyffe moved forward.

"Elisabeth's happiness is more important to me than anything else in this world," Henry declared. "If she remains with you, she will be unhappy." Odette's sobbing grew louder. "Come, Elisabeth." They turned to leave.

"Wait!" James's bellow stopped them. He had not moved since his initial entry and still stood by the side door.

Elisabeth gazed at him. "James?"

He folded his arms. "Sister, I would rather you marry Hampton, but if you will have Langdon, then take him."

"Take him?!" Odette shrieked. "James Stockwell, you are out of your mind!"

James shook his head. "No, only foolish enough to think I knew what was best for my sister. Come, Elisabeth, tell them all you know. Tell them what you told me. I know now it was not fancy as you claimed at the Red Boar."

Radclyffe sent a quizzical glance to her. "What is this?"

"While you were guests at Stockwell House, I had another guest. Someone terribly ill. A gentleman, badly wounded. He was kind, good, with but a hint of the rogue in him." Her smile grew reminiscent. "I found out his true identity afterwards. I did not lie when I told you, all those evenings ago, that nearly dying had changed his outlook. He told me so before I knew who he was, before he knew who I was. In London, he strove to prove it to you in every way."

"I cannot believe this." Radclyffe delivered an immeasurable stare. "Elisabeth, this is too close to us. We cannot welcome this man. We cannot approve of him as you wish."

"Even if he did save her life," Odette remarked.

"He what?" James exclaimed. "When?"

Henry spoke with some reluctance. "I believe Mrs. Radclyffe is referring to a certain evening at the opera."

"There was a thief with a knife," Elisabeth added. "I am indebted to Henry for that."

"Elisabeth," James said with new concern. "You are not marrying him in order to honor that debt, are you?"

"Of course not. Just as I will not allow him to marry me in order to protect my reputation."

"Your reputation!" Radclyffe exclaimed. He snarled at Langdon, "By God, if I have to call you out again, I will!"

"No!" Odette crossed to her husband and clung to him.

"I will not be drunk this time," Henry growled, his blue eyes glinting. At Elisabeth's touch upon his arm, he stilled. "I would not fight you in any case. I have done harm enough to you and your wife."

"And Elisabeth?" Radclyffe demanded, speaking over his wife's blond head. "What of her?"

"I marry her because I love her." His hands balled into fists. "I cannot live without her, dammit."

"Then marry her, Langdon." James spoke. He sketched a brief bow. "And if my sister would allow me to give her away . . . ?"

"Was that your plan in abducting me last time?"

"That was out of concern for your reputation," James told her, attempting a conciliatory smile. "I wanted to see you safely married. I did not believe then that Hampton had tried to force himself upon you at the Bradshaws. I got my first clue when you tried to escape, the way Hampton held you . . ."

Henry turned a querying look to Elisabeth. She shook her head. They would discuss it later. She reached out a hand to James. "It would be an honor if you would give me away." She smiled. "It is about time you took on some responsibility."

James did not rise to the bait, chuckling. "Only to give it away again, sis! Only to give it away again!"

Henry's arm rested around her waist. "Then perhaps it is time for us to leave, my dearest. We have not entirely achieved our aim, but enough of it, I think?"

She smiled into his eyes. "You are not succumbing to temptation, are you?" At his raised eyebrows, her smile widened. She turned to Odette. "Odette, if you could but send word to Maggie to pack my things? Have them sent over to Lord Langdon's home." She blushed. "My home now, I suppose."

"Anything you want from Stockwell House?" James asked, reaching for the bellpull.

"A few personal items. We can arrange that later. Will we be welcome there?"

James grinned. "To a man who almost won the place, I do not see any reason why not!"

"I would not intrude," Henry said. "Losing to me cannot have been pleasant."

"Your returning everything disturbed me more. Hampton had me convinced it was part of your intriguing. I should not have listened."

Satisfied, Elisabeth turned to the others. "We will not disturb you further."

Odette made one last rally. "You are not going to live in sin with him, are you?"

"I happened to have brought the special license with me," Henry told her, with a twinkle in his eye, his humor restored. He gazed down at Elisabeth. "Shall we be wed at once?"

Elisabeth flung her arms around his neck and hugged him. "Nothing would please me more," came her somewhat muffled reply.

His arms enfolded about her, he murmured in her ear, "Oh, I am sure I can find something."

Their gaze met. "I look forward to it," she breathed.

Henry chuckled. Their lips met in a brief kiss before they recalled they were in company. Henry actually blushed. Elisabeth smothered her amusement, aware of her own pink cheeks. "If you will excuse us. . . ."

James asked, "Am I invited to the reception afterwards?"

The three of them headed toward the hallway. Henry admitted, "I had in mind a quiet dinner for two."

James glanced sidelong at his soon-to-be brother-in-law. "Cannot wait a moment, eh? Very well, I will locate Hampton and tell him the news."

"Tell me what news?" Hampton opened the door on James's last words. Too late. Hampton had spotted his companions. "Elisabeth?"

"Good evening, my lord." She gestured he move aside.

He stood his ground. "Langdon's work, I see."

Heaving an impatient sigh, Henry replied, "On the contrary, it's all her work. Must we go through this again? Speak to the Radclyffes, they will explain all."

His face suffused with red, Hampton bellowed, "You are not leaving here with her!"

James lowered Hampton's arm. "I am afraid he is, Lamby, old boy. Do be a sport and let us pass."

Hampton shook off him off. "Over my dead body."

Henry shrugged. "That can be arranged."

Elisabeth stepped between the bristling pair. She poked

Hampton in the chest, to his utter surprise. "I do not love you. I have never loved you. I love Henry. Now. Will. You. Let. Us. Pass?" She accented each word with additional pokes in the chest.

Hampton stepped back. "You are mad. . . ." he breathed. He straightened his shoulders. "Wait until Society catches wind of this, you will be on the out-and-out!"

"I do not care," she declared, defiantly rising her chin. "I shall be perfectly content."

"Blow this," Henry muttered. Louder, he said, "Stand aside, Elisabeth."

She obliged. Henry swung his fist and planted a facer on Hampton. He went down, his head hitting the wooden floor hard. Odette cried out, leaping to her feet.

James knelt by Hampton. "He will be fine. We best hurry before he wakes."

Henry agreed, tucking Elisabeth's arm into his. "My carriage is outside."

"It did not have to be this way." Elisabeth tried to placate the Radclyffes. "I just wish you could see the goodness in him." She cast a sidelong glance at Henry, who examined his knuckles for damage. "Although it is a bit difficult to see that at present."

Before they disappeared from sight, Langdon left them with one last statement: "You have disappointed her, but I shall not."

The three of them were soon ensconced in Langdon's carriage and on their way. Elisabeth smiled. She slid closer to him and slipped her arm through his. "There is a certain appeal to this darker side of you," she murmured.

James chose to look studiously out the window, giving the couple some privacy.

"Miss Stockwell, are you flirting with me?" Henry pretended to be outraged. A glimmer of a smile betrayed his true feelings.

"You must admit it is useful," she pointed out.

"Flirting?" He raised a puzzled eyebrow in mock misunderstanding.

"No, your darker side," she replied. "If you had not got Hampton out of the way, I would have been married to him in a trice."

"I would never have let that happen, Elisabeth." He brushed her forehead with his lips. "Never," he murmured huskily. His hand cupped the nape of her neck. She tilted her head toward him, desiring another kiss. His lips met hers, her arms entwining around his neck.

## ABOUT THE AUTHOR

A 2004 Golden Heart finalist, Leanne Shawler has written for all of her remembered life (since she was eight). Always an Anglophile, she first became interested in the Regency period over fifteen years ago and has been researching and visiting England ever since. Leanne lives in San Diego, California with her husband, after he enticed her away from her hometown of Newcastle, New South Wales, Australia. Look for her next Zebra Regency release later in 2005. Visit her website http://www.leanneshawler.com/ for more information.

# More Regency Romance From Zebra

__A Daring Courtship       0-8217-7483-2      $4.99US/$6.99CAN
  by Valerie King

__A Proper Mistress       0-8217-7410-7      $4.99US/$6.99CAN
  by Shannon Donnelly

__A Viscount for Christmas   0-8217-7552-9      $4.99US/$6.99CAN
  by Catherine Blair

__Lady Caraway's Cloak     0-8217-7554-5      $4.99US/$6.99CAN
  by Hayley Ann Solomon

__Lord Sandhurst's Surprise   0-8217-7524-3      $4.99US/$6.99CAN
  by Maria Greene

__Mr. Jeffries and the Jilt    0-8217-7477-8      $4.99US/$6.99CAN
  by Joy Reed

__My Darling Coquette     0-8217-7484-0      $4.99US/$6.99CAN
  by Valerie King

__The Artful Miss Irvine     0-8217-7460-3      $4.99US/$6.99CAN
  by Jennifer Malin

__The Reluctant Rake      0-8217-7567-7      $4.99US/$6.99CAN
  by Jeanne Savery

## *Available Wherever Books Are Sold!*

Visit our website at **www.kensingtonbooks.com**.

# Embrace the Romance of
# **Shannon Drake**

**When We Touch**
0-8217-7547-2                           $6.99US/$9.99CAN

**The Lion in Glory**
0-8217-7287-2                           $6.99US/$9.99CAN

**Knight Triumphant**
0-8217-6928-6                           $6.99US/$9.99CAN

**Seize the Dawn**
0-8217-6773-9                           $6.99US/$8.99CAN

**Come the Morning**
0-8217-6471-3                           $6.99US/$8.99CAN

**Conquer the Night**
0-8217-6639-2                           $6.99US/$8.99CAN

**The King's Pleasure**
0-8217-5857-8                           $6.50US/$8.00CAN

## *Available Wherever Books Are Sold!*

Visit our website at **www.kensingtonbooks.com**.